THE
HORROR
OF
SUPERVILLAINY

By C. T. Phipps

"I'm sorry but are you Gary Karkofsky, the Superhero with¬out Mercy?" an obnoxious Italian by way of Jersey sound¬ing voice asked.

I was sitting back in the offices of MERCILESS: CA$H FOR $UPERHEROI$M, #MercilessForMoney. It was a large empty building in the middle of downtown Falconcrest City with a big neon sign across the front of the place. The metropolis voted "Worst City in America" fifty years running had suffered a zombie apocalypse, a fascist takeover by my alternate universe doppelganger, and a severe economic recession. That, thankfully, made real estate dirt cheap and allowed me to buy the entire city block for what I presumed would be a regular series of knock-down, drag out brawls with the city's supervillain elite. That hadn't happened.

Instead, I had my feet propped up on my desk for my second straight month of absolutely nothing to do. The large gray walled central chamber had the desk, a secondary desk for Cindy (who didn't show up for work), a firepole leading up to the second floor, a jukebox that played nothing but Eighties' punk albums, and a spiraling staircase. After the first month of nothing to do, I'd started bringing an e-reader to catch up on my reading as well as a bottle of Merciless brand alcohol. I was starting to debate leaving the e-reader behind.

"It's Merciless: The Superhero without Mercy," I corrected the voice, not looking up from my e-reader. "Hush now, I'm trying to see what happens to Dumbledore."

Foreword

Hey folks,

I'm pleased to introduce you to the seventh of Gary Karkofsky's amazing adventures with *The Horror of Supervillainy*! This is going to be my homage to things like *Vertigo*, *Ghost Rider*, *Blade*, and other horror comics that have sort of fallen off the radar in mainstream comics. It's been a long time since Alan Moore's *Swamp Thing* introduced characters like John Constantine or the original Giant-Sized Man-Thing.

Snicker

Yes, that was a real comic. Also, yes, I'm twelve years old. At heart, at least. Horror and comics have always had a relationship and it used to be one of the pillars of the medium. *Tales from the Crypt* got its start as one of the long-running horror comics and there used to be an enormous number of spooky horror stories to be found in their pages.

While growing up, I used to go down to the comic bookstore and regularly bought old issues of the Seventies *Tomb of Dracula*. I'd been brought into the medium by the short-lived Midnight Sons storyline of the early Nineties. It was Marvel comics attempt to do something akin to Vertigo before crashing and burning due to a variety of factors.

Gary Karkofsky, aka Merciless: The Supervillain without MercyTM, has always had an element of horror to his story. The Nightwalker was created as a combination of Doctor Strange and Batman with Falconcrest City envisioned as a kind of Lovecraftian Gotham City. It has all the problems of the Joker and Penguin but also Great Cthulhu.

Poor Gary's second book dealt with him having to stop a zombie apocalypse, a sinister cult, and a Great Beast all in one. It also cost him the life of his beloved wife, Mandy, who has been a continuing presence in his life ever since despite the fact she's lost her soul. That is a wound that never heals even though Gary has tried everything up to and including trying to move on to do so. This is going to be something Gary is finally going to confront, for good or bad, and I think longtime fans will enjoy it.

Another element is the fact that Gary has finally made his transition from antivillain to antihero. At least that's what he's trying to do. Becoming a superhero is something he wants to do for his kids because they change your life. He also wants to do it for Gabrielle in hopes of making right what he did wrong before.

Unfortunately, changing your entire nature is harder than it sounds. Gary has always fought for what he thought was right. Coloring in the lines and being a lawful hero is going to be a lot harder than it sounds. He's gone from Chaotic Neutral to Chaotic Good but could he ever be Lawful Good? Yeah, right.

This will be an important book in the transition of Gary's life. He's gone from being a guy in his late twenties trying to figure out his life to being a guy in his late thirties now dealing with the consequences of his decisions. Gary, unlike Peter Parker, has the option of aging into his responsibilities.

For better or worse.

Chapter One

Knocking on My Chamber Door

"I'm sorry but are you Gary Karkofsky, the Superhero without Mercy?" an obnoxious Italian by way of Jersey sounding voice asked.

I was sitting back in the offices of MERCILESS: CA$H FOR $UPERHEROI$M, #MercilessForMoney. It was a large empty building in the middle of downtown Falconcrest City with a big neon sign across the front of the place. The metropolis voted "Worst City in America" fifty years running had suffered a zombie apocalypse, a fascist takeover by my alternate universe doppelganger, and a severe economic recession. That, thankfully, made real estate dirt cheap and allowed me to buy the entire city block for what I presumed would be a regular series of knock-down, drag out brawls with the city's supervillain elite. That hadn't happened.

Instead, I had my feet propped up on my desk for my second straight month of absolutely nothing to do. The large gray walled central chamber had the desk, a secondary desk for Cindy (who didn't show up for work), a firepole leading up to the second floor, a jukebox that played nothing but Eighties' punk albums, and a spiraling staircase. After the first month of nothing to do, I'd started bringing an e-reader to catch up on my reading as well as a bottle of Merciless brand alcohol. I was starting to debate leaving the e-reader behind.

"It's Merciless: The Superhero without Mercy," I corrected the voice, not looking up from my e-reader. "Hush now, I'm trying to see what happens to Dumbledore."

"You never finished that series?" the voice asked, sounding surprisingly close. As if standing on my desk.

"I wiped my memory of it so I could experience the joy of it for the second time," I said, pausing. "Or maybe third since I don't remember how many times, I've read it. I can't wait to watch this new *Game of Thrones* show and see how awesome it's ending is going to be."

Mind you, I was reading the Harry Potter from Earth-B where the author wasn't transphobic and the *Game of Thrones* that was nine seasons long and had an awesome ending. One of the benefits of living in a multiverse where you could travel with magic was the fact that you didn't have to look far to see better versions of your favorite shows.

"Put down the tablet, Gary," the voice said.

I did so and blinked. "You're a bird."

"No, shit," the raven on my desk said. He was wearing a tiny fedora and had a striped tie around his neck. "What gave it away?"

"Say nevermore," I said.

"No," the raven said. "Also, that joke's been done to death."

"Who the hell are you?" I asked. "Also, why are you in my office?"

"To hire you, numbnuts," the bird said. "What the hell do you think I'm here for?"

"I don't work for chickenfeed," I said, adopting my best Humphrey Bogart. "Buzz off, birdbrain."

I really shouldn't have been turning down a paying job, but Falconcrest City had been eerily quiet for the past couple of years. It wasn't that it wasn't lacking opportunities to fight crime, we still had supervillains, it's just that the second Nightwalker (Amanda Douglas) took care of most of them alongside her husband, Mr. Inventor. Whenever I showed up to a crime scene, the criminals also turned themselves over to the police. Which, you know, is what they were supposed to do but that didn't give me any opportunities for epic fights. I'd made my business in hopes of some beautiful femme fatale walking in with a case I could investigate. As such, I wasn't interested in what a bird was bringing to the table.

"Are we going to make this conversation nothing but racial slurs, monkey boy?" the bird asked. "Because I can exchange barbs with shaved apes like you all days. Chimps like you don't frighten me. Also, I'm not offering you chickenfeed. I'm here to hire you with cold hard cash. Solid gold bricks. Two million. Untraceable. Not bananas."

I crossed my arms and leaned forward. "Alright, you had my curiosity but now you have my attention. Where did you get that kind of shiny, swallow?"

"Not by swallowing like your girlfriend, Cindy," the bird said.

I grabbed him with one hand and he immediately choked up. "Don't call my girlfriend a whore."

"Because she gave that up?" the bird asked.

I paused. "Yes? Don't insult any of my family. I'm fine with you running me down but don't insult the ones I love. I get real personable about that."

I was a married man with one girlfriend, two kids, a twin sister, a niece, and a mother I barely talked to since she wanted me to do the talk show circuit with her. Compared to the majority of superheroes, who were suspiciously mostly made of orphans and swinging singles, I was what approached a family man. If you were upset about the fact I was married and had a girlfriend, don't worry, they were the ones who came up with the idea. My wife, Ultragoddess, spent most of her time in space and had a alien prince husband on another planet. My girlfriend, Cindy, aka Little Red Riding Hood, was also someone with an open and expansive view of sexuality. Yes, she'd been a prostitute at one point but that was in her past. She didn't need to charge for it anymore. As for my kids? Well, no one made fun of them and lived. They were still rebuilding Twitter after someone looking like me nuked their servers. It seemed someone created a thread about how boneable my daughters would be when they reached adulthood. They were five and six now, by the way. Well, when they weren't time travelling. God, being a superhero was weird.

"Okay, okay," the bird said. "The chick and chicklets are off limits, Donkey Kong."

I let go of the raven. "So, what's your name or should I just call you Poe?"

"You already did the reference there," the bird said. "I am the Nightflier, animal sidekick to the Nightwalker! I also go by David Niall Wilson. It's the pen name I write under when I do horror novels."

The Nightwalker was my mentor, idol, and predecessor as a superhero. Lancel Warren, aka Cloak, had been a billionaire's police detective brother who had studied magic and gone on to become the most powerful wizard in the world. He'd worn the Reaper's Cloak and protected Falconcrest City for a century before dying of old age. I'd inherited the Reaper's Cloak, by accident, and spent my formative years being educated by his ghost. Cloak had sacrificed himself to rebuild a dead world and I'd been left without his influence. If the Nightflier was his friend, then I was willing to hear him out. It wasn't like I had anything better to do.

I blinked. "Animal sidekick?"

David sighed. "It was a thing in the Sixties to Eighties. Every major superhero had an intelligent super-pet. Ultragod had Ultradog, the Nightwalker had me, Guinevere had her kangaroo Punchy, and later, Gabrielle had Ultrahorse."

"You could talk but you were pets," I asked, making sure I was hearing that correctly.

"It was not a terribly enlightened time," David said. "Let's be honest, it's still not a great time to be me in America. I'm black."

I opened my desk drawer, removed the suspiciously Jack Daniels-shaped bottle of Merciless brand alcohol, and poured us both a glass. "Here, you need this more than I do."

"You realize this stuff is like the lowest grade cheapest imitation whiskey there is, right?" David asked, showing surprising knowledge of spirits for a raven. "I mean, this isn't even Tennessee whiskey. It's South Michigan whiskey, made in Satan's Hollow by redneck moonshiners."

"I know," I said. "I produce it. You pay like a hundred dollars a bottle and put it on your shelf to know that you contributed to my taking over the world."

"I thought you were a superhero now," David said.

"That's the least fraudulent thing about it," I said, pulling out a sucker from the drawer and putting it in my mouth. It was laced with pot, Red Dust, and magic. Cindy made them as the only cooking she did. They were only for dying patients, chronic pain sufferers, and rich addicts. Oh, and her boyfriend. "So, what's the gig?"

"Why are you talking like a noir private detective?" David asked. "Not even a real one but a parody of one you'd see in comedy skits."

"I'm trying to get into the mood," I said, conjuring a fedora on my head with my magic.

David shook his little bird head. "Only birds, Indiana Jones, and guys with problems with women wear fedoras today, friend."

I shrugged and removed the fedora, putting it on my desk. "Why don't you share the job then? My fee is five hundred bucks a day plus expenses."

I didn't need the money. As a supervillain, I'd won and lost fortunes. But due to Cindy being slightly smarter with money than myself, I'd invested in various properties at her behest. So, I had Super Pizza, Merciless brand whiskey, and a variety of other sources of revenue. Not to mention I'd given my sister the world's largest evil megacorp that she was busy dismantling the evil part of. No, I charged what I did to keep people with stupid problems from showing up. I didn't exactly want to spend all my time getting cats out of trees, especially when I was a dog man. Given I'd received absolutely zero work from the public, most of my neighbors moving away, I suspected I should just put out a FIRST SUPERHERO CASE FREE sign instead.

"Deal," David said. "The president's daughter has been kidnapped by an evil cult."

I blinked. "Well, I can see why you would come to me. Is it the Ultralogists? Tom Cruise always had the makings of a supervillain in my view."

"Funny," David said. "But can you take this seriously?"

"I am pathologically incapable of taking anything seriously," I said, fully committed to the truth of my statement.

David shrugged his wings. "Anyway, Dracula has taken Leslie Trust hostage in his castle around Slaughterhouse Swamp."

Karl Trust was the president of the United States after the fall of President Charles Omega after he was revealed to be a time-traveling Nazi. An American actor and businessman from New Angeles, Karl was a compromise candidate between the two major parties implicated in letting a lunatic take over the country. I wasn't a big fan of Karl since he'd sent troops to try and kidnap my children while his Chief of Staff turned out to be a PHANTOM operative. Leslie Trust was the youngest of his equally unpleasant family, She looked like an Olsen Twin and ran a fashion network across the globe.

"Dracula," I said, dryly. "The Lord of the Vampires."

"No, Dracula the Prince of Insufficient Light and Lord of Heck. Yes, of course I mean Dracula the vampire!"

I processed that. "Why would this fall upon me? I mean, there's the Secret Service, the Society of Superheroes, the Texas Guardians, the Shadow Seven—"

"Because the president is the one who gave her over," David said, disgusted.

Okay, the plot thickened. "I'm not sure that qualifies as kidnapped. Why would Karl Trust arrange for his daughter to be taken by Dracula?"

"Dracula has a bunch on him," David said. "Tapes of bleeding on vampire prostitutes, money payments, associations with organized crime, the works. She's been taken as a hostage to ensure his cooperation. At least that's my theory."

"Meaning you actually have no idea," I said.

"I'm a bird detective," David said. "Knowing and knowing are two different things."

"By which you mean you don't know," I replied.

"No!" David said. "Sheesh. But Karl Trust is rotten."

I stared at him, looking for duplicity. I didn't see any, not that I was well-versed in reading beaks. "Agreed. This is why I voted for the other guy."

"Pfft!" David said. "Like you vote."

I paused. "I got caught in traffic after a threesome. That is the best excuse ever not to."

"You could have done a write-in ballot."

"Those are hard to get!"

If a raven could roll his eyes he would have. "Listen, Curious George, I need an answer if you're willing to do this. There's a hidden castle in the swamps down below the city and its full of evil cultists planning to do something nasty to the president's daughter. We've got to go there and kill 'em all."

I blinked. "You realize this is the plot of *Resident Evil 4*, right? I'm not sure we're not going to get sued for this."

"I don't know what a resident evil is," David said. "But I believe in democracy and we can't let foreign governments, especially Transylvanian ones, impact our foreign policy. So I need you to go down there to kick ass and chew bubblegum."

"And I'm all out of bubblegum," I said, nodding at his Roddy Piper quote. "Still, I'm going to say something, here. I appreciate you coming to me first. Not a lot of people believed in me when I decided to become a superhero and even fewer have supported me since it happened."

The decision to become a superhero had come with a lot of costs too. My best friend, Diabloman, had turned on me to help his late sister Maria Gonzales, aka Spellbinder, try to resurrect herself. I'd ended up banishing her soul to hell as punishment for impersonating my vampirized wife Mandy (long story). I'd reformed for the sake of my lover Gabrielle, presently off in another part of the galaxy punching Space Nazis, and my two children. None of them seemed to particularly appreciate my actions and it was nice to get a chance to show off.

"Yeah," David said, looking to one side. "I totally came to you first."

I raised an eyebrow. "The others turned you down, didn't they?"

"Not so much turned me down as tried to arrest me," David admitted. "You're about fifteenth on the list of people I've visited."

I sighed. "Why, may I ask, did they try to do so?"

David spread out his wings. "I have a gambling problem, okay! It's an addiction! A sickness! Yes, maybe sometimes I make a few bets that land me in trouble. Maybe I've fixed a few sporting events. Maybe I associate with organized crime on a regular basis. Hell, maybe I'm under indictment in fifteen countries for securities fraud. Maybe I took money a few dozen times to look the other way during robberies. That doesn't make me a bad guy!"

I made a pair of finger guns at him. "I'm starting to see why Cloak never mentioned you."

"How is Lance anyway?" David asked.

"Dead," I said.

"I mean aside from that," David said.

"No, dead-dead," I replied. "His spirit has moved on."

"Oh," David said, looking down. "That blows. I was hoping he could help out on this. He was one of the few people to believe in me, even when the rest of the superhero world forgot they knew me."

"Yeah, he was," I said, lowering my head. "I miss him."

"Yeah," David said, nodding his head.

"So, out with the money," I said, rubbing my fingers together.

"What?" David asked. "You're a hero!"

"For hire!" I said. "Which isn't copyrighted if you don't say it all at once. It says CA$H FOR $UPERHEROI$M on the front for a reason."

Hey? If you're good at something, never do it for free.

Chapter Two

Facing an Undead Psycho Version of Your Mentor

Yeah, I didn't need the money, but I wasn't about to let the talking bird take me for a ride. I also wanted to know how serious he was about this and where animal sidekicks kept their wallets. Honestly, my reputation was so bad with the U.S. government that I'd do it for free. Karl Trust had agreed to not press charges against me for my anti-supervillain acts in exchange for not having him dragged off to hell by ghosts. But rescuing his daughter could go a long way to reducing my chances of being hit with a drone strike.

"Aren't you like a billionaire?" David asked.

"No, my sister is a billionaire," I said, pointing out a technicality. "I gave her all my stock in Omega Corp and bank accounts to keep them safe from the government. Instead, she started a bunch of charities and eco-friendly businesses to solve world problems. Oh and put me on a goddamned allowance! What am I supposed to do with two million dollars a month!"

The answer was to give it away. I really did receive a check from my sister every month and I spent it on trying to rebuild the various shops, homes, and businesses destroyed in Falconcrest City's various micro-apocalypses. It was slowly—and I do mean slowly—rebuilding the trust I'd lost due to my doppelganger briefly turning it into a fascist state. Goodwill was hard to gain but easily lost, ask any superhero. Indeed, I probably ended up giving away ninety percent of my yearly profits. The rest of my fortune I spent on such necessities as sex, drugs, and death rays.

I really needed to put back some of the money to buy a college or two for my kids when they hit adulthood, though. They were smart enough to get into one of the best already before kindergarten, but I hoped to bribe their way into one to show how much I cared. You know, like rich people were supposed to do for their kids.

"Oh you poor baby," David said, clearly not happy with my one-percenter First World problems. "I'm not going to pay upfront the whole thing."

"Then you don't have a hero," I said, going back to my e-reader. "Now if you'll excuse me, I have a knock-off Lara Croft erotica to read. I understand they're making a movie trilogy out of it. *Fifty Tombs in a Tank Top.* It's by Larry Karbowski and that's not a pen name for anyone I know."

"Ugh. Fine, I'll pay you," David muttered and then turned his head over the side of the desk.

Out from the raven's mouth popped out tiny bars of gold which proceeded to hit the ground and become regular sized bars of gold. He coughed up a good fourteen on the ground before stopping.

"Keep the change ya filthy animal," David said.

I reached down and picked up one of the bars of gold, immediately noting it was heavy enough to be the real thing. Then I noted the symbol on the top of the bar before slapping it down on my desk with a loud thump. "Are you frigging serious?"

"What?" David asked.

"*Nazi* gold?" I asked, barely containing my fury. "You're paying me in Nazi gold?"

"What's wrong with Nazi gold? They don't deserve it," David said.

"I'm *Jewish*," I said, sharply.

"Then you deserve it!" David said, flapping his wings. "Also, really? You don't look Jewish. More like one of those pretty boy male models that make me want to throw out my wife's underwear catalogs. How do you look like that and sound like the computer club kids the jocks beat up in Eighties movies?"

I felt my face and shook my head. "God, I'm going to have to contact my rabbi and cousins in Israel."

"You have cousins in Israel?" David asked. "Are they superheroes?"

"No, they're soldiers in the Special Forces, which makes them scarier than me by far," I muttered. "Fine, I suppose giving the Nazi gold back to its rightful owners is worth rescuing the president's spoiled daughter from vampires. Man, to think there was a time in my life that was a weird sentence."

"By rightful owners, we mean Jews, right?" David said. "Not the bird detective who found it in a lake near Count Schattenjaeger's castle?"

"Yes!" I snapped.

David bowed with his wings out. "Just checking. Don't get so hot under the collar, Seinfeld."

I raised an eyebrow. "The monkey jokes are funny. Jewish ones, not so much."

"Humans all look alike to me," David said. "Also, I'll have you know I'm a Jewish raven."

"Uh huh," I said, offering my hand. "Well, you've hired yourself a superhero."

David put his wing in it and we shook without me closing my grip. "Glad to hear it. Now just don't ask why I have two million dollars in stolen Nazi gold but still have significant gambling debts."

I stared at him. "Well, now that you mention it—"

David pointed at me. "There you are, you're about to ask!"

"It's an obvious question!" I said, stretching out my arms.

"Well, don't ask!" David said. "You wouldn't like the answer!"

"That just makes me more curious!"

I was about to ask him more when a figure walked in through the front door that I recognized. He was a tall, broad-shouldered man dressed in a thick, black, hooded cloak that cast shadows over his face as well as caused his eyes to glow like full moons in a clear night sky. Underneath the cloak was an extensive suit of body armor as well as a belt of wands, tiny magic portion vials, and spell components. It caused me to blink because it was a man whom I'd never seen alive but was unmistakable from his build and the many old pictures I'd seen of him standing with the Society of Superheroes.

"Lancel?" I said, aloud. "Cloak?"

"Boss?" David asked, equally stunned.

It was impossible because Lancelot Warren was, as I'd said, dead-dead. Resurrection was banned in our reality by an ill-fated cosmic wish I'd made. A wish designed to allow the never-ending stalemate between heroes and villains to end. Yet, here he was, right in front of me. Except it wasn't Lancel Warren. It was a horrific parody of him. An undead abomination that my Reaper's Cloak told me did not belong in this world. Some undead had souls and were just people walking around in corpses. This was a parody of everything my friend had been. It was the Nightwalker with none of Cloak's humanity.

Ah hell.

"Karkofsky," the Nightwalker said, opening his mouth to reveal a mouth full of shark-like teeth before his eyes turned blood red. "I've come for your soul!"

Ah hell.

I have had a very weird life. This isn't me bragging or even overstating things. Even among supervillains (dammit, superheroes), I have a complicated and bizarre history starting with the fact my brother was Stingray: the Underwater Assassin and ending with the fact my daughters occasionally visited me from the future to hang out.

My friend Jane Doe said it was like being friends with an actual comic book character and all his oddball continuity as well as melodrama. I had no idea what she was talking about since comic books in my world were all romances, Westerns, and pirate stories.

So, bear with me, that when I say that seeing my old friend Lancel Warren in front of me and turned into a hideous zombified monster was weird, I wasn't whistling Dixie. Dead was supposed to mean dead now. That was the whole reason I'd made my wish at the end of the Eternity Tournament. It was a wish that had cost me immensely and was something I bitterly regretted as often as I justified it.

"Holy George Romero!" David said, flapping his wings and jumping on top of my head.

"Please don't, Lancel," I said, standing up with the bird on my head. I really hoped he didn't take a dump there.

It was not one of the smartest moves on my part, doubly so because I'd already survived one zombie apocalypse. Zombies didn't have souls. They were just corrupt perversions of the person they were in life. Even vampires were closer to the person they were in life and I had extraordinarily strong feelings about nosferatu. The fact I was trying to reason with a zombie despite the fact it was threatening me in a manner of a Deadite didn't make my decision any smarter.

"I said I will swallow your soul!" the Nightwalker hissed before raising his hands and shooting out blasts of hellfire.

I turned insubstantial and slipped beneath the floor enough that the blasts struck against the back of my business' wall. The flame spread around the first floor of my building and I could feel the heat lick against the back of my neck. As much as my power had grown, I was still vulnerable to magic and advanced super science—both of which the Nightwalker had loads.

One thing his use of hellfire confirmed, though, was that this wasn't just any old ordinary zombie. It was able to use magic and that was a sign it was a higher order undead at the very least. Most of my knowledge of monsters may have come from *Dungeons and Dragons* but that wasn't an entirely bad source of information. If this creature was casting spells, that meant it had some serious juice behind it, like an archdemon or evil god. It also meant it might really be the Lich King or Ringwraith version of Lancelot Warren. If it came down to a conflict between our shared mastery of sorcery, well, I was a self-trained hedge mage with some overpowered artifacts, and he was once the Supreme Archmage of Earth. In other words, I needed to cheat like hell if I wanted to win this.

"Hot stuff, hot stuff, hot stuff!" David said, flying.

"I'm sorry, Lancel, but I'm going to have to blast you," I said, apologizing to a zombie corpse.

I proceeded to unleash hand blasts of frost, creating a chilling block of ice around the Nightwalker. No sooner did I freeze him that he burned it all away around him and let out a menacing laugh.

"You are a rank amateur, Karkofsky," the Nightwalker said. "A minor warlock without a single day of formal training in the Art. I, however, was the Supreme Archmage of Earth!"

"I was just thinking that!" I said. "By the way, how are you not dead-dead?"

"You shall burn!" the Nightwalker hissed, firing a lightning bolt at my head.

"I can see that this is going to be a wonderfully deep conversation," I said, creating my own lightning bolt that just barely managed to cancel his out.

The Nightwalker gestured to the ground beside him and a pair of flaming hellhounds emerged from the shadows, barking and gnashing as they looked like creatures made of cracked magma. The heat was now pressing on my back as well as front. Both the hellhounds charged at me, only for me to conjure two pistols in my hands and fire into their heads, sending them flying backwards and exploding. My pistols were creations of the Primal Orb of Death and were capable of destroying anything short of a god.

"Imposter!" The Nightwalker hissed. "Cheap imitation!"

"I never claimed to be anything else, Lancel," I said, dryly. "I also know you're just an ugly rotting fake. The real Lancel Warren never talked like a supervillain. He was a super*hero*."

"Which you never will be," the Nightwalker hissed as a horde of featureless shadowy figures emerged from the ground, each of them reeking of hellfire and brimstone.

Ghosts. Damned ghosts or what we in the business called lemures. I hated lemures. It was technically my job to send them back to their proper resting place, but I'd mostly cleared out Falconcrest City of them. These seemed directly summoned from hell, which implied not only was Lancel full of otherworldly juice, but he had access to the Lower Planes too.

The lemures charged at me and I shot each of them with one round, causing them to explode into hellfire as they were disintegrated. As powerful as this version of the Nightwalker was, the stuff I wielded was cosmic. It was time to end this farce.

"I don't know who created you, but I know Lancelot Warren went to heaven," I said, only ninety-nine percent sure. "So, I'm going to destroy you and make sure whoever sent you after me follows real soon."

The Nightwalker laughed, right before he took two bullets in the face, only to regenerate the damage instantly. "I come for the Primal Orbs, Merciless. I will deliver them to my master and undo the horrid mistake you made. The dead will reclaim the Earth."

Uh oh. The Primal Orbs were pretty much the most powerful objects in the universe but had a "One Ring" clause to them in that they only provided you with as much cosmic power as you could use. You know, like Smeagol turned into Gollum but Galadriel would turn into Sauron 2.0. There were eight of them and together they could make anyone omnipotent. I had two of them, the first being the Death Orb that I was supposed to have according to, well, Death and the Chaos Orb that I'd taken from veteran supervillain Tom Terror.

I was pretty much the worst guy in the universe to have a Primal Orb, let alone two of them, outside of someone like Tom Terror or Hitler. However, I couldn't think of anyone else who could safely keep them, and the biggest defense of that decision was the fact no one knew I had them. If Lancel Warren's undead doppelganger here knew then I was screwed. Every cosmic baddie in this universe and several adjoining ones would come for them once they found out. Some of them wouldn't hesitate to blow up the Earth and sift through the wreckage as fast as you could say Alderaan. I needed to find out where the Nightwalker had found out, who he'd told, and then kill them all. Looks like my brief career as a hero for hire was over.

David flew over to the jukebox and tapped it a few times before the Clash's "I Fought the Law" started to play.

"Nice music choice," I said, cheerfully, as I started firing at the Nightwalker.

"Thanks," David said, saluting me with one wing. "Try not to die!"

"I'll try not to!" I shouted, jumping on my desk, and then leaping over the Nightwalker with a minor boost of levitation. You keep trying the same thing over and over again expecting a different result, but I didn't think that applied to bullets.

The Nightwalker's cloak swirled and twirled, extending its length before becoming a shield that absorbed all the magical bullets I was firing out of my enchanted pistols. Even worse, the entirety of my office was on fire and I could feel the heat against my skin. Hellfire wasn't something I could guard against by turning insubstantial. I could hear the wailing of the damned around me and it sucked at the power that my magic provided me.

"The Primal Orbs aren't going anywhere," I said, coughing in the sulfuric smoke that was being created from my place of business. "I stole them fair and square!"

That was when the Nightwalker lifted his fingers. "By the Crimson Bands of Zul-Barbas, I paralyze you!"

"That's a stupid spell," I said, right before I was suddenly wrapped with magical bindings and collapsed on the ground.

Paralyzed.

Ah hell.

Chapter Three

Where I Lose My First Wizard Duel

Well this sucked.

I was wrapped in the Crimson Bands of Zul-Barbas, which was one of the strongest spells for binding someone. It prevented you from being able to move, do magic, or speak. The spell was designed to allow the caster to torture the subject for the hours it lasted, usually as part of a ritual to appease the titular Zul-Barbas. I'd killed Zul-Barbas permanently, erasing the god from reality, but the magic named after him still worked. I wondered if one of his Great Beast brothers had sent the Nightwalker after me.

Mind you, I was choking to death on the horrible smoke coming from my burning building and the flames were getting more intense around me. Unless the Nightwalker intended to transport me out, he wouldn't have time to torture me long. As if my juke box was haunted by a particularly malevolent spirit, the next song that started to play was "Disco Inferno" by The Trammps.

The Nightwalker advanced on me, opening its mouth impossibly wide as a long demonic tongue slithered out. "Your soul will be sucked into my own personal hell dimension. Then I will deliver it to Lord Dracula. We will extract the Primal Orbs from you, and we will rewrite this reality to fix it."

I wanted to say, "Would they do something about your underbite? You've got a serious case of python jaw there, friend." Unfortunately, the Crimson Bands of Zul-Barbas were still holding me and I couldn't say anything. On the plus side, I knew who was responsible for my problem: Dracula.

"You stay away from Gary, you rotting imitation!" David shouted, flying down, and clawing at the Nightwalker's face. It snarled and hissed, distracted for a few precious seconds as I tried to figure out what could possibly get me out of this situation. It occurred to me that I was probably overthinking it and there was one way I might be able to save myself: brute force.

Closing my eyes and concentrating, I was able to picture the Primal Orbs inside my heart. I was crazy enough to store the two objects in the space in-between my atoms. If that made no sense to you, then congratulations, you have a working knowledge of physics. The thing about the Primal Orbs was they were designed to beat up physics and take its lunch money. It helped that the Primals were the Elder Gods who created physics in the first place.

"Get off me you stupid bird!" The Nightwalker smacked David and sent him crashing into the juke box, ending the disco accompaniment to my imminent death.

That was when I managed to absorb the energy of the spell and found myself once more able to move. I was sweating like a hog and felt my flesh licked by the hellfire around me. So, of course, the first thing I did was make a quip. "Man, I hope the real Nightwalker had better lines than that. You are vicious but have no finesse. Just attack, attack, attack."

"Die!" the Nightwalker shouted, charging at me with a running leap. It was a classic comic book attack, but it didn't work out for him here.

I turned insubstantial and lowered down six feet before he crashed into the desk above me. I grabbed him by the leg and pulled him halfway into the ground. "You can't kill what's already dead, but I can certainly try."

The rotting corpse of the Nightwalker stared up in shock before I concentrated on burning the Reaper's Cloak around him. The original Reaper's Cloak, the one I'd worn, had been reclaimed by Death long ago but I'd created my own. The one on the Nightwalker poseur felt similar, but I had the power to destroy it the same way I'd destroyed all the other ones.

"Argghhhhh!" The Nightwalker hissed as the zombie suddenly found itself without the source of its powers. I didn't stop burning the monster and countered the heat around us by creating my own flames. Seriously, that's a thing in science. Even magical science.

"How do you know about the Primal Orbs?" I shouted, pouring on the heat. "Tell me who else knows!"

The Nightwalker tried to raise his desiccated skeletal hands at me and cast another spell instead of answering. I ended up throwing him into the flames behind me and watched the figure disintegrate into the pyre now surrounding me. The hellfire flames were consuming the walls, most of the floor, and separated me from the outside. The Nightwalker didn't scream but disappeared into the fire and presumably returned to whatever hell he'd been conjured from.

"You probably should have focused on getting out of here over beating the undead Nightwalker," David said, flying over and landing on my head. "You know, I do think the Good Lord can get me out of this but I'm pretty sure you're borked."

"Borked?" I asked, looking up to the raven.

"I think swearing is a sign of an unintelligent mind," David replied. "That and all the soccer moms won't buy my horror novels if I say anything badder than butt."

"That's borking stupid," I said.

"Tell me about it," David said. "Well, talk to you later. I hope you don't mind if I have someone dig out the gold near your burned-out dead body. I mean, waste not, want not."

I was really starting to dislike that bird. "Yeah, well I'm not dead—oh, bork! That stings!—Yeah, well I'm not dead yet."

"Got any ideas how to get out of here?" David asked, watching part of my ceiling collapse, exposing the levels above.

"In fact, I do," I said, concentrating and levitating above the flames. The second floor of my building was full of giant props from when this was a factory for them in the Sixties (don't ask me who bought them) and the third was just empty apartment space. I didn't stop levitating until I reached the rooftop above both. David flew behind me, keeping up with my serendipitous escape.

The fresh-ish air of Falconcrest City was something that filled my lungs and I was surprised that I wasn't entirely sarcastic. Falconcrest City used to be such a toxic hellhole that you might have done a better job getting fresh air by smoking a pack of cigarettes. Most of the smog was gone now, at least by comparison, and it was only about as awful as Downtown New Angeles these days.

It was early in the morning and there was a fog laying out over the city streets below with the sun barely visible. I had a fairly good view of my hometown. It was a shame that said view was coming from on top of my burning office building, but that was a small price to pay for surviving an undead version of my old friend Lancel.

Falconcrest City used to look like one Gothic Art Deco skyscraper after another. When I was growing up, the Thirties buildings were covered in gargoyles and you couldn't cross the street without running into a decaying slum. Things had changed in the past few years, time compression or not, and half the city was now modern glass buildings that looked like they were built in the twenty-second century rather than the twentieth or twenty-first.

The City of Nightmares—yes, that was its actual nickname—had changed because of the efforts of heroes combined with the dozen disasters that had hit the city one after the other. It no longer looked like Cthulhu was going to team up with the mafia to kill everyone. Now it looked like Cthulhu, the mafia, and cyberpunk gangs were going to kill everyone. I'd done my best to rescue my city from being called the Worst in America fifty years running. Now it was just in the bottom twenty. Progress, am I right?

David plopped himself on the top of my hood as I looked out to the metropolis below. "Well, our goose was almost cooked or raven in my case. I can't believe that Dracula sent a zombie version of Lancel after us."

"It wasn't a zombie," I said. "I know zombies. It was something much worse. Like a lich and a wight combined. A Lich-Wight."

"That's not a real thing," David said.

"It is if I say it is," I replied. "In any case, Dracula has made the mistake of coming after me so I'm going to have to take him down now."

"You were already going to," David said.

"Yes, but it's more ironic if I pretend that I wasn't going to accept until he attacked me," I replied.

David cawed in a way that I assumed was him laughing. "You're alright, Merciless. You're the second-best Jewish mobster I've ever met."

I frowned, both irritated at the misidentification as well as wondering who the best was. "I'm not a Jewish mobster."

"Sorry, Jewish supervillain," David said.

"Superhero," I said, unhappy.

David made a snort-like sound that was slightly different due to the fact he was a bird and had a beak instead of a nose. "Sorry, chum, but you ain't no Hebrew Hammer. He was the baddest Heeb since Tel Aviv. You're mid-tier Arnold Rothstein at best. Now there was a guy who knew how to run the rackets of Falconcrest City."

I was getting the distinct impression my talking bird was racist. "Listen, David, if you're going to be my familiar then you're going to have to cut it with the language. I'm not a mobster and even if I was, I'd be the best mobster in the city period versus the best Jewish mobster."

"Actually, I think Cindy and her dad are the best Jewish mobsters in the city," David said. "In my day, the Kosher Nostra were professionals. You're a fairly good heist man and I applaud you taking a hit out on all the baddies you've eighty-sixed. But as a boss? I don't think so. Fuhgeddaboudit."

"How are you an Italian raven again?" I asked.

"Sicilian!" David said.

I felt we were about to start a Monty Python sketch and debated going with the dead parrot or swallow with a coconut one. I didn't get a chance to, though, because my right leg was grabbed by a bony hand that reached up from underneath the roof. Levitating up and carrying me up into the air was the Nightwalker, his Reaper's Cloak having regenerated, and his mummified form burned but otherwise unharmed. He turned me upside down as the edges of his cloak became unnaturally long tendrils that lifted me upside down in front of his face.

"Motherborker!" I shouted.

"You cannot kill what is already dead," he said, his eye sockets now empty except for a pair of flames like eerie Saint Elmo's fire. "I am immune to the power of Death. I am beyond her, I am beyond life, I am—"

"Web!" I said, making the heavy metal horns with my fingers and covering his face in a bunch of steel hard goop.

"Gah!" the Nightwalker said, his prehensile cloak dropping me on the ground.

"Where did you get that power?" David said, flapping about.

"Long story," I said, aiming at the Nightwalker with both hands. *"Prismatic Spray!"*

A glowing rainbow blast of a half-dozen spells released at once and struck the Nightwalker, sending him flying over the side of the roof. He was taking everything I was throwing at him and proving damn near unkillable. I was going to have to think of something better than my usual bag of tricks if I was going to defeat him. Leaping off the roof, I levitated down to follow him just as the building behind me collapsed. The hellfire had eaten away its interior and I would have been buried alive if I'd remained inside. Well, I would have been burned alive, killed by smoke inhalation, and then buried alive.

I landed in the middle of the alleyway behind my now-destroyed place of business. It was next to two abandoned warehouses and a mob-owned recycling center. There were no workers or homeless people around so I could cut loose. Still, it said something about Falconcrest City that a building could go up in literal hellfire and there was no sign of either the police or fire fighters. As Wang Chi said in the immortal *Big Trouble in Little China*, "Cops got better things to do than get killed."

The Nightwalker was already ripping away the webbing on his face, tearing pieces of his skull away and regenerating them almost instantaneously. The *Prismatic Spray* spell, which was seventh level in *Dungeons and Dragons*, had only managed to injure it for a short while. I needed to inflict damage so great that it would prevent the Lich-Wight from repairing itself or figure out something it couldn't regenerate.

"I do not recognize that breed of magic," the Nightwalker said. "Tell me the secret of it and I will make your end a short one."

"Uh, no," I said, debating returning to the Primal Orbs to unmake this scumbag. Even if I could do it, I wondered if it was designed to rip them from me. If they fell into this monster's hands then it would probably teleport away, and I would have just handed Dracula two of the most powerful objects in the multiverse.

"So be it," the Nightwalker hissed. He then started making elaborate gestures and muttering in languages I didn't understand. Glowing red runes and circles of symbols I didn't recognize appeared all around me. I found myself once more unable to move but this time it was accompanied with pain that prevented me from concentrating enough to access the Primal Orbs again.

"Dammit!" I said, struggling to force past the pain.

"This world should not exist," the Nightwalker said. "You have created one where the struggle between good and evil is determined as much by blind luck as the value of the struggle. Kings and heroes die due to random chance. Great monsters die at each other's hands as often as due to the chances of fate. Fools like you live when geniuses, saints, and sinners fall. It is an abomination."

I started summoning flames capable of incinerating atoms. Fire that was hotter than the flames that had destroyed my office. "Tell me... something I don't know."

It was strange but the Nightwalker was sounding a lot more coherent now. The Lich-Wight had acted like nothing more than a parody of his previous self when it wasn't outright acting like a monster from a Bruce Campbell movie. Now he almost sounded like the real thing, brought back to life to judge my sins. I didn't like it.

"Goodbye, Merc—" The Nightwalker didn't get to finish his statement because there was a gunshot that caused his head to explode in golden heavenly light. The rest of his body crumbled to dust and the magic he was weaving vanished.

"Huh, that was anticlimactic," David said, flying down onto the edge of a nearby dumpster.

I collapsed on the ground, my vision blurry and my head pounding. "Not that I'm not grateful for the assist but who, exactly, just saved my ass? Could you come out and identify yourself? Also, why did your weapon work and not mine?"

"Is that important now?" David asked.

"It is if there's another of those things coming!" I snapped, shaking my head free of the pain.

"Hopefully, there isn't," a familiar female voice said. "As for what killed it, my bullets are forged in Heaven. Almost as good as New Detroit for ammunition."

Stepping out from behind a garbage bin where she'd taken her shot was Jane Doe, aka Weredeer. Jane Doe was, as her name stated, a weredeer. She was a beautiful twenty-something girl with a bowl haircut, brown hair, freckles, and a lithe yet toned body hidden under clothing that immediately identified her as a hipster.

She had ripped blue jeans from the Eighties, an out of season Christmas t-shirt with a reindeer hunting Santa on it, and a bedazzled jacket covered in flair that hadn't so much gone out of style as never been worn by anyone over the age of fifteen. In her hands was a WW2 American pistol that glowed with heavenly power that was the antithesis of the kind I had wielded with the Reaper's Cloak. I didn't wield the power of Hell like the now deader-than-dead Nightwalker did but mine was the power of darkness while hers was, well, light.

Jane Doe was from an alternate reality, one where superheroes had never emerged and the supernatural was predominant instead. It had vampires, shifters, mages, and more living openly among mankind instead of Supers. Circumstances had dumped her in my reality for a time, but I'd sent her back to her home universe once I'd mastered how to use the teleportation powers of the Primal Orbs. I hadn't asked her whether she wanted to go first, and it had cost me one of my few friends. I wasn't sure how she was back in my universe and in that moment, I didn't care.

"Jane!" I said, walking up to her. "I am so glad to see you."

She promptly slapped me in the face, thankfully holding the gun in her other hand. So, at least she wasn't pistol-whipping me mad.

"Ow," I said, rubbing my face. "Usually, I've slept with a girl before she does that. Also, it's usually Cindy."

"We need to talk," Jane said.

I stared at her. "Also, a line usually coming from women I've slept with who are usually Cindy."

"Nevermore," David said, taunting me.

I glared at him.

Chapter Four

Where Jane and I Catch Up

"You hit me!" I snapped at Jane Doe, miraculously returned from her home dimension.

"You get hit all the time," Jane said, putting her hands on her waist. "Don't act like it's a big deal."

"I just got my ass kicked by a Lich-Wight, so I'm feeling particular," I said.

"There's no such thing as a Lich-Wight," David said, flying around in a circle above us like a vulture. "That was a Greater Zombie at best. Maybe a Higher Revenant."

"You shut up," I said, pointing at the raven.

Jane did a double take at the talking raven then shrugged. "Eh, it's not like I haven't seen weirder. Are you a wereraven?"

"Pfft!" David said, offended. "As if I would be something so lame. The only shifters that have any dignity are werewolves and weresheep."

"Weresheep?" I asked.

"They'll pull the wool over your eyes," David said, nodding his head. "Every time."

"Ugh," Jane said, "and I thought I made bad puns."

"You do. Also, how are you back?" I asked, simultaneously elated, and confused. "You got sent back to your home dimension by an evil wizard impersonating me!"

Jane stared. "Uh-huh."

"Okay, it was me who sent you back," I said, sighing. "I was terrified you were going to get killed fighting Tom Terror."

Jane and I had shared many adventures together while she

was here inside my world. Time passed differently between parallel realities so while she was projecting herself through time and space at a sweat lodge on her world, she got to spend an entire year with me and her cybernetic lover Case. I called it "Narnia Time." The thing was that events had gotten deadlier and deadlier until I was pretty sure they would get her and Case killed. I'd then made the unilateral decision to use my orbs—which isn't a euphemism—to return them to their respective universes. In the end, it had cost me my best friends and done little to ensure their safety if what I'd seen of their worlds was any indication. Seriously, both came from planets every bit as dangerous as mine and we regularly had a giant space god try to eat our sun.

"You could have asked," Jane said. "Case and I were ready to fight beside you."

"And maybe die," I replied, feeling sick to my stomach. "I was sick of losing my friends. Still, I reiterate, how are you back?"

"I don't think that's ever something you get used to," Jane replied. "In any case, I have no idea how I'm back."

"Excuse me?" I asked.

Jane put her enchanted gun away in a holster sewn into her jacket's interior. "I'm saying I don't know how I ended up in Comic Book World—"

"Please don't call it that, Urban Fantasy Worlder," I replied. "I'm from Earth-A, you're from Earth-USOM. Don't ask me who made these designations or why I get to be the first letter. Because then I'd have to say it's because I'm the one giving the designations."

"Do you want to hear what I know or not?" Jane asked. "I'd like to learn how I got back here myself and, Goddess help me, you're the most knowledgeable wizard I know in this dimension."

"Man, you are screwed," I said. "My doctorate in magical studies is from a correspondence course via the University of Bangladesh. Which would not be so bad if not for the fact that it is from their Cleveland, Ohio campus. A campus which consists of a storage unit and internet router."

"Gary—" Jane started to speak.

"I think you can refer to me as Doctor Merciless now," I said. "Man, Cindy screwed up bothering to take actual classes and getting accredited. The internet can sell you everything you need to know about supervillainy doctorates."

"Gary!" Jane said.

"Sorry," I said. "I also have an honorary degree in supervillainy from Londonium University of Evil. Which is a real campus and that bothers me more than you could know. I would never take a degree from a university that would graduate me. Except, you know, the one from where I actually graduated. If only because Falconcrest U taught me such valuable skills as casual hookups, beer pong, and coding."

Jane rolled her eyes. "One day I was just driving my Hummer—"

"You have a Hummer?" I asked. "Way to protect the environment, Deergirl. Those things consume two gallons per mile."

"They're also indestructible and it was a gift from my granddad," Jane snapped. "Anyway, I ended up driving into some fog and I emerged outside of Falconcrest City, which pointedly does not exist in my world. You replace New Detroit and Chicago."

"We have a Chicago," I replied. "That's the little port city with the really good pizza. Al Capone used to use it to smuggle whiskey into South Falconcrest."

Jane rolled her eyes. "I've been here about a month trying to figure out how to get back."

I opened my mouth in horror. "You've been back here a month? And you didn't contact me?"

Jane stared at me.

"Oh right, I sent you back to Kansas with your little dog too," I replied.

"No, Emma didn't come with me," Jane muttered. "I admit, I was pretty mad at you, Gary. I've only been able to keep up with your adventures by reading the comics about them in my world. It's pretty damned expensive even if I only buy them digitally. You and Cindy have like eight series between you. It'd be easier to follow what Spider-Man and Batman are up to."

I blinked. "You know, I'm never going to get used to the fact I'm a fictional character in your world."

"Ditto," Jane said, shaking her head. "I read the entire Bright Falls Mysteries books while I was your world and that C.T. Phipps guy is creepy in his insights."

"Yeah," I said. "He wrote my biography and it's just full of errors."

"Anyway, I tried to get in touch with you but couldn't. I've been traveling with the Society of Superheroes Dark and their kind of nonstop evil fighting adventures."

"Society of Superheroes Dark?" I asked.

"Yeah, they're the branch of the Society of Superheroes that deals with occult happenings," Jane said. "Nightgirl, Mr. Inventor, Black Witch, Human Tank, John Henry Booth, and Mercury."

"And they couldn't come up with a better name?" I asked, knowing most of the people on that team. "Also, why the hell am I not on that team?"

"Because no sane person would have you on a team?" David suggested. "A joke would have been way funnier if you hadn't already done it with your universities joke. Leave some comic material for the rest of us."

I glared at him. "No one asked you, Bird Brain."

"Bird Brain, really?" David said, looking at me with pity in his beady little eyes.

"They can't all be winners," I muttered. "So, if you're traveling around doing the superhero thing, why come to me now?"

"Realities are merging," Jane said, pointing to the dust where the Nightwalker used to be. "That guy, there, was actually the Nightwalker from the *Zombies vs. Amazing!* comics crossover event. In his universe, all the heroes were turned into Lich-Wights by the Wicked Witch of the Westside. They killed everyone and devoured the rest of the universe. It was so damn depressing, you'd think Garth Ennis wrote it."

"Ha!" I said, pointing at David. "I told you Lich-Wights were real."

"Their reality got unmade in the—" Jane started to say but my attention was already wavering.

"Hold on, I need to upload this to CrimeTube," I said, taking a moment to turn my cellphone around. "Wassup, CrimeTubers! It's the Supervillain without Mercy, Grandmaster M, Merciless with the less-ness! I just hooked up with my main gal here, Weredeer, and we just trounced a Lich-Wight version of the Nightwalker from another dimension!"

Jane blinked. "Please don't say we hooked up. Ever. Also, I'm sure that's no way anyone over thirty should talk. Anyone under it should be smacked for it."

I ignored her. "Remember folks, I'm doing the hero thang and saving the day! Team-up central! More vibes coming as we work on untangling where this unhappy Deadite came from! I have another mission I'm working on too but it's hush-hush for now! Ya dig!"

"Literally, no one in the world talks like that except maybe guys on MTV reruns," Jane replied. "I also may classify it as racist against white people."

I rolled my eyes and turned off my cellphone. "Listen, CrimeTube is the only way I can promote myself as a superhero. People think of me as a supervillain and the only way I can reach out to them is social media."

Jane stared at me. "You opened up by describing yourself as a supervillain."

I blinked. "Goddammit."

"I'm also processing the fact you have a YouTube, sorry, CrimeTube, channel," Jane said. "Can't you do something normal with that channel like review video games or insult women and minorities for ruining science fiction?"

"In addition to promoting the Merciless brand, I also review old episodes of *Murder, She Wrote*," I said, proudly. "Do you know that if we catalog the number of episodes set in Cabot Cove and assume that they took place over the same period of time as the series that Jessica Fletcher's hometown has a higher murder rate than Baghdad?"

Jane stared at me then shook her head. "The horrifying thing is that I actually find that interesting. What's your channel called?"

"Merciless' Big-Ass CrimeTube Channel," I said. "I used

to review gangster movies but not everyone appreciated how I laughed through most of them. I still don't know how anyone takes the ending of *Scarface* seriously. Dude didn't have any superpowered security whatsoever? Come on."

"Of course," Jane muttered. "Now, Gary, I need to talk to you. Introduce you to the SOSD. You think you can do that?"

I nodded. "Sure, sure. There are some universal laws and one of them is that I owe you for saving my ass. The Lich-Wight would have swallowed my soul if not for you. That means that an oath of fealty is needed."

"That's not necessary," Jane said, perhaps knowing I was going to make a big deal out of this.

"The Gungan and Wookies both speak of the Life Debt with great reverence," I said. "I shall now have to be your co-pilot and best friend until you're horribly murdered by your son because Harrison Ford hates Han Solo."

"Kylo Ren," Jane said, getting a dreamy look in her air. "So hot yet so lame."

"I do need a second to repair all my broken bones, though," I said, not actually joking. I hadn't even noticed how much damage the Crimson Bands of Zul-Barbas had done to me until now. One of the benefits of the Reaper's Cloak, the one I made with the Death Orb to replace my old one, was a heavy resistance to pain. "I've got a punctured lung, three cracked ribs, and my ankle is shattered."

Jane stared. "How the hell are you not screaming? How the buck did you do a podcast?"

I grimaced and lifted one of my cloak's sleeves. "I've sussed out about eighty percent of what the Reaper's Cloak can do, which is more than Lancel Warren did. Now I can take a beating and keep on ticking."

"That commercial hasn't been on in decades," David said. "Find some newer material."

He had me there. "Now I can take a beating and get up to take even more of a beating."

"Better," David said.

Jane blinked rapidly. "Your cloak only suppress the pain but not heals the injuries? Wait, no, then you'd be useless. Do you regenerate it like Wolverine, or do I need to take you to a hospital?"

"Wolverines regenerate in your world?" I asked, not getting the reference if reference it was.

Jane sighed. "I am never going to get used to the fact that everything is the same in your world except comics."

I reached into my cloak's extra-dimensional pockets and pulled out a bunch of spiral notebooks as well as a couple of yellow pads. "As for regenerating? No. I'm just going to cast *Cure Serious Wounds* a couple of times using the MMOS."

"I'm going to regret asking this but what?" Jane asked, walking closer. "Also, you look like you're studying for finals and have lost your laptop."

"The Merciless Magical Operating System," I said, flipping through the documents. "Have you ever noticed that when you need to cast a spell, you have to invoke a bunch of ancient gods and/or have a bloodline that dates back thousands of years?"

"Being as I'm a wizard, yes," Jane said. "Well, shaman technically."

"Well, that system is busted," I replied. "Magic could be used for so much more than just tossing fireballs in the name of Yog-Sothoth or Cthulhu. So, I've decided to create an open-source system."

Jane stared at me like I'd grown three heads and started breathing fire. "Open-source *magic*."

David reappeared by flying up on a nearby parking meter. "That sounds simultaneously awesome and stupid at the same time."

"Oh, hey," I gestured. "Jane, this is David Niall Wilson. David, this is Jane Doe."

"Like the guy who publishes the Supervillainy Saga books in my world?" Jane asked. "He's not a raven there."

I shrugged. "I dunno. I'm still surprised the husband of Supreme Court Justice Michelle Obama was the president in your world."

"Yeah, I miss him," Jane sighed. "Anyway, Gary, there's no way to create an open-source magic system. Magic is a raw, primeval, chaotic force that we can only channel because gods—i.e. the most powerful beings in the universe—serve as a medium between us. They purify and detox the raw chaotic stuff into something we mere mortals can harness in exchange for our prayers empowering them. Even then, it's limited because there's not so much power in prayer that most gods can exchange—"

I threw up the horns with my fingers and shouted, "CURE SERIOUS WOUNDS! CURE SERIOUS WOUNDS! CURE SERIOUS WOUNDS!"

A glow appeared around me as I felt my bones knit back together while the internal damage healed itself. It turned out my injuries were a lot more extensive than I thought and would need more spell work. If not for Jane and my magic, I'd have most assuredly died.

Jane stared at me. "I'm not sure what confuses me most: that you actually have created open-source magic or that you needed to look just reciting the spell's name three times while throwing up the horns."

I shrugged and cast the spell again before answering. "Why make magic difficult?"

"Because it's a universal cosmic force and you don't want every idiot to be able to harness it?" David answered for Jane. "I mean, bad enough that someone like you has access to it."

"I resemble that remark," I said, doing the spell a third time and finishing up my healing. "In any case, there's some limits on the MMOS. I must individually inscribe each spell into the laws of the Multiverse using the Primal Orbs before they'll work. I've only got about half of the latest edition of *Dungeons and Dragons'* core book spells. They're limited to ninth level, though. No epic level stuff. I mean, I'm not stupid."

David covered his face with a wing then shook his head behind it. Apparently, not everyone here agreed with my plan to make sorcery something the common ordinary citizen of the multiverse could use.

Jane just opened her mouth and closed it for a few seconds. After going through a variety of reactions, she sighed. "I don't suppose you have a spell book for this. I'm kind of terrible at magic."

I reached into my robes and pulled out a copy of *The Book of Merciless' Madness: 5th Edition.* "Here ya go. It's also available on Drive Thru Tabletop and Amazing Books' Print on Demand service."

"My aunt always said RPGs would corrupt my soul. I guess she was right." Jane took the book and started flipping through it. "Why does every page have naked elves?"

"I don't understand your question," I said. "Anyway, I wonder what the archwizards and gods will give me for democratizing magic."

"A horse's head in your bed?" David suggested.

I looked up at him. "Honestly? Probably. If they're feeling generous. I have no illusions this is going to go over like anything other than a lead balloon."

"Then why do it?" Jane asked, still flipping through the book.

I shrugged. "I'm an anarchist. I have issues with authority. Even when it's my own. It's why the worst thing that could ever happen to me would be to successfully take over the world."

"Says the guy altering the laws of physics," Jane said. "Well, meta-physics. You're aware that magic is supposed to be hard, right?"

"Is it?" I asked. "I'm a terrible wizard. Harry Potter could beat me up and take my lunch money. However, I do kind of have a pair of magic rocks that contain infinite power. Oh and a bunch of objects given to me by Death herself. I should probably stop using them for trivial projects."

"Ya think?" Jane asked.

"As soon as I finish my next trivial project: making the stars spell out my name!"

Jane and David stared at me.

"I'm kidding," I said. "Probably. I mean, it would only work from specific parts of the universe. I'd get a lot more oomph out of moving galaxies. Which I understand from my orbs that I could do but it would take two billion years of charging."

"Ugh," Jane said.

"Well, you've got the orbs for it I guess," David said. "A real pair of 'em."

"Wait 'til ya hear my wand jokes," I said.

Jane proceeded to grab me by my arm and start dragging me. "Come on, Gary, we need your help to save the Multiverse!"

"Again?" I said. "I just got done saving the Multiverse a year ago!"

"Well, it needs saving again!" Jane said, pulling hard.

"No, you can't make me!" I said, pulling against her. Unfortunately, the shifter was much stronger than me and was dragging me away by inches.

"Your daughters need help!" Jane shouted.

I stopped resisting immediately.

Chapter Five

Only I Can Save the Multiverse... Again

Jane and I headed to my car that was, thankfully, parked in the parking garage across the street and wasn't destroyed by the fire that had eradicated my place of business. Jane was, of course, impressed by my replacement for the Merciless-Mobile.

"This is your car? What are you, having a midlife crisis? Did you die and become replaced by Tom Selleck?" Jane asked, looking at the 1965 Blue Corvette I owned. I called it the Blue Meanie.

"No, I don't have a mustache," I replied. "This was a gift from Cindy's dad to her. I'm just driving it around."

"She lets you?" Jane asked. "I thought she'd watch the odometer like Ferris Bueller's dad."

"It was his best friend's dad," I replied. "That movie taught me the value of slacking off and disobeying authority."

Jane shook her head and slid into the passenger's seat. "Well, it's still a weird car to drive if you're avoiding attention."

"I'm a superhero now, I don't need to avoid attention," I replied, turning insubstantial and sliding through the door into the driver's seat. Across the street the fire department was finally arriving to put out the ashes that were the sole remains of my building. I didn't have much attachment to the building, but I felt there was something symbolic about this.

David flopped himself in the back. "Plenty of superheroes and supervillains have switched teams over the years, Gary. The majority of heel-face turns don't end up sticking. Larceny Lass tried being a hero a dozen times because she was in love with the Nightwalker. In the end, she always ended up going back to being a thief."

"Maybe that's because switching sides for a guy is stupid," Jane replied, buckling her seatbelt.

"I always thought Larceny Lass was playing the long game," I replied. "Being a beautiful Eartha Kitt type, you pretend you're not so bad. Then they try to save you and you get away with murder. Because they can tell themselves that they're trying to do the right thing by you rather than just being in deep lust."

"Is that what you did with Ultragoddess?" Jane asked.

I stared at her, narrowing my eyes. "No."

Jane shrugged. "No skin off my back if you are. My boyfriend is a crime lord. That doesn't prevent me from being the protector of my hometown against evil spirits."

"So, you do have superheroes in your world," I said, starting the car and driving off into the morning mist. The police didn't even try to stop us.

"No," Jane said. "This is completely different. We don't wear costumes or have codenames."

"Uh huh," I said. "You just use your superpowers to fight evil."

Jane flipped me the bird and I just laughed. "So what happened to the Merciless Mobile?"

"I donated it to the Nightwalker Museum," I said. "That and my sister stopped buying me replacements whenever I wrecked one. It turns out that maybe you should leave the autopilot on when you're piloting a land vehicle with a jet engine."

"It's amazing that you haven't killed more innocent people," Jane said.

"I'm just lucky that way," I replied. "Mostly I just maim and cripple them. However, it's a net win because I can cure that."

Jane looked like she didn't know if I was serious.

"I'm joking. Like, ninety percent joking. My expression turned serious. "So, my daughters are involved in all this?"

"Yeah," Jane replied. "Leia and Mindy showed up, the adult ones, and told us to seek you out."

"Why didn't they seek me out directly?" I asked.

"I don't know," Jane said. "Maybe because I'm their former babysitter."

"I swear, my life is like the Terminator sometimes," I muttered. "My adult children regularly come to visit me from the future."

I had two daughters by different mothers: Leia and Mindy Karkofsky. Leia was Cindy's daughter and had been born a Super with the power of hyper-cognition and telepathy. The short version being that she could build spaceships when she was a toddler and knew what sex was as "That icky thing adults are always thinking of." Mindy was Gabrielle's daughter and a genius herself with the power to lift small planets as well as light-based telekinesis. In the future both grew up to be time police in the latter half of the twenty-first century. Apparently, that was a thing when humanity got its crap together.

Despite the fact I was one of the worst time criminals ever, they regularly showed up to get my help. I got the impression both were eager to spend more time with their father. Which meant that I probably was not around while they grew up. I had to admit that was part of the reason I'd switched to being a superhero. I wanted to see my kids grow up and give them the horrifying example that would hopefully scare them straight. Unfortunately, that had been the exact motivation my brother Keith had when he'd retired and gotten himself killed by Shoot-Em-Up.

"So, your relationship is like the X-men," Jane said. "Rachel Summers and Cable."

"The who?" I asked. "Never heard of them."

Jane glared at me. "I sent you those comics! Like I wasted a wish from a genie to send you them."

I rolled my eyes. "Listen, it's hard to keep up with your fake superhero comics."

"Fake comics?" Jane asked, appalled. She looked like she was about to seize the steering wheel.

"We have historical comics for the Society of Superheroes but those aren't as popular," I replied. "I don't see why people would want to go read about a bunch of made-up superheroes when we have the real thing."

Jane shook her head. "Oh my Goddess, I'm in a goofier *Watchmen*."

"Is that a comic too?" I asked.

Jane looked at me strangely. "Okay, what does Alan Moore do in your world?"

"The wizard?" I asked.

"Okay, that fits," Jane said. "Stan Lee?"

"The science fiction writer from the Fifties?" I questioned, wondering where all this was coming from. "The guy who made the Incredible Mister Hyde and Fantastic Force novels? That Stan Lee?"

"Huh," Jane said. "Steve Dikto?"

"The Objectivist cult leader?" I said, now curious how all these people related.

"Ugh, poor guy," Jane said. "Jack Kirby?"

"Nazi Basher?" I asked, remembering the Jewish superhero. "He retired to Hollywood and made a bunch of psychedelic movies about alien gods."

"Okay, your world is both a little bit cooler and still lame for not having superhero comics," Jane replied. "I'll have to go on a shopping spree before I go home. By the way, if David Bowie or the Beatles have any extra tracks they put out in your world, I'll be stealing them to make a vast fortune."

I blinked, confused. "Is something wrong with David Bowie in your world? I mean, I just saw him last week at the alien-human friendship concert."

Jane gasped in stunned surprise and clapped her hands together. "I take back everything bad I said about your world!"

I was glad to have Jane back in my life but nervous at her statement about returning to her world. Maybe it was selfish—and I was one of the most selfish people the world had ever produced on a good day—but I wanted here to stay here with me. I was the one who sent her away for her own safety and regretted it every day. I also regretted sending away G because he had been forced to return to his crappy cyberpunk dystopian world where no one flew or thought of superheroes as anything other than a thing that children believed in.

The car eventually reached an abandoned factory not too far

from where my office had burned to the ground. Merciful had demolished most of the traditional supervillain hideouts in the city during his brief reign as First Citizen—no more abandoned amusement parks, haunted houses, or underground sewer palaces—but there was a decent number of factories left. Blame the economy not being something even my evil doppelganger could fix overnight.

"This is where you are hiding out?" I asked, not overly impressed. "I mean, it's not even a factory with a theme. I think this place just used to make aglets."

"What now?" Jane asked.

"The little plastic things on the ends of shoelaces," I replied.

"Ah," Jane said. "We're just holding up here after destroying the Left-Handed Bokkar's army of zombies. We're going to move on to fight the Demon Satano in a few hours, but I stopped by to help you."

"I killed the Left-Handed Bokkar," I replied, offended. "He's not coming back."

Jane looked at me. "It's another guy using the name. You kill one villain another takes up his name."

Yeah, that was another thing we were dealing with. "Right."

Driving my car through the chain-link fence's broken gates, I parked the car and headed on inside. The interior of the factory was dark, dust-filled, and had more than a few magical runes drawn on the wall in blood. All of them had been defaced, though, in order to deprive them of power. I caught a glimpse of Amanda Douglass, aka Nightgirl, in the rafters looking down and wondered if I'd see any of my other old friends here. She was a hooded Asian American woman with glowing eyes that had done her best to slip into the late Nightwalker's shoes. Even on my best day I'd never be half the hero she was.

"Where is my daughter?" I asked, finally looking at Jane. David was sitting on her shoulder, looking nervous as if something about the factory unsettled him. He was being quiet, and I appreciated that.

"Over here." Jane gestured with her head and I followed her around some equipment to see a makeshift hospital bed where I saw Mercury Takahashi and John Henry Booth standing over

Mindy. Mercury was a short, red-headed, Korean woman who dressed like classic Lara Croft and John Henry Booth was a tall black man who wouldn't be out of place in an Idris Elba remake of *The Good, the Bad, and the Ugly.* There was no sign of Leia and I had to wonder where my other daughter was.

"She's injured," I said, looking over at Mindy.

"Yes," Jane said. "Pretty badly. Where's Gizmo?"

"Out for supplies," John replied. "She'll be back soon. Probably. Time travelers are like that."

"Leave us," Mindy said, coughing on the bed. "I need some time alone with my dad. Well my dad and Jane."

Mercury nodded and turned to John as they departed.

"Hi," I said, deeply concerned about Mindy. I walked over to her and took her hand before looking down at her. Mindy appeared a couple of years older than me now and looked like she'd come out on the losing end of a war. She was lying there, one eye bandaged and missing one arm. She had all the strength of her mother but looked like she'd been beaten within an inch of her life.

"Merciful Moses, Mindy, what the hell happened to you?" I asked, unable to keep my opinion of her condition to myself.

Jane elbowed me in the gut.

"Sorry," Mindy said. "It's just I've been fighting in the Great Crisis."

"I think that's copyrighted," Jane said.

I elbowed her back for that.

"The Great Time War?" Mindy suggested.

"That's *definitely* copyrighted," I replied. "The BBC's lawyers are scarier than mine and he's a literal demon."

Jane glared at me. "Focus, Gary."

Mindy rolled her one good eye. "Fine, let's call it the Big Ass Time Disaster."

"That works," I said. "What is it?"

"Diabloman destroying the universe," Mindy said. "He's using the power of Entropicus and the Seven Beasts to unmake reality. It's the Norse Ragnarok, the Christian Armageddon, the end of the Aztec calendar, and a dozen other ends of everything. It's taking all the heroes of time to fight it."

"Diabloman is destroying the universe again?" I asked.

"Not quite," Mindy said. "This is the first time he's doing it."

I blinked. "I hate time travel. It should only be used for killing Hitler and sleeping with historical celebrities. You know Jack Kennedy was almost your sister's father."

Mindy looked amused, though that quickly faded away to more pain. "I understand Julie d'Aubigny and you almost gave me another half-sister."

"Awesome lady, people reading my memoirs should look her up," I said. "So, you got seriously injured fighting a war that's already happened."

"Not quite," Mindy said. "The Big Ass Time Disaster—"

"Are we really calling it that?" David asked, sitting on a nearby crate.

I shot him a deadly look. I'd hoped he'd keep his opinions to himself during this conversation.

"Shut up, David," Mindy said, with surprising venom in her voice. "Call it the Time Disaster."

"Oh you know him?" I asked.

"All too well," Mindy said. "The conflict is taking place outside of time. Therefore it can't ever really end as long as it's ever happened. As long as it has happened, Entropicus can continue to summon reinforcements to try to change the result of the battle. The consequences of this are damage to the fabric of space-time that are constantly being felt in your world as well as others."

"I have no idea what the hell you just said," I said, nodding along.

That wasn't entirely true because I knew about Diabloman destroying the universe in the Time Disaster, which was a much better name for it anyway. The Society of Superheroes, Superhero Legion, and Club of Champions, among many others, were gathered by Death to battle the forces of entropy. In the end, the universe was destroyed but they rebuilt it. Unfortunately, the universe had become a darker and nastier place. The beautiful Silver Age Earth my archnemesis Merciful came from was replaced with the gritty Iron Age Earth I lived upon. I'd eventually killed Merciful and brought his world back as the tenth Planet in our solar system (or ninth depending on your opinion of Pluto). It was a crazy bit of storytelling but, as Jane was wont to say, "It's a comic book universe out there."

"I know how to explain it," David said.

"You do?" I asked.

"Remember in *Back to the Future* when Marty lifted up the picture of his siblings and they started slowly vanishing?" David said. "Reality was in the process of changing but Marty had a grace period to fix things. It's kind of like that."

"Oh Goddess," Jane muttered, feeling her face. "We're actually using *Back to the Future* as an example."

"If it works, it works," Mindy said. "I'm the time cop here. Well, was while there were time police. They've all been killed except for me and Leia. Your little thing about banning resurrection allowed us to defeat the Great Beasts and capture President Omega, but it was at a heavy cost."

I still wasn't following the logic here. "Just so we're clear, this Time Disaster is screwing with things in my reality. Causing… what, people to vanish?"

"More," Mindy said. "It's what causes time compression in your reality."

I blinked. "Holy crap. That's not normal?"

I knew of time compression only because I had done a lot of time traveling and had come back a few times to find things changed. I also stored my journals in extra-dimensional space that let me keep things out of the effects. Even then, I probably wouldn't have remembered if not for the fact that I was Death's Chosen.

"What the hell is time compression?" Jane asked.

"It's a thing that happens in superhero worlds like Gary's," David explained. "Basically, say, superheroes appeared in the Thirties. They save the day, get old, get married, and then have families before dying. Time compression results in them suddenly moving to the Fifties when they appeared. Their families vanish. Their children appear later. Events that took place over a decade happen over the course of a month. It screws with people's sense of reality."

Jane stared. "In my world, that's just comic book companies

mucking with continuity so they can keep Spider-Man single forever."

"A spider man is a terrible idea for a superhero," I said. "No one likes spiders."

"I will force you to watch the Tobey Maguire movies if it kills me." Jane rubbed her temples, looking like she was getting a migraine. "So, comic book time is a thing in your world? Or what my mom would call soap opera time?"

"Hell yes it's a thing in my world," I said. "It's been screwing with my life for a while now. I can't say how long either. That's the result of this Time Disaster? To think all of the retcons and weirdness in my previous memoirs were actually foreshadowing."

Mindy gave a short nod. "It even exists in your world, Jane. It's called the Mandela Effect there."

The Mandela Effect was in my world too. Basically, someone mentioned they remembered hearing Nelson Mandela died in prison despite the fact Ultragod forced the South African government to release him after defeating the Afrikaaners. Dozens of other people reported remembering the same thing. While some people—sensibly—assumed this was a sign of people remembering things wrong, others believed it was proof that multiple realities were crashing into one another.

Jane's eyes widened. "What can we do to stop it?"

"Gary needs all of the remaining Primal Orbs," Mindy said. "Only with the combined power of all eight can he end the Time Disaster and save the multiverse. Then this universe will no longer suffer time compression, retcons, and other horrors."

I stared at her. "You know, every time I'm required to help the cosmos reset itself, it always seems to make my universe more boring."

Mindy frowned. "For history to move forward, the Age of Superheroes must end."

"I object to this plan," Jane said.

"Good," I said. "I like the Age of Superheroes."

"No, I object to making you God," Jane said.

I shrugged. "Can I really do a worse job?"

"Yes!" Jane shouted.

"Well too bad," Mindy said. "Dad is the only person in the world who is willing to give up the power after getting it."

"Well, then we're screwed," I muttered. "Do you know where the other orbs are?"

"Yes," Mindy said. "You're going to have to retrieve them, too."

Great.

Chapter Six

Superheroism Ain't Easy (Like Pimpin')

I looked at my daughter. "Have you considered calling the Society of Superheroes?"

"No," Mindy said.

"The Shadow Seven," I replied. "Which is now the Shadow Seventeen as I understand it. The New Texas Guardians—"

"He literally gave me this speech when I tried to recruit him," David said.

"Gary is not dealing well with the pressure of being a superhero," Jane explained to Mindy, apologetically.

"I am too!" I replied, before frowning. "I just don't want the responsibility of people's lives depending on me."

Mindy looked at me sideways. "Dad, that's the very definition of being a hero."

I stared down at her. "That's part of the reason why I didn't want to be one."

I knew some true superheroes in my time. Ultragod, Splotch, Gabrielle, the Nightwalker, and even Guinevere—despite her loathing of me—were the real deal. So was Mandy. God, poor Mandy. Most superheroes were good people, don't get me wrong, but they were flawed rather than the paragons the media tended to portray them as. They killed, they made money off their name, and they occasionally went the easier route than doing the right thing. It was just like most supervillains were not the psychotic evil doers who would never do any good.

One of the big reasons I'd chosen to become a supervillain was because I never wanted the responsibility of trying to live up to the example of the big heroes. Supervillains did what they wanted when they wanted, good or evil, and didn't worry about the responsibility. I was pathologically allergic to responsibility, great power or not. Yet, being a supervillain had lost its allure after Mandy had sacrificed herself to save Cindy's life. I'd done everything in my power to bring her back, but it hadn't been enough and all I'd achieved was to inflict misery on her vampire remnant.

"Is he okay?" Jane asked, looking at me. "He's kind of drifted off."

"He's brooding," Mindy said. "Dad does that a lot. When you're a superhero you either are a bright and cheerful paragon or some tortured vigilante with a dark past."

"Gary has a dark past?" Jane asked. "Really?"

"You'd be surprised," David said. "He's a lot more similar to the Nightwalker than you might think."

"Uh-huh," Jane said. "Gary. The guy who can recite *Monty Python and the Holy Grail* verbatim."

"Lots of people can do that," David said, looking aside. "It's a classic movie."

"I can't do it," I said, sighing. "Listen, I've already got a job to do right now. I have to rescue the president's daughter from Dracula. That's closer to my level of doing things. No more big cosmic battles, no more fighting archdemons, or zombie apocalypses. I just want to do street level stuff."

"Dracula kidnapping the president's daughter is street level stuff?" Jane asked. "It sounds more like the plot to a bad Eighties beat-em-up arcade game. Are you bad enough to rescue the president from ninjas?"

"It sounds like the plot to an awesome Eighties beat-em-up arcade game," I corrected her. "But, I just can't. I'm worn down."

Truth be told, it was the lack of support that had really done me in as a superhero. When I'd been a supervillain, I'd had Cindy and Diabloman backing me up. Gabrielle was there and I had believed that I would eventually have Mandy by my side again. Now everyone had gone their separate ways and while Cindy was there, she was also doing her own thing. I didn't pry but the weight was heavier now than it had ever been before. It turned out that I wasn't meant to be a solo act and was practically paralyzed without the others. Maybe that was why I hadn't gotten any work here in Falconcrest City—I subconsciously didn't want it. Okay, now I was getting a little too Freud.

"It's okay, Dad," Mindy said.

"Thank you," I said.

"No, you still have to do it," Mindy replied. "All of reality is at stake."

"Oh," I said.

"It's just the other six Primal Orbs are in driving distance," Mindy replied.

I blinked. "Excuse me?"

"What?" Jane asked, clearly surprised that the whole "saving the Multiverse" thing was a local job.

"Where are they?" I asked.

"Satan's Swamp," Mindy said. "Either with Dracula or someone around Dracula. It could be why there are dimensional rifts popping around. Just a few hours ago I had to deal with Mercirat and Cindy Woofkowski."

"Mercirat?" Jane asked.

I frowned. "Yeah, he's my cartoon doppelganger from Earth-Toon."

Jane stared at me. "You have *living cartoons* here?"

"Yeah?" I asked. "What?"

Jane shook her head. The expression on her face was one of pure disbelief. "*A frigging rat.*"

I stared at her. "Like that's so much worse than a deer."

"Yes!" Jane said, throwing her hands up.

"Speaking as a bird, you're all just hairless monkeys to me," David replied.

"No one can enter Satan's Swamp without potentially alerting the other holders of the Primal Orbs to their coming, which will escalate things considerably. You're the one exception, Gary. You won the tournament," Mindy said, "You're linked to them. You can do this."

"The only problem is that if I head into Satan's Swamp, I'm going to get my ass kicked," I said, feeling more embarrassed than troubled. I'd fought gods and supervillains, but it was the only place I'd well and truly gotten my ass kicked.

"Okay, Satan's Swamp?" Jane asked. "Really?"

"It's the most haunted swamp in the world outside of New Bourbon and a lot of that city's ghosts came to live here after Hurricane Bedalia," I replied. "Satan's Swamp is the bayou that exists just outside of Falconcrest City and is full of every conceivable problem you can run into. It's got mutant hillbillies, will-o-wisps, inbred Great Beast cults, weregators—"

"Hey!" Jane said. "Don't be racist against shifters."

"Cannibal demon weregators," I said. *"The Hills Have Eyes* version of shifters to your CW Drama."

"Okay, you can racist against these," Jane said.

"Plus, Sheriff Injustice has it in for me," I said.

"Sheriff...Injustice," Jane said. "Is that his real name."

"Don't be ridiculous," I replied. "His name is Sheriff Integral Nordbert Justice."

"So, Sheriff I.N. Justice," Jane replied. "I hate your world so much."

"Says the weredeer named Jane Doe," I replied.

Jane glared at me. Then she looked confused. "Wait, you've killed literal gods, why are you afraid of a redneck sheriff?"

"You're not questioning how there's a bayou in Michigan?" Mindy asked. "Also, why the Deep South is apparently in the Far North?"

"One problem at a time," Jane replied.

"It's a leftover from the Second Civil War when General Terror revived the Confederacy here," I replied. "Thankfully, John Henry and Ms. Steam stopped him with some time traveling Society of Superhero members."

Jane blinked. "Now I kind of want to hear that story. But let's stick with the sheriff."

I frowned at the memory. "Sheriff Injustice is the duly elected Sheriff of Satan's Hollow and Satan County. I was full of excessive confidence after beating Tom Terror. I decided to throw my weight around. Nordbert is a kind of magic parasite who absorbs the strength of those he fights. He kicked my ass, peed on me, and left me to drown in the swamp. It was the most humiliating defeat of my life."

The truth was I'd been lucky a lot of times in my career. I'd managed to take down a lot of powerful foes with the help of others: Diabloman, Cindy, Mandy, Jane, G, Amanda, and Alex to name a few. Other times I'd managed to succeed against my foes because I'd been underestimated or through sheer dumb luck. Nordbert had stripped me of my powers, humiliated me, and given me the worst beating I'd had since high school. I'd been alone and he'd taken advantage of that. I'd also been stupid.

I had the Death and Chaos Primal Orbs but even they didn't make me feel invincible—mostly because I didn't know how to use them for small projects. They were made for epic godlike feats, not precision work. If I used them on Nordbert, I'd probably make him a god rather than show him up. Wow, there was an emotion I didn't often admit to: fear. I was afraid of the guy. The only other ones I'd ever been afraid of were Entropicus and Spellbinder. One because he was a god and the other because she screwed with my head worse than anyone else I'd ever faced.

"Satan County?" Jane asked.

"Don't question it," Mindy said.

"It's hard not to!" Jane said.

"So, let's go kick the conspicuously northern-located southern redneck sheriff's ass," David said. "Then stop Dracula, rescue the princess—err president's daughter—and then get your balls back."

"Orbs," I said.

"Same difference," David said.

Jane looked skeptical. "Let me understand this, there's a cosmic quest to protect the multiverse by ending the Time Disaster—"

"The Big Ass Time Disaster," I corrected her.

"I'm not calling it that," Jane said. "Yet, the way to do it with the omnipotent Primal Orbs is all possible within a fifteen-mile radius."

"More like thirty but yeah," Mindy said.

"And our primary opposition is Dracula, which is terrifying even if he was once killed an ordinary cowboy with a knife, and a crooked alien sheriff." Jane blinked as if processing something that doesn't make sense. "This seems like it should require five or six movies. Maybe a cosmic space god or two as the villain."

"Not all superhero stories are *Avengers: Endgame*," Mindy said, making a reference I didn't get. "We don't have to worry about satisfying the House of Mouse's hunger for cash."

"It just seems suspiciously easy," Jane said.

"Maybe it's like *Spider-Man: Far from Home* and this is all a trick to get Gary to steal the Primal Orbs that will only obey him because he won the tournament," David said. "By the way, Earth-USOM has the best version of that movie. Making MJ a vampire was a great call."

Jane did a double take.

"I watch a lot of alternate universe television back at my nest," David said. "Technology was so much cooler back during the Silver Age. Alternate reality televisions, casual space travel, and time treadmills. The internet really ruined super-science. Now it's quantum this, atom that. No imagination."

"I both love and hate this world," Jane said. "Mostly love but hate whenever I think about all the cool spoor I'm missing."

"You can say 'shit'," I replied.

"I prefer to use deer swearing," Jane said. "Buck off."

Mindy reached out and took my hands. "Dad, you can do this."

"I'm not afraid," I said, lying to my daughter.

I wasn't afraid of being killed. No, I'd just had my throw-down with my Lich-Wight former mentor and that hadn't been a problem in the slightest. I was the Chosen of Death, for whatever that was worth, and knew an afterlife existed. No, I was afraid of failure. I'd failed Mandy, Cloak, and Diabloman, too, after a fashion. I'd instituted an "all deaths final" rule on superheroes and villains too, which had seemed like a good idea at the time but now seemed to remove the best of us while leaving the worst to carry on.

"So, what happens if I get all my balls together?" I asked.

"Now you're doing it," Jane said.

"Yes," I admitted.

"The Big Ass Time Disaster never happens," Mindy said. "The bad guys lose and life returns to the way it's supposed to be."

"Who decides what it's supposed to be?" Jane asked, suspicious.

"Clearly we do," David said. "Caw, I say. Caw."

"Did you just say caw?" Jane asked.

"I had to remind you I was a bird," David said, waving his wing. "Too bad deer don't have a recognizable animal noise. What do you do, anyway?"

"We bleat," Jane said.

"Sounds dirty," David said.

Jane lightly smacked David and sent him flying.

"Oh, the deermanity!" David said.

I sucked in my breath. "I have a bad history with trying to fix my past mistakes. I've been trying to move forward. Badly. Still, I would do anything for you and Leia. I'll go get the balls full of magic and rub them down."

"In front of your daughter, really?" Jane asked.

"She was raised by Cindy and me," I replied. "We're lucky she's not like the child from *The Exorcist*, and I mean that literally."

"Oh Great Deer Jesus," Jane said. "You poor woman."

"I learned from your example, Jane," Mindy replied, smiling. "You were the best babysitter since Elizabeth Shue."

"That's not a movie reference by the way," I replied. "Cindy and I kidnapped Elizabeth Shue to save her from a vampire stalker. She was really nice to the girls."

"I feel like I've missed some issues of your comic," Jane said. "To be fair, I work in a diner and it's not like I have the disposable income to pick up your entire run as well as crossovers. I'd like to help here too. I feel like a third wheel with the Society of Superheroes Dark."

Mindy gave an enigmatic smile.

I sucked in my breath. "Okay, I'll head to Satan's Swamp and take care of this for you."

"We'll send reinforcements when you're ready," Mindy replied. "Good luck, Dad. We'll be seeing you."

"Well, I hope you'll stick around. I've barely gotten to speak with Amanda for the past year and I miss Mr. Inventor too. I want to talk to Adult Leah and—"

That was when Mindy disappeared along with everyone else but Jane and David. The warehouse was cold and empty.

"Or, you could just disappear," I replied. "Does she normally do that?"

"All the time," Jane said. "I'm going to say, I expected a bit more from being part of a superhero team."

"Well at least you've got the health insurance and weekly check," I replied. "The Society of Superheroes benefits are top notch."

Jane blinked. "Wait, superheroes get *paid*?"

I smirked. "Let's get going, Jane, I'll buy you lunch on the way out."

"As long as it has mushrooms and lots of meat," Jane said. "Oh and cherry pie."

"So pizza," I said. "Also, aren't deer herbivores."

"We're opportunity omnivores," Jane said. "Most herbivores will eat anything if it's available."

"So noted," I said, smiling and glad to have my friend back. "Well, let's eat up before heading to Omega country."

"Omega Country?" Jane asked.

"There's Blue Country, Red Country, and Nazi Black country," I replied. "Satan County is the latter. There's no place more antithetical to a middle class suburban liberal than the last remaining Sundown town in America."

Jane grimaced. "Great."

"Last remaining? You sweet summer child," David said. "You have no idea."

Chapter Seven

Small-Town Sheriff Blues

Creedence Clearwater Revival's "Born on the Bayou" was playing as I drove down the dirt road leading into Satan's Hollow. The transformation of the temperate forests surrounding Falconcrest City's suburbs to the hot, muggy swampland was like someone flipping a light switch. Despite still being in the state of Michigan, we might as well have been transported to Northern Florida.

"How the hell is this even possible?" Jane asked, consulting a map in the front seat. "I think this is Ann Arbor. My hometown doesn't even exist in your world. Also, why the hell are you wearing that goddess damned hat?"

I was wearing a big RCA cowboy hat that was deliberately modeled on the one Burt Reynolds had worn in Smokey in the Bandit. I'd discovered the Reaper's Cloak could imitate almost any piece of clothes and used it to adopt a black button-down shirt, jeans, plus a necklace of fake gator teeth. I deplored the hunting of rare animals in real life but thought the look was good for journeying here in the Blue Meanie. Jane didn't exactly have room to talk since she'd changed into a pair of Daisy Dukes with a flannel shirt tied above her belly. I suspected she was already making use of my open-source magic to warp her fashion.

"It's a stylistic choice," I said. "As for why there's a massive swamp outside the city, the answer is always magic. Swamp Beast and his daughter Nightshade are supposedly the reason Satan's Hollow is the way it is," I replied. "It's like when an area is inhabited by a unicorn. It's always temperate and pleasant, even in Alaska."

Jane stared at me. "Unicorns?"

"You don't have those?" I asked.

"I kind of shot one once," Jane said, putting down the map. "To be fair, it was a jerk."

"They always are," I replied. "Never trust anything that has a fondness for virgins. Are you okay with leaving behind the rest of your group?"

Jane put her bare feet on the dashboard and crossed her arms. "I could ask you the same question. Don't you have an entire crew to go with you?"

"Gabrielle is in space," I said, dryly. "There's like a royal wedding or something on the asteroid city of Vargo where the last Ultranians live. Diabloman and I haven't spoken since I kinda murdered his sister and sent her to hell—"

"What was that?" Jane asked.

"Diabloman and I aren't speaking," I replied. "Mandy, well the vampire Mandy, is off doing her own thing. Sometimes I see her hanging around the mansion's gardens, looking in on us. Cindy, I gave a text too, but she said she is working on her own project right now. Apparently, it supersedes saving the Multiverse."

"So who's watching your kids?" Jane asked. "The small versions, not the adult ones we just left behind. I mean, I did for a year but I'm not an easy to replace babysitter."

"One benefit of being a superhero is that your access to decent childcare services goes up. They attend Guardian Super Elementary School, which allows me to try to be a superhero during the day, and when I'm off at night I can set them up with the Ultragod Robots at the Observatory. They haven't murdered any superheroes or tried to take over the world since Gizmo reprogrammed them to obey only her. I'm sure they'll be great guardians."

Jane stared at me in horror.

"Or they're with their grandmother," I replied. "My mom's house is protected by General Sherman's ghost army according to Kerri. I don't know because then I'd have to send them all away and that would mean I'd have to find new protectors."

Jane looked at me like I was crazy. It had been a common look when she had first come to our world. Still was to an extent. "I literally don't know which answer I prefer."

"Clearly, you haven't met my mother," I replied. "Then you'd definitely think they'd be better off with the robots."

Jane snorted. "It'll be good to see them again."

"You plan on staying long?" I asked. "You also didn't ask why you're with me rather than your team."

Jane looked sad. "They don't need me. Not really. It was nice returning to this world after I was unceremoniously banished—"

"You mean sent home," I replied, keeping an eye out for Sheriff Injustice or his deputies.

"Banished," Jane replied. "However, I'm not a superhero. Everything is just so vast, cosmic, and weird here. Being a weredeer just feels like small potatoes."

"Heroes come in all shapes and sizes," I replied. "Some don't even have any powers or specialized equipment."

"How long do they last?" Jane asked.

I grimaced. "About a week before they die horribly, usually. Things have gotten even worse since my wish after the tournament."

"Do you regret making it?" Jane asked.

"Sometimes," I replied, honestly. "So are you here permanently?"

Jane looked at me. "I don't want to be. It's tempting, but I have a boyfriend back home now. Friends, family, and loved ones. This is the magic land of Oz for me, but I have to eventually click my heels and return home."

"You know Dorothy actually returned to Oz, took her aunt and uncle, and stayed permanently. I'm also fairly sure she began a lesbian relationship with the fairy queen Ozma but that's just my interpretation of the books," I said.

"Oddly mine too," Jane said, scrunching up her nose. "I can't stay here permanently, Gary."

"But what if you could visit?" I asked. "Like, say, with the ninth level *Plane Shift* spell that is included in your Merciless' granted spell book."

Jane looked at me. "You want me to regularly commune to *another dimension?*"

"I don't have that many friends, Jane," I replied, neglecting to point out that plenty of television shows had alternate dimensional travel: *Fringe, Sliders,* and *Doctor Who.* I just wanted one that hadn't been cancelled. "It'd be nice if I had one more."

I regretted sending Jane away. I regretted it from pretty much the moment I did it. I also regretted sending away Case, but it seemed like he'd made a life for himself in the cyberpunk hellworld he came from. I also thought he might actually kill me if we ever saw each other again. I'd been afraid of losing both of them to Tom Terror and in the end, I'd lost them to myself.

Jane didn't respond immediately. "I'll think about it. You really need to talk to Diabloman, though. Even if you did send his sister to hell."

Ouch, she heard that. "I don't think that's the kind of thing you forgive."

"Maybe if you got her out," Jane said.

I paused. "She did things to me, Jane. Things that I will never forgive."

"Yeah," Jane said. "I know. You forgave Diabloman for a lot worse, though."

"That was different. It was crimes against other people but not me!"

Jane gave me a sideways glance.

"Yeah, yeah, I'm a hypocrite." I sucked in my breath. "I dunno, maybe I'll send her to another planet. Compromise."

Jane smiled. "You okay, David?"

David was sitting in the back of the Blue Meanie, a seatbelt covering both his wings as well as well as his belly. A bottle of Jack Daniels was half-drunk beside him and I was curious how a bird managed to hold the bottle, let alone drink its own body weight of it. Then again, he was a magic bird so maybe that explained everything.

"I'm doing fine, toots," David said. "All we need to do is head into Satan's Swamp, find Dracula's castle, and rescue the president's daughter. Then we'll be heroes."

"I'm already a hero where I'm from," Jane said.

"Yeah, I don't think rescuing the president's daughter will get me off for killing a previous president," I said.

I knew killing President Omega would have some fallout, but I figured since he was sending giant robots to attack the rest of the world, I would have gotten more breathing room. Instead, a lot of people had actually agreed with his extremist views. There were already Omega apologists and people who were trying to claim he had some hidden motive before Super supremacists assassinated him. Well, they were right, he had the hidden motive of wanting to kill a bunch of people for fun. He'd been a time traveling Nazi from the future who'd come back to make sure his utopian future never came to pass because it was too boring. I mean, I was a crazy anarchist who misused time travel and even I found that disgusting.

"Hey, President Omega's presidency was annulled!" David said. "He's like, an anti-president. A Jefferson Davis, not a Lincoln."

"Well, given he wanted to kill all the Supers in the world, you could say he's more a Hitler," I said. "I think I've gotten all of the alternate universe versions of him in my immediate Multiversal cluster."

"You are so goddess damned weird," Jane said, shaking her head. She'd developed a case of freckles since I'd last seen her and they were adorable on her. According to a couple of people, we were alternate versions of each other due to some quantum physics logic I didn't understand. Personally, I didn't see the resemblance, but I felt a strong brother-sister bond with her that rivaled the one I had with my actual twin. Or maybe I was just desperate for a friend. I'd driven away a lot of my old ones and lost others to vampirism or death.

That was when my driving was interrupted by an enormous cypress tree falling down in the middle of the road. I slammed on the brakes before we hit it, only to immediately hit the reverse. In the bush around the road, I saw a trio of eight-foot-tall alligator men pulling on ropes that were attached to the tree.

"What's going on?" Jane asked.

"Ambush!" I shouted.

I didn't get a chance to move very far before another cypress tree smashed down right behind us. This time, I didn't hit the brakes fast enough and the back of the car struck the second tree. Both my taillights broke as I cursed under my breath.

"Weregators?" Jane asked, finally catching up to speed. "They're like dragons!"

"Clearly spoken by someone who has never fought a real dragon," I said. "No, it's not them I'm worried about."

Jane's unspoken next question was answered by the sound of a police siren going off from behind the front cypress tree. A light rain started pouring down as a pair of sinister-looking lights turned on, outlining the modified cruiser that Sheriff Injustice used. He stepped out of the driver's side as a much shorter woman stepped out of the passenger's side. She wasn't that short, it was just that Sheriff Injustice was huge.

Media has made most crooked sheriffs fit a certain mold: short, fat, Southern, and ugly. Sheriff Injustice didn't fit any of these categories, at least in appearance. He was about six-foot-seven and built like a tree trunk. He didn't look to be any older than his thirties despite there being records of a Sheriff I.N. Justice dating back to the Sixties. I remembered reading an article about him being investigated by the Foundation for World Harmony eight times, only to have all-local juries dismiss the charges. He spent a few years in prison for voter intimidation before President Omega had pardoned him. Somehow, the sonofabitch had gotten himself elected again in the wake of my archenemy Merciful's brief takeover of the state.

Strangely—and this is a quality that I am weirded about noticing—Sheriff Injustice was also a good-looking man. He had that kind of modern country music star thing going on with long blonde hair and stubble. A part of me could not help but imagine him sucking dry people of their magic in order to maintain his youth a la Dracula. Mind you, I was coming here to hunt the actual Dracula, so maybe I should be focusing on the real vampires.

The girl I didn't recognize looked to be a teenager, about five foot four, with long blonde hair and a bright smile on her face. She was dressed in a deputy's uniform despite her age and was carrying a modified cattle prod that sparked like a firework on the end. On her lapel, I could see the name "Carrie Anne Justice" sewn under her badge.

"I take it this is Sheriff Injustice?" Jane asked.

"Yep," I replied. "In all his redneck glory. I think the younger one is his daughter."

"At least her name isn't a pun," Jane replied.

"Ms. Carrie Anne Justice?" I said, letting her put together the wordplay in it. "Miscarriage of Justice? Come on, work with me here."

"Goddess, I hadn't even thought of that!" Jane said, grimacing.

"I thought weredeer liked puns," I said.

"That's a vicious stereotype!" Jane snapped. "Even if it's true."

"Listen, this probably isn't the best time to reveal this," David the Raven said, "But I'm like high as a kite right now. I've got like a brick of reefer hidden under the seats and more than a little LSD hidden under my feathers."

Both Jane and I looked back at David in confusion. That was when both of us felt Sheriff Injustice's anti-magic field hit us simultaneously. It was difficult to describe for someone who had no talent for magic. I'd spent most of my life as a Muggle and it was only the Reaper's Cloak that had introduced me to magic. However, once I had magic, I could not live without it. It was like the internet or regular sex.

The Justice family's auras washed over me like a pair of wet blankets. I could feel his daughter's power add to her father's. It made me feel dizzy and nauseous at once. Looking at Jane, who had grown up with magic, I saw her look like someone had given her a bad set of mushrooms. Worse, there was something about draining our magic that made both seem taller as well as more menacing. I'd cut myself off from the Primal Orbs out of fear for what their power would do to Sheriff Injustice. It would be giving phenomenal cosmic power to, well, someone worse than me.

Sheriff Injustice made his presence unambiguously known by first smashing out a headlight with one of his steel-toed boots. He then proceeded to swing his fist down on the front of the Blue Meanie's hood, caving it in and destroying the engine underneath. The car, predictably, stopped running and we were left trapped in the middle of the road.

"Looks like you're having some engine trouble," Sheriff Injustice said, speaking with a thoroughly non-Michigan Southern drawl.

"Looks like it," I said, grimacing.

Jane looked at me and mouthed, "What's the plan?"

I shrugged. I had no idea.

Sheriff Injustice proceeded up to the front driver's side tire and kicked it out of its frame, causing the vehicle to lean to one side. He then walked up to the driver's side and looked down at me. "Well, if it isn't Gary Karkofsky, aka Mercilass."

I wasn't sure if he was mispronouncing my name due to his drawl or a deliberate attempt to mock me. He needn't have bothered. I wasn't that petty. I was much too scared to be. Weird how I was more afraid of this guy than Entropicus. "Hello, Nordbert."

"It's Integral," Sheriff Injustice said. "Nordbert is my middle name."

Miscarriage moved up behind him and shoved her cattle prod onto the side of the vehicle, causing me to jerk away.

"Don't you forget it!" Miscarriage hissed.

I was feeling all too human now and they were superhuman. Still, I did my best to control my emotions. A part of me was wondering if they were psychically generating fear or it was just the reptilian portion of my brain that knew how much danger I was in right now.

Speaking of reptiles, the four weregators moved out from behind the fallen cypress trees to surround us. They were all huge, scaly, and unpleasant looking things that were pretty much what you'd expect to see when someone described the word "weregator." They had the long mouths of their animal sides, tails, and a hunched-over bipedal body covered in scales. Strangely, they were wearing custom-fitted deputy outfits with little sewn-on stars. None of them had names, though, but just letters patched onto them.

"New hires?" I asked.

"Not really," Sheriff Injustice said. "Shifters have always been a problem in the Hollow. Shape-changing vermin making it hard for poor put-upon humans."

I resisted the urge to point out he and his daughter were about as human as the creature from *The Thing*. They were Supers at the very least, and more likely aliens. "Ya don't say."

"Yep," Sheriff Injustice said. "I did my best to rid the Hollow of them and was making good progress until that damned Swamp Beast ruined things. Still, I managed to get their Big Mama in the swamp and all her eggs. I raised them as One, Two, Three, and Four. They've helped me track down their awful scum of a race."

Jane stared daggers at Sheriff Justice. He knew what she was and was baiting her.

"You don't say," I replied, trying to figure out how I could take out someone like him without my magic. I'd brought a few trinkets and tricks with me, but I wasn't sure any of them would actually work against him. Still, I reached into the space between the corvette's seat and grabbed hold of the grenade I'd hidden there.

"You remember what I told you when I first beat your ass?" Sheriff Injustice said. "Never come back here or I'll kill ya."

"You tried to kill me and threw me in the swamp," I said. "You never said anything."

Sheriff Injustice smiled. "Oh well, in that case, let's just cut to the chase."

That was when Jane pulled her gun and fired first.

Oh hell.

Chapter Eight

Southern Hospitality Is a Boot to the Head

Goddammit, Jane.

I'll be honest, there was no chance of this not ending in violence and it wasn't like Sheriff Injustice didn't have it coming. I generally tried not to kill cops, but I'd met plenty over the years who were just another flavor of criminal themselves. There was a reason that Falconcrest City's Police Department had been listed as the eleventh most dangerous gang in America three years running. Sheriff Injustice gave them a run for their money, and I meant the entire department.

Jane's pistol fired and went off against the side of the Sheriff's cheek. It burned a hole against it, only for it to immediately heal over. I could feel there was magic inside the bullet but the very remnant she'd probably been counting on pushing it past Nordbert's defenses had empowered his healing.

"You are guilty of assaulting a police officer, Pocahontas," Sheriff Injustice said, grinning like it was Christmas. "I am authorizing use of deadly force against you and your Jew boyfriend."

"Do you want to point out he's a frigging alien or should I?" Jane asked.

"Racists are not big on ideological consistency," I replied, dryly. "Russian Nazis, Irish white supremacists, alien rednecks."

Sheriff Injustice didn't wait for me to finish my quip—which was just rude—and grabbed me by the throat. He proceeded to rip me from the Blue Meanie and hoist me up to his face. "It's time to make America last, son."

That was President Omega's slogan by the way, just in case you didn't get it. I regretted not permanently killing that scumbag. All I'd managed to do was dissipate the jerkass for a few millennia, which was a questionable obstacle to a time-traveler. It galled me to know the jackass still had supporters who felt he'd been railroaded by the Jewluminati baby eating cult of pizza-rapists. Which was like, literally, the only bad guy group that didn't really exist. Believe me, I'd know as I belonged to the proper Illuminati and was deeply annoyed there was no Jewish conspiracy to take over the world beyond myself.

"You're certainly making America last," I muttered, trying to figure out what ways I had to deal with a guy who could trade blows with Ultragod.

"Funny, boy," Sheriff Injustice said, before punching me in the stomach and cracking two ribs. "But who's laughing now?"

I was completely drained now but that didn't mean I was helpless. The Nightwalker had confiscated literally hundreds of super-technology gadgets from various supervillains over the years and I'd swung by the rebuilt Falconcrest City Clock Tower in order to pick them up. Unfortunately, the kind of objects I'd brought along were mostly the kind of things that fit into small containers around my belt. I couldn't even rely on the Reaper's Cloak's magic pockets since that was the sort of thing Sheriff Injustice was capable of draining the power from too. Instead, what little gizmos and toys I had were all tied in a golden metal belt that served as a Swiss Army knife for superheroes. Sort of a "utility belt." Huh, I was going to have to remember that name for the future.

Reaching down, I picked a metal ice cream cone "toy" and then shoved it onto Sheriff Injustice's face. The thing exploded with highly corrosive acid that was capable of melting through even hardened superhuman flesh and caused the Sheriff to cry out in pain. He dropped me to the ground, and I hit it with a thud. My chest was still hurting tremendously but I'd developed a remarkable tolerance to it over the years as I was getting my ass kicked.

"Red, White, and Blue Neapolitan," I replied, reaching for another device on my utility belt. "Courtesy of the Ice Scream

Man. Who knew he'd ever had a patriot phase."

"Daddy!" Missy shouted, ripping the door off the Blue Meanie to get at Jane. "I'll kill her for that, you hooded freak!"

I threw Jane an ice gun that had belonged to Mrs. Chillingsworth and which would fit easily into the palm of her hand. She caught it and fired a glowing white beam right into the face of Missy. The evil deputy's head was encased in a huge block off ice before cracking to pieces, decapitating the alien being.

"I thought ice beams disabled people, not killed them!" Jane said, shocked.

"Who told you that?" I asked, dodging out of the way of an enormous kick from Sheriff Injustice that smashed through the side of the Blue Meanie. It was a shame that my classic car was taking such a severe beating, especially since it was technically Cindy's, but at least it was dying for a good cause.

Missy's human form, meanwhile, warped to reveal the gross purple abomination underneath. A huge gaping maw with dozens of spike-like teeth, all of them the size of steak knives, was in the center of its chest with three long tongues licking inside. Hideous tentacles burst out of the sides of her body and red eyes blinked across her limbs. She looked like an anime version of The Thing crossed with *Hellsing*'s Alucard in his monster form. Seriously, if you haven't seen either of those then you definitely should.

"What the hell?" Jane shouted, aiming her ice gun again only for a tentacle to knock it out of her hand. "I just blew off her head!"

"Undifferentiated nervous system!" David said, sitting in the backseat without a care in the world. "Pretty standard for a Purple Venusian."

"Why are aliens so much stronger than us humans!" Jane said, jumping out of the car as another tentacle impaled the front seat.

"Speak for yourself, monkey girl," David said, slipping out and into the sky. "Or is that deer monkey girl. Also, that comment is inherently prejudicial."

"Shut up!" Jane said, backflipping like a cheerleader to grab the weapon and use it again.

Unfortunately, I was back to getting my ass kicked. Sheriff Injustice grabbed me by the arm and gave it a squeeze, shattering bone inside it as well as marking me with his power. I could feel him start to drain away my life-force rather than my magic. It was like burning from the inside out, every organ in my body seizing up with nightmarish pain.

"You are yummier than a BBQ on Saturday night," Sheriff Injustice said, tightening his grip. "I've got to admit, I went easy on the first time you came to my hollow. You thought you could kick me out and rescue them trespassers that were stirring up trouble with their 'Supers Are People Too' and other nonsense. I coulda killed ya then—came close, too—but I let you live."

I remembered the horrifying failure that had been my last attempt to come to Satan's Hollow. It had been my first and only attempt to be a hero on my own as well as a miserable failure. A group of protestors against the treatment of Supers had come down to try to bring attention to the human rights violations happening just outside of Falconcrest City.

They'd vanished almost as soon as they'd arrived, their phones going offline, and their families had hired me to investigate. Not only had Sheriff Injustice kicked my ass but he cleaned up every bit of evidence that might have proven his culpability. He'd gotten away with murder and I'd been left humiliated and unsure of myself. I wasn't going to let that happen again.

"You didn't *let* me do anything," I said, trying to figure out what gadget to use next. The pain was excruciating, and I could barely move. "I survived on my own."

Experience was the best weapon any superhero or villain had during combat. Every second's hesitation and decision cost you against a more seasoned opponent and allowed them to get their own hits in. It was the only reason why super-speedsters ever lost battles. They were very often faster than thought and that made them vulnerable.

"I let you live because your power is so damn tasty," Sheriff Injustice grunted, his breath smelling rancid and with just a hint of sulfur. "You came in here and I became stronger than any hero other than Ultragod or the Nightwalker. They were scared of me, scared of what I might become, and you made me reach my full potential. I think I'm going to run for governor, boy, and start my own super team. The White Knights. Maybe I'll start their career off by burning you on a cross."

Okay, I had one advantage in the fact that Sheriff Injustice was a talker. That gave me time to reach down to my belt, pull out the Weather Witch's wand, and lift it up into the air. "Do you have any personality other than being a racist stereotype? I remind you we're not even in the frigging South, Nordbert."

The skies over Satan's Hollow were always covered in storm clouds, even during advanced global warming before Doctor Aeon fixed that, and the wand called down a bolt of lightning that struck the deranged alien in the face. He cried out again and I kept summoning down bolts onto him. A second struck him, a third, a fourth, and then a fifth before the wand lost its charge. Electricity was one of the few ways to harm regular Blue and Red Venusians, so I was lucky the same rules applied to Sheriff Injustice.

Even so, the guy mostly just staggered back and dropped his human form. Like his daughter, the result looked like something H.P. Lovecraft would have come up with during one of his fevered, xenophobia-driven dreams. Unlike his daughter, it was still mostly humanoid in shape with his tentacles wrapped together and twisted into limbs. I'd managed to injure the monster, but it was still too powerful to defeat. I was also rapidly running out of tricks in my utility belt and wished I'd packed it with more miniature nukes and less Nightwalker shark repellent.

"Alright," the monstrous mouth in Sheriff Injustice's chest spoke, his voice guttural as well as nightmarish. "Now you've officially pissed me off."

Sheriff Injustice unfurled one of his arms at me and it wrapped around my chest like a whip before hurling me through the air. I was already in tremendous pain from the beating he'd given me and that only increased as I landed, rolling around in the mud. My weather manipulation triggered a full-on storm that soon left me drenched. He could have easily taken my head clean off but, apparently, he had something special planned.

I took a moment to check on Jane and saw she was still managing to stay ahead of Missy's attacks like a champ. She moved around like Chun Li during the original Street Fighter 2, bouncing against trees and moving with dance-like motions even as she continued to fire her ice beam whenever possible. Unfortunately, while Missy was now missing a few pieces, she was nowhere near defeated.

I considered my options and wondered if retreat was still even a possibility. The only place to flee was Satan's Swamp and I didn't put my chances of escape very good. I also wouldn't abandon Jane, yet, which was impressive. Aside from my family, there weren't that many individuals for whom I would give my life. Risk? Hell yes. I risked my life for fun three times a day. Give up? That was a different matter entirely. There were Cindy, Mandy (which made her absence all the worse), my daughters, Kerri, and Diabloman. Gabrielle was sort of a non-issue since she'd once survived a nuclear missile. It only left her head ringing for days. Now the number of people I was willing to die for apparently included Jane. Which was a shame because after I died, she'd be next.

"Too scared to keep fighting me, huh?" I said, slowly crawling to my feet. "Well, I'm willing to accept your surrender."

That was when I heard four growling noises behind me. I looked over my shoulder and saw the four alligators were gathered behind me in their war forms. Each of them was an enormous lizard man with armored skin and massive jaws capable of biting someone's arm clean off. Their eyes were feral, and devoid of conscience, having been raised as nothing more than Sheriff Injustice's attack animals.

Oh yeah, those guys.

"I'm tired of beating on the Jew. Do with him what you will," Sheriff Injustice said, slowly regrowing his skin which was apparently part of his transformation. Unlike other shapeshifters, his clothes didn't seem to be a part of the package and he was now a huge, *naked* redneck. I had to admit, his idea of Earth equipment was severely exaggerated, or he'd procreated with a giantess. Remember, bigger isn't necessarily better. It's better to find compatible partners. Oops, that was a bit of a diversion wasn't it? Sorry, I was just preoccupied with my imminent demise.

"Have you guys considered learning martial arts?" I asked, turning around. "I know the Adolescent Viking Battle Boars and they would happily take you under their wing. I mean, their name's not accurate anymore since they're all in their fifties but they're Cindy's frenemies. She tried to blow their houses down for some reason."

All four of the weregators descended on me at once and I would have been torn to bits if not for the fact the largest of them had an arrow shot into its throat. That would normally not stop a rampaging werebeast—no offense, Jane—but this particular arrow was glowing with unnatural white energy that caused him to burn away as if he was an exorcised ghost. The remaining three weregators instantly stopped in their tracks. That was when I heard the powering up of a chainsaw.

Turning, I saw two figures coming out of the other side of the swamp that commanded my attention despite the fact I was surrounded by a bunch of mutant lizard men and two racist aliens. Wait, were crocodiles lizards? I needed to look that up on my cellphone after this.

The first of the newcomers was a beautiful thirty-something Eurasian woman with her hair in a ponytail, wearing not so much a superhero uniform as leather pants with a tank top. A pair of goggles rested around her neck but that was the only concession to anything resembling a costume. In her hands was a bow and arrow that I recognized radiated the holy Ultra-Force energy of an Artemis. They were a cult of warrior women that had been blessed by the gods to hunt demons and serial killers. Guinevere had been part of their Celtic branch and was technically their leader on my Earth. A halberd was resting on her back, humming with an equal amount of holy energy, and I gave her props for it. The poleax an underrated weapon.

The second figure was about six-foot-three, wearing a hockey mask, and carrying a chainsaw that radiated unholy magic of a kind that I recognized as like my own Nega-Force. Rather than dress like Jason Voorhees or Michael Meyers in practical overalls, though, the guy was dressed like an accountant at a particularly high-end firm. His suit wasn't new either, with numerous blood stains just barely visible alongside the sides. There was something cold and soulless about him that made me think he was every bit as empowered by Death as I was. A cute little Halloween pin was resting on his lapel and I swore the thing grinned at me.

David rested on a nearby branch next to them. "Hey, I brought help! You wouldn't believe the kind of weirdos you'll find out here. This is the Accountant and the Final Girl. I'd have called the cops but when has that helped anyone?"

Sheriff Injustice, naked and glaring, stared at them. "You two have just opened yourself a serious can of whoopass. You're going to feed my daughter and me for a long time."

Realizing that more magic wasn't going to help our situation, I tried to warn the two superheroes (?) I wasn't familiar with. "Get the hell out of here! You don't know what you're facing here."

Sheriff Injustice charged at them, only to have the Accountant bring down his chainsaw into the crooked cop's body. The weapon went through all of Sheriff Injustice's defenses and purple gore went flying in every direction. Jane and Missy stopped their fight mid-step to look on in shock while the weregators fled in terror.

Huh, that was unexpected.

Chapter Nine

Psycho Killers in Love

"Have you ever fought anyone who could actually fight back?" The Accountant asked, his voice dry and patient. It was the kind of voice that would have made him the world's most terrifying math teacher or school principal.

"Argh!" Sheriff Injustice shouted, pulling back and flailing his tentacles in every direction.

"Daddy!" Missy shouted. It was kind of funny hearing that from the monstrous creature form she currently had.

The Final Girl aimed her bow and arrow before firing into Missy's arm, sending her spiraling backwards. The holy arrow seemed to be yet another thing they were unable to absorb and bought us valuable breathing room. Mind you, it felt like they were cheating because their magic worked and mine didn't, but I was not going to look a gift horse in the mouth. Well, mostly.

I felt my magic return to me as the pair stopped draining my power away. Even then, I didn't feel strong enough to cure my injuries. It was more like I was no longer being actively bled dry. I was still running on magical empty and if I tried to conjure fire, I probably wouldn't have been able to light a cigarette. There was also the fact that I had multiple broken bones and probably looked like I'd aged a few years.

"You are guilty of countless murders, Xanda'gar of Venus. You have absorbed the ideology of a failed state and passed that horror onto your children. Death is the only punishment you deserve," the Accountant said, continuing to attack him with his chainsaw.

Sheriff Injustice screamed. "That is not my name!"

The corrupt hick wrestled the chainsaw from the Accountant before hurling it into the nearby swamp. He then began to grapple with him. That was when, much to my surprise, the Accountant managed to start pounding the guy left and right. Sheriff Injustice's blows were clumsy and frenzied, which made me think the newcomer's assessment of his previous fights were correct. Bullies preferred prey that didn't fight back. They didn't enjoy battles, they enjoyed slaughter that they called victory.

The newcomers weren't fans of fair fights themselves as Final Girl shot another arrow into the side of Missy before drawing her halberd and hacking into Sheriff Injustice's back. I felt bad about not being able to join in the fight but moving to engage, I ended up stumbling on the ground before landing face first in the mud. Not my finest hour, this.

"I'll save you, Daddy!" Missy shouted, severely injured and yet still flinging herself with her tentacles out at the Accountant.

"You do that," Sheriff Injustice muttered before using his tentacles to grab some trees and flinging himself away. I should not have been surprised that Nordbert was cowardly enough to abandon his own daughter, but he was. You'd think even a racist ignorant asshole like him would have at least one redeeming quality, but apparently not.

Final Girl stepped in front of the Accountant, a glowing white nimbus appearing around her as well as her halberd. She swung the weapon faster than Missy could move and then cleaved the sheriff's deputy in half. Missy let forth an ear-piercing, unearthly scream as her entire body was consumed in witch fire. The only remnant of her body remaining being a few disgusting leach-like parts that inched along the ground. One of them crawled up the side of my leg before stabbing me in the leg, burrowing in.

"Bork!" I shouted, slapping my hand down on the injury and burning it inside and out. It took every bit of my remaining magic, but I fried the sucker. It did, however, cause me to fall to the ground again after I'd worked so hard to stand. All of my body tensed up and I found myself unable to move. "Oil can. Oil can. Anyone got some oil for a man without a heart?"

"Please, you're obviously the Scarecrow," Jane muttered, walking over and helping me up with one hand. "Though, I kind of wish Emma was here to be Toto now."

David flew over to the remnants of my destroyed car and set himself up on the rear fender. "I think recent events have proven that I am the most valuable player on this team. I think we should renegotiate my contract."

"I work for you! You hired me!" I snapped, spitting out some mud and feeling like my blood was on fire. I wasn't sure if I'd gotten that last parasite out in time before it had poisoned me. It turned out, despite what *Star Trek* taught me, alien and human biology tended to be incompatible.

The Accountant walked over to me. "You have killed hundreds of people, Gary Karkofsky. There is much blood on your hands. Most people you have slain were the guilty and irredeemable, but some innocents have lost their lives because of your choices. You have misused your gifts as well, using them for selfish gain when you could have helped others. Vengeance must be satisfied."

I looked up to him. "And who the hell are you? The Ghost of Christmas yet to Come?"

The Accountant reached down and put his palm on my forehead. In an instant I felt my agonizing pain become worse. I felt a dark presence enter into my brain and a series of images flashed through my brain: killing Shoot-Em-Up, my failed attempt at robbing a second bank that got a bunch of people killed by the Extreme, my failure to save Mandy, my use of dark magic to bring her back as a vampire, my attempt to give her back her soul, and killing my doppelganger Merciful within a few yards of his restored family. Finally, there was my wish after the Primal Tournament to end the revolving door of life and death on my world. Every day I hated the consequences of that decision more and more.

Why couldn't people come back from the dead? Yes, it led to constant never-ending fights between superheroes and villains, but who the hell cared? The world was better off with more heroes and fewer monsters. Why did it have to be both at the same time? Maybe it meant the world was wrecked every other week, but we could rebuild, goddammit! I couldn't help but think of the people I'd lost and now would never see again. What kind of world was I leaving to my children that it was growing a little less wondrous and magical every day?

The Accountant pulled his hand away from my head, no expression on his face. "There is nothing I could do to you that you are not already doing to yourself."

"William!" Jane said. "Nancy! What the hell are you two doing to my friend?"

"Jane Doe the Weredeer?" Final Girl, apparently named Nancy (because of course she was), asked.

"I was testing his soul with the Mark of Cain," William said. "It is my purpose to judge the guilty."

"Says who?" I snapped, pushing my way up off the ground despite the pain I was in. It was getting worse rather than better and I didn't feel strong enough to heal myself. In fact, I didn't feel like my magic was coming back. That was going to be a serious issue since I needed my magic to access the Primal Orbs and if I didn't have it, I didn't have them. They were stuck in the Reaper's Cloak's pocket dimension.

Crap.

"The Red Goddess," William replied. "I am a servant of the Living Spirit of Murder. However, unlike other slashers, if I must be compelled to shed blood then let it be the blood of the guilty. The blood of those who deserve to die."

I was not a big fan of antiheroes. The difference between a superhero and an antihero was generally how they reacted to killing people. A superhero, despite what the media might tell you, was usually willing to kill in self-defense or the defense of an innocent. Antiheroes were executioners who set on assassination missions or outright military operations that could end up with severe collateral damage. During the Nineties, a bunch of antiheroes had risen to become extremely popular and helped permanently stain the reputation of superheroes forever. It had also resulted in the death of my brother, Keith, at the hands of the first. I had a bunch of blood on my hands, but the difference was that I didn't claim to be a hero. Well, until now. Crap.

"Uh huh," I said, replying. "Ask a stupid question, get a stupid answer. Jane, you know these two?"

"Yeah," Jane said, looking embarrassed. "This is William Englund—"

"England," William corrected. Apparently, the a versus the u sound was important.

"And Nancy Loomis," Jane replied. "They're slasher hunters. William uses his power as an immortal serial killer and Nancy as an Artemis to hunt the worst of the supernatural. Not weredeer like me, but demons or Lovecraftian monstrosities."

"Sometimes vampires too," William said. "Sometimes humans. All monsters are our prey."

"Nice job with the first impressions, lovebug," Nancy said. "I'm sure he doesn't think we're psycho killers."

"Aren't we?" William asked.

Nancy rolled her eyes.

I blinked. "So Buffy and Angel are randomly in Satan's Hollow."

"That's... not an entirely bad comparison," Jane said. "How the hell did you get into this reality?"

"Magic," William said. "People are disappearing across our world and appearing on this one. The same is happening on this planet. There are people from other realities as well. Some places where superhumans do not exist, have had their world destroyed by monsters, or are great space-faring civilizations."

"It's like *Crisis on Infinite Earths*," Nancy said. "Which would be a funnier joke if not for the fact we're on an Earth with real honest to goddess superheroes."

I stared at them. "Said the superpowered man and woman who fight crime."

"That's completely different," Nancy said.

"Who have codenames," David said, entering the conversation for the first time.

Nancy looked abashed. "Codenames are cool."

I glared at Jane. "So your world *does* have superheroes."

Jane looked sideways. "Not ones with capes. Capes are cool."

I snorted. "So, you guys are investigating the same disturbance I am?"

"I thought we were rescuing the president's daughter!" David whined. "Listen, man, I paid for you to be a hero and I expect you to live up to our bargain. I mean, yeah, the gold bar is buried under a ton of debris and would just barely pay for repairing your building, but a deal is a deal. This is America. What would our country be like today if we broke our treaties with the Native Americans?"

Jane glared at David.

"Oh, right, sorry there," David said. "Forgot you were of the *Last of the Mohicans* persuasion."

Jane grabbed David and started throttling him with her bare hands.

"Help, animal abuse!" David shouted.

I ignored them.

"No, actually," Nancy replied. "The fact that this seems to be the center of everything weird going on is a complete coincidence."

"Except for the fact the majority of people appearing on this world seem to be appearing around Falconcrest City," William replied. "You didn't attempt to investigate?"

"I didn't know!" I replied. "Mind you, maybe if I paid attention to the news, I would have but it's so depressing these days."

Jane stopped strangling David to stare at me. "You are a terrible superhero."

"I know!" I said, admitting it. "I'm not good at this."

"We've been working with some of the local… superheroes to apply our skills to help," Nancy said. "We have a training camp nearby."

I blinked. "Other local heroes? Training camp?"

There were not that many places to train superheroes in the world. There was the Guardians Academy, the Society of Superheroes moon base, the Temple of the Flaming Fist in Shamballa, and the Evo-Lutionaries' various secret bases. Basically, people hated Supers and were generally not too inclined to let them train in the use of their powers. Finding out there was one in my backyard was yet another sign I was really botching this superhero thing. There were also no other local heroes if Mr. Inventor and the second Nightwalker were off with the Society of Superheroes Dark. That was when everything started to get blurry.

"Uh, Gary," Jane said. "You don't look well."

"Yeah," I said. "I think I was poisoned."

"What?" Jane asked.

"Sorry," I said, seeing everything start to get blurry. "I don't think I'm going to be able to join you on this final leg of our journey."

It was a relief, really.

"You're not dying, Gary," Jane said, sounding less confidant than I did. She still had her fist wrapped around David's neck.

"I'm sorry," William said. "I can feel your essence leaving."

"Jeez, sorry man," Nancy said, not knowing me that well. "Is there a hospital nearby?"

"Sorry, no," I replied.

"I want a refund!" David squawked.

"I'm not afraid of dying," I said, sighing before sitting down on the ground. "Sheriff Injustice already killed me once before, so I know what waits for me on the other side."

"What?" Jane asked.

I took a deep breath. "Dying is a part of the dangers in being a superhero. While I made the rule that all deaths are permanent, there's a little leeway between the moment of death and permanent brain death, do not pass go, do not collect two hundred dollars. It was enough that I had a glimpse of my afterlife before I managed to revive."

"That seems like cheating but whenever comic book editors say that deaths are final, you know they're lying," Jane said.

"You do realize I'm not a fictional character and that editors actually don't determine my fate, right?" I asked, almost done.

"I'm still debating on that," Jane said. "It would explain a few things about my life too."

I paused, smiling. "Sometimes my life does read like fanfic. Then again, I suppose it's mostly just that nerds are naturally sexy and thus irresistible to beautiful Amazon superheroines. That and a wealth of pop culture knowledge is a guarantee of success in life."

Jane rolled her eyes. "So, what afterlife awaits you?"

I puffed out my chest. "I was sentenced to Heck, the Realm for the Insufficiently Good! I was darned there by forces beyond comprehension! You get cable but only Cinemax, bad covers of your favorite songs, and the internet but only dial up. All the bottled water is tap and the food is pre-prepared! Oh, the humanity! It is truly the most unexceptional place in the Multiverse!"

Jane frowned. "You just stole that from *The Good Place.*"

I shrugged, almost done. "Kristen Bell was the runner up for playing Cindy in the Merciless movie. She lost to some Italian assassin chick."

I would miss seeing my children grow up, as well as Cindy, and Mandy. Strange how those were the three things I regretted most.

"What's your real afterlife like?" Jane asked, looking terrified and wanting to hug me. She finally let go of David and he flew away.

I sucked in my breaths. "An endless road paved in regrets going nowhere."

Jane put her hand on my shoulder. Her eyes were tearing up. "I'm sorry."

"Eh, it's okay, I plan to haunt you all as a ghost. Either that or ascend to godhood. I think that's still allowed under the rules I imposed," I replied. "Either that or take over my own hell dimension like Jackson Blackwell or Henry Kissinger."

"Do I want to know about the last one?" Jane asked.

"I'm getting sued for reaping his soul," I replied. "The Republican Party took it personally."

With that, I died.

All deaths final.

What a stupid rule.

Chapter Ten

What It Means to Be a Superhero

Death was an old friend.

I meant that literally. There were eight Primals in the multiverse and they were each a fragment of God, though the One Above was perhaps less like my rabbi had described him than I was strictly comfortable with as an observant Jew. Death ruled over all afterlives and customized them accordingly to your spirituality, sins, as well as virtues.

I was the exception.

For whatever reason, whenever I died, I tended to relieve my past and find myself wallowing in both my regrets as well as triumphs. I hadn't been lying when I told Jane that my personal hell was a boulevard of broken dreams. Which, yes, outs me as a Green Day fan. God, I just realized that "American Idiot" was sixteen years old. That would have been music from the Seventies when I was in high school. I was getting old... er. Yes, older. Not anywhere near old, just older. You were only as young as you felt and your magic kept you.

Anyway, I found myself back just a few months during the start of my career. I was not in Falconcrest City but hanging around in Atlas City, Ultragod's old pad. There was a billboard just outside of Atlas City, Florida that stuck with me. I often came out there to look at it when I needed time to think about what being a hero meant.

It was a cheerful, bright, and optimistic portrait of Ultragod and Ultragoddess standing before an art deco skyline of the city. Underneath their smiling heroic poses were the words,

"Welcome to the Hope of Superheroes." It was a transparent reference to the Magic Kingdom that was about forty miles due East of the city called the "New Amsterdam of the South" and unnecessary since until recently it was one of the most thriving cities in America. Well, circumstances had changed.

The brightly colored billboard was now cracked and faded with pieces peeling off in the smog-laden air. Graffiti had marred the optimistic portrait with the words ULTRAGOD IS DEAD over Ultragod's features in neon pink and WHORE over Ultragoddess in purple letters. The slogan at the bottom was further changed with a strike through its last word, changing it to WELCOME TO THE HORROR OF SUPERVILLAINY.

Title drop.

The skyline of Atlas City had changed from a bunch of beautiful WW2-era structures designed to show the best of human achievement to glittering cyberpunk-esque towers of steel and glass. The sun was setting behind them and made them look like dark and menacing black obelisks. They loomed over the increasingly large slums of the city as alien, Super, and regular old human refugees crowded the city out.

Atlas City was a refugee center a la Ellis Island designed to process people fleeing from their home planets. Unfortunately, that no longer was viable due to the backlash following President Omega's coup with alien mercenaries. Worse, the economy of Atlas City had tanked following the death of Ultragod and investors no longer trusted it to be a safe place for their money since the only superhero watching over the city was, well, me. Well, me and the Super-Duper Splotch Man.

"You suck, Merciless! Get the hell out of our city!" A teenage boy shouted before hurling a glass bottle at my head. "We don't need your kind here."

I was sitting on the guardrail of Highway 333 leading into Atlas City across the street from the abandoned tourism board building. I had my dinner of power bars and a bottle of water in my lap. It turned out waiting for crimes to happen in order to stop them was a lot less satisfying than committing them.

I turned insubstantial and let the thrown bottle pass through my head. "My kind, really? Do you mean Jewish, superhero, supervillain, or devastatingly handsome geek? Where did you learn your taunts? The terrible book of bullying clichés?"

Truth be told I was just tempted to ignore the group of teenagers that were dressed like some Eighties politician's idea of a feral teenager. They were wearing leather jackets, had punk hair styles, and were (gasp!) multiethnic (sarcastic shudder!). Honestly, I was not concerned about them and sympathized with their anti-authoritarianism. I just bored and trying to figure out what a superhero did. Atlas had a rocketing crime rate, but it wasn't like the police had any desire for my help and my powers weren't really designed to be non-lethal.

The kid didn't respond well to my taunt and pulled out a gun. "Yeah, we'll see how smart your mouth is... ah!"

I heated the gun and he dropped it on the ground. "Yes, because it's a great idea to assault the guy who has fought actual space gods. Also, really, assault with a deadly weapon? Do you know what they do to pretty boys like you in prison? I'll tell you. They bake you a cake and treat you with great dignity and respect."

"Huh?" The kid asked, looking confused.

"Except not!" I snapped. "Now leave me alone or I'll turn you into toads. Which I can do, because magic!"

I made several elaborate but meaningless hand gestures. I couldn't actually turn people into toads because I hadn't yet adapted *Polymorph Other* into my new magical system. I was only to second level spells.

"Let's get him!" Another one of the teens shouted. He was an obese Asian kid taller than the rest. "Superheroes can't hurt people!"

"I heard he's actually a supervillain!" A young teenage Asian girl with pink hair said. She was a good deal younger and reminded me of my niece. I suspected she was the fat one's sister by their similar faces.

Another picked up a crowbar.

I conjured a wand made of ice and pointed it at their direction. "Avada Krev—"

"Ah! It's the killing curse!" the obese kid shouted and ran.

Everyone else joined him except the pink-haired girl who stopped to look at me.

"Thanks for saving the world a couple of times! My mom has your poster!" Pinkie said, before running away. "She'd totally give you a BJ!"

I waved back, not bothering to look at her. "Uh, thanks."

"Reduced to harassing street kids now?" Cindy's voice spoke in my earpiece. My daughter, Leia, had constructed it from spare parts to keep in touch with everyone on missions. I hadn't had the heart to tell her that cell phones already existed.

"Hey, they were harassing me," I snapped. "Also, what ever happened to the lost art of tagging? There should be elaborate murals and social critiques on the walls here. Instead, we've got some insults to Ultragod and Ultragoddess. It's like no one takes any pride in their work. Hell, the abandoned tourism board next to me still has unbroken windows."

"You are terrible at this," Cindy said.

"Says you," I said, shrugging. "Listen, I don't want to harass people. I'll save lives and go after professional criminals, but these guys are harmless."

It was conveniently ignoring one had tried to shoot me in the face. That was a sign he was probably not going anywhere but prison or the morgue. There was nothing I could do about that, though. It's not like I was qualified to inspire people to be their best self and any "scared straight" speech about avoiding juvenile delinquency would be undermined by the fact I was a billionaire due to disorganized crime. You can grow up to be anything you want to, kids, as long as you take advantage of systemic bias or rob the people involved in it.

"Gary, how much crime are you ignoring?" Cindy asked.

"Well, I don't go after drug dealers. I don't go after prostitutes. I stopped three cops from shooting a guy they thought had a gun, who turned out to actually have a gun and had just robbed a gas station. He really needed the money, though, and the gas station was a front for human trafficking! So, I stopped that!"

"That's good, I guess," Cindy said, sounding skeptical. "You know this city has several dozen supervillains operating in it, right? That's part of the reason you chose it. Gabrielle apparently has better things to do than protect her father's old city."

"The Super-Duper Splotch Man has that mostly under control," I replied.

"You don't have to say Super-Duper Splotch Man, you can just say Splotch," Cindy said.

"I don't think I can," I replied. "Otherwise people might not use my trademark when I call myself Merciless: The Superhero without MercyTM. Which is not a great brand for a hero but I'm not changing it."

The Super-Duper Splotch Man was the hardest working superhero in the business and the least appreciated. He'd been empowered with obscuromancy, or shadow magic, by bonding with an alien being from a lightless dimension. He could conjure extra limbs, shoot blasts of mystical darkness, and even make crude constructs. He was a man of living inky black energy but one of the brightest most optimistic heroes in the world. You know, when the papers were not calling him a menace or trying to blame him for the crimes he stopped.

Atlas City had grown accustomed to a special kind of hero in the Ultragod family and just did not warm up to its other hometown hero. He was too flawed, too weak, and too street level compared to their champion. Then again, given how they were mourning Ultragod, maybe it was just that the people of Atlas City were assholes. Mind you, this was technically the third Splotch as father had passed it down to son since the Sixties. They were all wise-cracking, heroic, and self-sacrificing types, though.

The Super-Duper Splotch continued working day and night, seven days a week, to protect the city, though. Sometimes he failed and people died. Sometimes he got beaten and hospitalized. He'd had his secret identity exposed a few times too. I wasn't sure how he put that particular genie back in the bottle, but it was a reminder that not everyone had an unbroken record of wins to losses. I admit, I was one of like ten kids growing up who bought his merchandise. I still had an adult pair of Splotch underoos I'd bought on sale at Ultramart.

"That's not the point, Gary," Cindy said. "Superheroes beat up supervillains. It's kind of our thing."

"Eh, I got a bunch of the C-Listers jobs at Omega Corp: The Brown Anemone, the Soccer Ball (known as El Football everywhere else), the Purple Hippo, and the Leapin' Leapfrog are all doing pretty well. I paid off Sexy White Rabbit Girl's legal fees with *Playboy* too. Really, she just needed to change to Sexy Brown Rabbit Girl. It's really got down on the redactivism in the city."

I could hear Cindy feeling her face. "You've been getting supervillains legitimate jobs, Gary?"

I shrugged. "They work in corporate security so I wouldn't say legitimate. Mind you, a couple of them tried to rob the place but that's what insurance is for. I'm actually supervising about forty more applications from other ex-cons. The problem is convincing them that I'm *not* starting a crew."

It helped that, having been on the other side of the curtain, I could tell the difference between which supervillains were professionals trying to make a dishonest buck versus the hardcore monsters. The former might—and frequently did—end up hurting people because of bad luck or trying to stay out of jail, but the latter got off on mayhem even when it made things worse for everyone. It was like the movies *Heat* or *Reservoir Dogs*. There was always that one psychopath you never wanted to work with. I had a reputation for killing those guys in the supervillain world and it actually left me with some lingering goodwill despite my turn to heroism.

"Want me to give you something actual evil to fight?" Cindy asked, sounding surprisingly happy.

Cindy had decided to go semi-straight rather than fully straight, which was good because she was anything but. Cindy targeted the rich, powerful, and corrupt in the city before robbing them blind with an unknown partner. I didn't bother to question her on this because, well, I didn't care. If she wanted to tell me who she was working with then she could. The fact we didn't need the money was immaterial as sometimes the heist was its own reward.

"Ooo, how evil? Murderer? Child abuser? Guy who leaves his dog in a hot car? Because that last one is murder-worthy offense."

"Kidnapping," Cindy said, cheerfully. "The mayor has been kidnapped by the Red Condor."

"Which Red Condor? There's been like five."

"The original! He came out of retirement last year. Apparently, a vast fortune of stolen goods runs out eventually, especially with today's medical bills. A million dollars in the Seventies isn't the same as a million dollars today."

"Cool, cool," I said, not particularly concerned about dealing with a mid-level crook like the Red Condor. "What's the ransom?"

"It's not a ransom thing. He's going to take the mayor out to the swamps and feed her to his pet alligators."

I blinked. "Well that's just not in theme at all. Also, why is he in Florida? Shouldn't he be based in California or Arizona?"

"Eh, you go where the work is. I figure this is a chance for you to get some good publicity."

"It's not about the publ—"

I was interrupted from saying more by an armored limousine flying down the highway at ninety miles per hour while a jetpack-wearing, armored, orange birdman zipped behind it. Police cars were following them, only for the Red Condor to spin around and fire half a dozen micro-rockets that caused the vehicles to explode.

I looked over at the sight. "You could have told me they were right next to me!"

"Oh, are they? Well maybe I would have if you'd just shut up and let me speak!"

I smiled. "Love you."

"Love you too," Cindy said. "Now don't tell anyone or I will hunt you down and kill you."

"Even our daughter?" I asked.

"*Especially* our daughter. She might grow up respecting me and that's just asking for trouble. Now go chase the bad guy as I have a Ming vase to steal. Someone else here wants to say they love you."

"Who?" I asked.

"Shut up!" a female voice on the other line said. "I'm not ready."

The phone connection cut out.

"Okay, that was weird," I muttered and took off into the air. Flying wasn't really one of my powers, but I could levitate and if you levitated sideways, well, that was flying. I also had learned to pump up my speed significantly since acquiring a couple of obscenely powerful magical artifacts that I couldn't use but gave me a niece boost.

"Ha, ha, ha! No one can stop me now, not even Ultragoddess!" The Red Condor said, laughing.

The Red Condor (aka Jose Juan Cortez) was a sphere bald man in his seventies, wearing a pair of aviator goggles that worked well for his fire-colored costume. I recalled reading about him fighting Ultragod growing up with my father's 'history comics' only to have him transition to being one of Gabrielle's (aka Ultragoddess) rogues. Personally, I felt that a guy with a jetpack and explosive feathers was a poor match for people who could move the moon out of orbit but that's how the game worked these days. Sometimes you were the underdog and sometimes you were the boot instead of the ant.

"Uh, actually she's in Afghanistan right now," I said, coming up behind the man. "Props for the classic villainy lines, though. You're a bit dated in your slang, though. Maybe it's an Atlas City, though, though. I think I heard a gang of thugs call murdering a guy a swell way to pass the time."

"Ugh, Merciless," the Red Condor said, like I was a roach crawling across his shoe. Well, if he had shoes and was not flying at high speeds I could barely catch up with. Indeed, I was having to turn insubstantial while we flew just so the wind didn't blind me. This was why flying superheroes tended to be invulnerable. There was no real point to it if you blinded yourself with windburn.

"Yeah, sorry to disappoint," I said, glad to be dealing with an honest-to-god supervillain again. I wasn't invited to the parties anymore and I hadn't realized just how much I'd miss it until I wasn't anymore.

"You can't get in on this. This is my plot!" the Red Condor shouted back.

"Wait, what?" I asked.

"I am going to kill Ultragoddess! You got lucky by killing her father. Personally I don't believe it, but I am going to cement my legacy by killing his daughter!"

I blinked. "Wait, you think *I* killed him?"

"Yes, obviously," the Red Condor as he turned along the edge of the ocean with the limousine beneath him. "Didn't you?"

I was so used to no villains taking me seriously, I'd forgotten it was still a rumor that I'd been the triggerman for Ultragod's death. You know, instead of the guy who looked identical to me. Given Moses Anders had been my close friend, I was engaged to Ultragoddess, and I didn't want everyone who wasn't a supervillain to hate me, I wasn't inclined to confirm it. As such, plenty of other people had filled in the gaps with stories about secret government conspiracies, lone gunmen, new supervillains, or jackasses like the Glue Man willing to take the credit.

"Let's put a pin in that for a moment," I said, pausing. "Your plan is to kidnap the mayor and kill her in order to lure Ultragoddess into a trap so you can kill her, too?"

I mentioned earlier the Red Condor was an old guy in an armored flight suit. The guy was in decent shape for his age and probably could tear into most superheroes who, you know, weren't able to fly or were invulnerable. However, this seemed a bit like the mouse going after the lion. Ultragoddess had a few weaknesses like her father—Ultranium and magic—but nothing that was readily available to even your above average crook. It was about the only reason that I didn't feel inclined to break the guy's neck since I didn't take threats to my loved ones well. (Finger wag) Superhero (finger wag) or not.

"Obviously!" The Red Condor said. "She has Ultra-Hearing so I can lure her back to the city via the mayor's murder. Also, the jackass has promised to be tougher on supervillain crime. You know who that's prejudiced against, right?"

"Minorities?"

"Supervillains!" The Red Condor said. "So, once they're both dead, we'll run this town!"

I debated telling the Red Condor that whenever a

supervillain killed a superhero, that resulted in the entirety of superherodom descending to kick your ass. It had happened to me and I was about the only one still alive. Superheroes tended to be unable to save the villains from collapsing buildings, fires, or suspicious takings of their own lives. Funny how villains committing suicide seemed to happen most often when it couldn't be verified.

"Yeah, well, I'm afraid I'm going to have to stop—" I started to say.

I was about to take the guy down when an energy blast sailed right into his jet pack before another one went through his head.

Then they started being fired at me.

An arrogant synthesized spoke behind me. "PREPARE TO BE TERMINATED, SUPERVILLAIN."

Oh shit, the government had sent their Super Hit Squad after me. Yeah, did I mention one of those existed now?

Chapter Eleven

My Favorite Superhero (After Gabrielle)

"Mother puss bucket!" I said, feeling the heat of an energy blast that sent me flying out of the air.

I was insubstantial but some frequencies of energy should penetrate my magic. Yes, Super-Science was catching up with sorcery—isn't that great? Yaaay. It burned the side of my cloak and against my flesh before sending me spiraling down toward the ground at speeds I was not terribly comfortable with hitting the ground.

"Ouch, damn, crap, hell, fudge!" I said, bouncing into a lesser city park near the highway. The ocean was visible beyond the edge of the highway and I had to admit a certain fondness for the view even as I felt like every bone in my body was aching.

Who the hell was attacking me? Who killed the Red Condor? That was when my attention turned to the sight of the person I'd come here to rescue. An explosion occurred right in front of the limousine containing the Condor's henchmen and the kidnapped mayor. The attack, probably a missile, sent it flying over the guardrail before doing three flips across the ground. It landed about thirteen feet away from me with its driver's seat completely crushed and henchman juice leaking out the side.

"Yeah, I'm pretty sure the mayor is dead," I muttered, spitting up some blood on the ground. "You know, ever since I got my healing factor, I get my ass kicked a lot more."

That was when I heard a jetpack settle down behind me. I turned my head and saw a chrome armored figure with a smooth faceplate. He was also wearing a cape. In his hands was an energy rifle with a rocket launcher attached to his rocket pack. Honestly, he looked like a just barely copyright friendly version of Jango Fett.

"Well if it isn't Merciless," a familiar voice spoke on the other end. It had a thick rural Florida twang filtered through a voice synthesizer. It was rather unmistakable. "This is going to be a red-letter day down at VICE."

I coughed. "Scarab?"

The voice was of the Chrome Scarab, aka Jim Jameson, a C-List supervillain that wasn't even up to the Red Condor's level. He was also one of the people I'd recruited to serve on the side of good. He'd railed on me for being a snitch, traitor, turncoat, and other nastier words until I pointed out he actually made less than minimum wage after expenses as well as jailtime. Maintaining jetpacks being expensive, no matter how many ATMs you robbed in a day. I'd set him up with Darklight Security and a new job to get him off the street.

Unfortunately, the Chrome Scarab had proven to be one of the latter in the professional criminal versus psychopath distinction. Even being a mercenary for an organization that regularly broke international law hadn't been enough to satisfy his inner bloodlust. Last I'd heard, he'd accepted a government contract and hopefully would put his inner psychopath to good use. I should have remembered there was no such thing under a government still rebuilding after President Omega's takeover.

"It's Rocketdeath now," Jim said, his voice low and threatening. "I'm getting top of the line superhero technology now that I work for the government. Also, I get to keep the toy money and t-shirts. You did me a solid. Too bad I have to kill you now. You're still registered as a supervillain, ya know?"

That was another thing making my days (as well as nights) harder. The Society of Superheroes and the Department of Supernatural Security were not on the same page these days. Superheroes had been briefly outlawed under President Karl Trust and while he'd rolled that back, they were still under pretty strict guidelines. I might have a pardon and be on the right side of the law with the SOS, but the cops didn't see it that way. Indeed, some jackass had actually posted a million-dollar bounty for bringing me in. The only reason more supervillains didn't try to do it was because, well, as stupid as some were, most realized that when you call the Feds you get pinched too.

However, as bad as the DSS was and a pain in the ass for superhumans, there was one group within it that was even worse: VICE. The Variant Intelligence Collective Enforcement agency. Which was one of those acronyms that came before what it supposedly stood for. They were guys who existed to track down Supers, search for their families, and tag anyone who could gain superpowers. They also went after aliens, magic-users, shifters, what few undead remained, and anything else that qualified as a variant from mundane humans. Lots of them were interred without trial, others deported from the planet or dimension, and even more separated from their families. It was the group that would have tried to take Leah and Mindy from me and Cindy.

"Rocketdeath?" I asked, getting up slowly. I felt like I was on fire and hated the fact that Jim had weapons that could hurt me. I'd help get him those, goddammit. "That's what you're going with, really?"

Jim's back straightened and he looked to one side. "Listen, on the street you can just choose whatever codename you want, but all of the good ones are taken when you're a hero. Literally millions of them have been trademarked. Some heroes have to rent theirs out from any dweeb who has five hundred bucks to reserve the rights. They even have a form online."

"Why did you kill the Red Condor?" I asked, already knowing the answer.

"Uh, duh, because he's a supervillain. It's my job as a cop."

"You're not a cop," I said, disgusted.

"Close enough," Jim said, chuckling.

I felt my face. "Wasn't he your friend? You were part of the Syndicate Seven a while back?"

"You know what they say, all's fair in love and making a lot of money. The bounty for the Red Condor was fifty grand."

"You can't collect a bounty for a dead man," I said, sighing. "This isn't the Old West. Also, you just killed the mayor."

I wasn't about to point out that as a government employee,

he wasn't allowed to collect the bounties that the United States had put up for supervillains either. The government had tried to come to my mansion to collect both me and my child last year, part of the reason why I was in Atlas City now, and I'd successfully managed to intimidate them. Unfortunately, that had also resulted in the death of at least one Federal agent after he'd threatened my kids. It was why I wasn't going to be a part of the Society of Superheroes anytime soon.

I'd live.

Honestly, facing down Rocketdeath here made me excited. He wasn't the evil that Cindy had sent me down here to face but was one I would have absolutely no difficulty beating the living hell out of. I couldn't put him in prison, but I was pretty sure breaking every bone in his body would keep him from anymore murder sprees. Maybe that was my problem: I was too focused on guys on the wrong side of the law when the real nasties hid behind money and power.

"Eh, I'm pretty sure my bodycam will show *you* killing the mayor," Rocketdeath said, raising his rifle. "The benefits of dummy AI editing. Now, I must bring you in alive to get paid. Stupid laws, but I'm fairly sure I can do that without you having limbs."

See what I mean about the DSS not being on the same page? Therefore I kept having to kill the guys I wanted to redeem. "That's not how anatomy works. At all."

"Too bad," Jim said, pulling the trigger as I prepared to blast him with the full power of my magic.

I didn't get to, much to my surprise, as Rocketdeath's rifle was pulled from his arms by a inky black tentacle of pure Nega-Force. It was, apparently, something quite a lot of heroes wielded these days. Standing nearby, using insect-like legs to push himself twenty feet off the ground, was the Super-Duper Splotch Man.

"Oh, Jim, you can take the murderous mercenary out of the suit but not the suit out of the murderous mercenary. Wait, no, that makes no sense," Splotch said before launching himself forward with his extra-appendages and kicking Jim in the helmet. "Oh well, they can't all be winners."

Using my magic, I conjured a little white placard with a six point five on it. Just like if we were at the Olympics.

"A six point five?" Splotch said, shocked. "That was at least an eight and a half."

"I'm sorry but I'm not easily impressed," I said, watching Jim aim the rocket launcher on his back at us.

I proceeded to freeze it over and the object misfired, becoming a burned-out useless wreck. Really, it's impressive when you can get an object to freeze on its top when it's so hot it melts through the backpack of a "superhero" below. Jim swore a blue streak before aiming his wrist gauntlet lasers.

"So, how did you get here, Super-Duper Splotch Man?" I asked, ignoring Jim.

"You know you can just call me Splotch," Splotch said.

"Do I have to?" I asked.

"All my friends do! As for how I got here so fast, your girlfriend, Red Riding Hood, called me. I was already on my way to rescue the mayor, which, honestly doesn't seem like it's going to be happening." Splotch fired a shadow blast over his shoulder and clobbered Jim in the helmet.

I felt a little irritated at that and said so in my earpiece. "Cindy, I could handle it."

"Sure you could," Cindy replied in my ear. "Besides, with Splotch distracted, I can now rob the Atlas City Museum! Bwhahahaha."

"She sounds like a real keeper," Splotch said. "Does she have a sister."

"Not that I know of," I said. "Mind you, I'm in a polyamorous relationship."

"Ah," Splotch said. "I have three sisters. I would not surround myself with that much female energy to save my life."

"Technically, Gabrielle's dating some other dudes, but I don't know them," I replied, not entirely happy about it and feeling hypocritical.

"Fascinating!" Splotch said. "You could do a reality show."

"Kill you!" Jim shouted, pulling out a laser knife and charging at me. For an intergalactic bounty hunter and government assassin, he was awfully emotional.

I conjured ice under his feet, and he slipped on the ground like we were in a cartoon. I had to admit, I hadn't had this much fun fighting in years. "Cindy tried but it got cancelled due to her attempt to market it on that cellphone only network. She's the mother of one of my children and I love her dearly."

"And Gabrielle is the mother of your other daughter," Splotch said. "Plus, you're involved with Nighthuntress?"

That was Mandy's codename. "That's...complicated."

"More so than dating three of the most dangerous women on the planet?" Splotch said, doing a backflip then conjuring four Nega-Force tentacles with fists on their end to slap around our opponent.

"Yes," I said, not about to explain that Mandy had been my wife before she'd died, become a vampire, gotten herself possessed by the ghost of my ex-partner's sister, and then I'd sent said ghost to hell.

Rocketdeath pulled out a miniature nuclear grenade, which looked suspiciously like Boba Fett's thermal detonator, and turned it on to a six second countdown. I proceeded to grab it from his hand using my phase powers and shut it off.

"Hey!" Rocketdeath shouted. "No fair!"

"So is nuking the city!" I replied. "Area of effect attacks are cheap! It's like camping and kill stealing!"

Don't worry if you didn't get that reference, Rocketdeath did and it pissed him off as he let out a frustrated scream. He had bigger problems, though. Splotch conjured an enormous paddle, attached a Nega-Force string, and then used Jim as a ball before bouncing him back and forth.

"Well, she's in the city," Splotch said. "Apparently, she's part of some sort of heist crew that goes after the rich and evil. Maybe you should talk to her."

I didn't immediately respond to that. The wound between me and Mandy was still too raw. It didn't exactly take a rocket scientist to figure out she was probably working with Cindy. It also explained why Cindy was keeping her business to herself. You know, that and plausible deniability about her crimes while I was ostensibly trying to be a superhero. "Hmmm."

"How noncommittal!" Splotch said, finishing his defeat of Rocketdeath.

The bounty hunter fell onto the ground as his armor was now beaten to uselessness. "I give! I give!"

"Aren't you married?" I asked, walking over and looking for his armor's off-switch. Shockingly enough, the Darklight-83 combat armor had them. This is why you never hired advertising firms to design your death machines. Switching off Jim's weapons, I proceeded to remove his helmet and check to see if he was still alive. He was but he looked like was concussed all to hell.

Poor baby.

"Ten years now," Splotch said, covering the nonsensical Jim in a bunch of inky goop to hold him. I understand it dissolved after a few hours. "She's the light of my life but also why I must keep my identity secret. I'm not throwing around my name like you and Red Riding Hood."

"Yeah, well, we were criminals before we were heroes," I said, simply. "It's hard to keep a secret identity after your first arrest."

I wasn't about to tell Splotch I knew his real name was Stanley Okitd, that he was Japanese American, and that he was one of three Splotches who shared their powers across family lines. Hiro Okitd had been Splotch during the Sixties to the Eighties, his eldest son Steve had taken up the mantle from the Nineties to the New Millennium, and then Stanley replaced his brother from 2001 onward. Diabloman had figured out the secret identities of most superheroes during his days as a villain. He'd left all his notes at the Warren Estate and I'd gone through them as part of my plan to be a better superhero.

It bothered me that, if Diabloman were to go off the deep end, then there would be nothing stopping him from going after all the heroes with secret identities. Generally, people who were invulnerable like Gabrielle or Guinevere didn't bother with them. Also, most "rational" supervillains knew that as lethal as it was to kill a superhero, it was ten times worse to go after their families. Aquarius had his child murdered by Whipray the Undersea Executioner and fed the guy to a shark.

Since then, he'd personally killed virtually every supervillain who went after people's families. Some people had gotten the message, others hadn't.

"Yeah, I heard about you giving up the supervillainy thing," Splotch said. "Why?"

"Excuse me?" I asked, surprised by that.

I saw the Red Condor's corpse had landed—well crashed—nearby and decided to go check to see if there was anything salvageable. He had been a crazy old buzzard and a murderer, but no one deserved to be executed from behind like that. Well, nobody who wasn't a Nazi, slaver, or guy who abused animals.

"Well, you weren't really much of a villain, Merciless," Splotch said, continuing to talk only with our codenames. I suspected it was just force of habit at this point. "You did a lot of good for a lot of people while pretending to be a bad guy."

"I wasn't pretending," I said, simply. "It's just I wasn't quite as bad as the people around me. Being a hero isn't that far from being a villain."

Splotch didn't accept my logic. "Actually, it is literally as far from the concept as possible. It's what's called an opposite or antithesis. You learn about these things on Sesame Street or the first grade usually. Bad is not good. Up is not down. Football is not soccer, despite how many other countries get it wrong. You know."

"Yes, well I wanted to be a hero-hero," I said, pausing. "But it turns out being a hero is actually hard despite me not being much of a villain."

"Tell me about it," Splotch said. "The Splotch Family has three generations of being hated, hounded, and treated like crap. I think the one time that Ultragod ever got a negative review in the press was when he said my dad was a good man."

Much to my surprise, I found the Red Condor wasn't dead. Mostly because he was never alive. He was just a busted up and damaged android. "Well, this is weird."

"Yeah, Old Man Cortez died years ago," Splotch replied. "He's had his work carried on by Real BoyTM dolls programmed to act like him. Another one will probably pop up in a week, just as cranky as the previous ones. Personally, I'm not sure what the benefit of carrying out petty acts of terrorism and theft are as a legacy but I'm not a supervillain."

"If you love something, do it professionally," I said.

"I doubt my wife would appreciate a career as a professional lover for me," Splotch said. "I'm also not sure whether it's possible to make a living surfing the internet for news about yourself."

"Such a shame," I replied. "But yes, I want to help Atlas City but I'm just not doing a good job. Technically, I'm supposed to be undercover, but the supervillains think I'm a cop and the cops think I'm a supervillain."

"A clever plan!" Splotch said. "Well, if you'd like to go patrolling, I can show you some of my tricks for rescuing civilians while a hated rogue."

I blinked, processing that. Truth be told, I didn't have that many friends in the superhero world. I also didn't have many friends back in the normal world. I could blame it on the cold, solitary life of a supervillain but truth be told it was a combination of the fact I was an enormous jackass with the unfortunate business back at the Hollow Earth driving most of my friends away. It would be nice to be friends with someone who, masked menace or not, was a guy I'd admired since childhood.

"Yeah, I think that would be good," I said. "I'm doing something wrong and I could use some advice on making it right."

"Being a hero is *trying* to do what's right, not necessarily succeeding."

"That sounds like terrible advice."

"What did being a supervillain get you?"

"Billions of dollars, true love, and two children. Oh, and I saved the world on multiple occasions."

Splotch paused. "I feel like there's a lesson here but not one I necessarily want to learn."

"Evil will always triumph over good because good is dumb."

Splotch laughed and made finger guns. "Ha-ha. You made a reference to a movie and that is somehow funny because it's a thing I recognize."

Yeah, there was a wee bit of criticism there.

"I'm sensing I may have to up my humor game," I said.

"Welcome to the big leagues, kid," Splotch replied, ignoring that he was my age. "It's not about how strong, fast, or heroic you are. It's all about the quips and I am the Master."

"See, I'd have said I am your Mister Miyagi."

"And that is why you fail," Splotch said, adopting a Yoda voice.

We didn't get to talk more because Mayor Melanie Spencer crawled out of the wreckage of the car, seemingly no worse for wear. The woman stared daggers at both of us and began shouting at a level I didn't think possible for someone of her frame. "This is what's ruining our city! Criminal hooligans like you two! I'll see you all arrested! Do you think Atlas City has problems with superheroes now? Well, just wait—"

Splotch pointed at her. "See, this is why I don't bother trying to get people to like me."

"My history with politicians is mixed," I said. "You know, what with the time traveling Nazi president."

"We don't speak of him anymore," Splotch said, taking off. "Last one to the center of the city is a rotten egg."

"And you're supposed to teach me about quips?" I said, taking off behind him.

"Hey, don't leave me here!" Mayor Spencer shouted from behind us.

Chapter Twelve

Friendly Neighborhood Merciless Man

The glittering part of Atlas City was called New Town and it was a place where the rich had every advantage of super-technology, alien cuisine, and private security that specialized in dealing with all manner of dangers the police couldn't deal with. While Ultragod was alive, he'd done his best to guilt the one percent into donating enough of their fortunes to keep the destitute from starving in the streets or dying from untreated diseases.

That time had passed.

Now most of the city's poorer citizens dwelled in Old Town with a minimum amount of attention from the rest of the city. Yeah, I know, what original geniuses the city planners were. Old Town was where the city's poor had been gradually driven by rising housing costs, prejudice, and the influx of refugees. There were Supers who thought Atlas City would accept them, aliens feeling from wars, and the old-fashioned kind of displaced person who had struggles going on at home.

It was here, unsurprisingly, that superheroes could make a difference. It was also a reminder of what I used to use my money to try and alleviate. It had done wonders in Falconcrest City, but I'd lost the way somewhere and ended up focusing on having wild adventures more than trying to make the world a better place. It was doubly embarrassing when Splotch and I passed by a billboard for Omega Corporation showing my sister's face. In six months', time, she'd turned around the corporation I'd stolen from President Omega and turned it into the world's number one eco-friendly techno-solutions firm. I had no idea what that meant but apparently, they did a lot of good with science.

"So, what do you do down here?" I asked, watching Splotch use his black tentacles to cling to the side of the walls like a fast-moving centipede.

"It's a mistake to assume the majority of superhero work is fighting supervillains," Splotch said, leading me deeper into the region. There was a pulse and energy to the community below that surprised me. Contrary to New Town's depiction of Old Town as a crime-ridden cesspool in need of bulldozing for a richer, paler class of citizen to come in, I saw a lot of people just living out their lives. Aliens, humans, Supers, and children of some mixture were just getting along. There was even an enormous graffiti art picture of Ultragoddess giving a thumbs up on the side of one apartment building.

"Yes, there are also mobsters, muggers, and mimes," I replied, flying behind Splotch. I'd been able to temporarily keep up with the Condor, but I was much more comfortable flying at a speed of around thirty miles an hour. Which, frankly, was fairly good given the traffic in this city.

"Punching mimes is important," Splotch said, cheerfully. "However, I come from a school of thought that even if there weren't supervillains or criminals in general then there would always be a place for superheroes."

"How's that?" I asked.

That was when I heard a ringing underneath Splotch's "costume" that I understood to be a second skin of Nega-Force energy. "Oops, some of the locals have sent me a Chitter."

"You have a Chitter feed?" I asked.

"Yep!" Splotch said. "Two actually. One that is my public one and is full of spam and hate messages as well as my private one. That I pass out to people around town I trust. They tell me when something bad is happening and I need to help."

"Like a Splotch Signal?" I asked.

"What do you think this is, a superhero movie?" Splotch asked.

I snorted.

"But basically, yeah," Splotch said. "One of my friends just told me there's a fire nearby and the fire department was mysteriously blocked by traffic. A lot of people are in danger."

"Mind if I help?" I asked.

Splotch chuckled. "No, Merciless, I would not like the help of someone who can turn insubstantial, fly, and conjure ice in evacuating a burning building."

"Just to be clear, that's sarcasm, right?" I asked.

Splotch just headed right. I followed him and saw the apartment complex was something like thirty stories. It was ridiculously large and like something out of Judge Dredd. It had also multiple fires burning from different points throughout the building and looked like someone had set off several incendiary devices. There were probably a couple of thousand people living inside the place and they were in deep need of help. I ended up catching someone who was trying to get out through her window before depositing her to the ground.

I'd like to say there was something heroic or glamorous about the whole thing, but it was actually hard, nasty, and gritty work. There were already places where people had died of smoke inhalation, burned to death, or perished in the initial explosions. Lots of the building was uninhabitable by the end and I didn't do nearly as much to make things better as I wanted.

Still, at the end, I had to say there were few times in my life that I'd ever felt more satisfied with what I'd done. In the end, Splotch didn't stay for the accolades and departed as soon as the city's services had things under control. I ended up following him, exhausted, and a little lightheaded. It was past sundown, and I was late in returning home.

"How often does that happen?" I asked.

"What? The local crime lords trying to burn out the locals so they can buy up the land or rescuing people in general?"

"Err...both?"

"More often than I'd like," Splotch said, moving through the night as the moon hung above. "Mind you, tomorrow morning the papers will probably say I set the explosives."

"Why do they hate you so damned much?" I asked. "You being the bad guy seems the definition of fake news."

Splotch stopped on top of a building with a large neon sign that said ACME WAREHOUSING. "That's a long story."

I checked my cellphone. "Well, I'm about two hours behind and my daughters are going to be extra mad I missed story time. So, I might as well be late."

"That is terrible parenting," Splotch said.

I shrugged. "Probably but I wasn't going to abandon a bunch of other parents with their kids."

Splotch paused and leaned up against an air conditioning unit. "The short version is my dad made a lot of mistakes in the Sixties. One of them was betraying himself."

I blinked. "The original Splotch was a supervillain?"

"No," Splotch said. "My father was scientist who wanted to be a superhero more than anything else in the world. He was a nerdy science wiz and being both poor as well as Japanese American came with its own issues. He made an experiment to give himself superpowers and tapped into the Nega-Force."

"The opposite of the Ultra-Force," I said, making a note for any readers in other dimensions. "What gave Ultragod his powers."

"Yeah, that made people suspicious when they heard about it. Also, the fact that powers associated with darkness meant that people tended to be suspicious. It didn't help my father was always challenging other superheroes to fights."

"I thought that was what every superhero did. There's just an innate need to kick each other's ass whenever you meet a new superhero for the first time."

Splotch paused. "Oh my God, you're right. We completely forgot the pointless throwdown part of our first meeting!"

"Dammit!" I said, slapping my head. "We totally screwed this up."

"We need to fix it immediately," Splotch said, making a fist.

I did too. "On the count of three?"

"You got it," Splotch said. "One, two, three. Shoot!"

"Scissors!"

"Rock!" Splotch said.

"Dammit," I said. "You win this time, Splotch, but I will have my revenge."

He chuckled. "Yeah, well, you'll win the rematch. That's usually how these meetings go. You don't just get one fight. You have to fight twice in one day."

"We can do a dance off next," I said.

"Oh, no, there's no way you're winning that," Splotch said. "You are the whitest supervillain I know."

"In Florida? I'm pretty sure that's Johnny Rebel or the Klansman." I, of course, had them on my hit list. Not that I had a hit list. No sir. That wouldn't be a very superheroic thing to have at all.

"Fair enough," Splotch said. "I'd still kick your ass in a dance off."

"It still doesn't explain why your father and you are hated," I said. "It sounds like he just would be considered a bit edgy."

Splotch didn't respond.

"It's a personal subject," Splotch said, looking up at the sky. "Pretty hard to share."

"Well, my brother was killed by Shoot-Em-Up in front of me and I ended up killing him at age fourteen. It's left me permanently traumatized."

"Okay, that may be oversharing," Splotch said. "Especially for a first team up."

"I'm sorry, I always come on a bit strong."

Splotch sucked in his breath. "My dad's first wife was killed by a supervillain. Samhain got lucky and killed her with a jack-o-lantern bomb. So, Dad made a deal with the Crime King to find him. He beat Samhain to death."

"Sounds like justice to me," I said, being honest. "I'm not a guy who judges the person who kills a murderer the same as the murderer. Black and white morality is not my thing."

"Then maybe superheroism isn't for you," Splotch said. "Better to be a good supervillain than a bad hero."

"There's more to the story isn't there?" I asked.

Splotch nodded. "My dad did a lot of things to make up for the favor he owed the Crime King. Never anything overtly evil. Go beat up these criminals here, go avoid these areas where things are victimless crimes, and maybe just distract Ultragod. In the end, when my father finally said enough, the

Crime King revealed all his activities. He'd kept meticulous details and proof that showed my father was dirty. After that, everyone just took the worst interpretation of anything we did."

"I'm sorry," I said, meaning it. "I know what it's like for a good person to get caught up in events beyond their control."

I wasn't sure if I meant Keith, Diabloman, Cindy (okay, that was stretching it), or myself. My brother had failed the test to become a Navy SEAL but he'd put that training to use to become a thief. First because it was a way to provide for his family and later because he was good at it. I used to think he was the coolest man on the planet when he was Stingray: The Underwater Assassin. Instead, he'd died ashamed of the path he'd took and unable to make amends for what he'd done.

"It's okay, I don't do this for the fame or glory," Splotch said. "I do this because I want to help people."

"You're the real deal, Splotch," I said. "You remind me of Lancel and Moses."

"You're on first name bases with the Nightwalker and Ultragod?" Splotch asked.

"The first was trapped in my cloak for years and the latter was my father-in-law," I said, ignoring the fact Gabrielle kept finding reasons to delay our wedding. It was starting to give me a complex. If she didn't want to marry me then I wish she'd just say it. I did want to get married, but I'd understand if it wasn't something she could do.

For whatever reason.

"I feel like you maybe should be the one mentoring me," Splotch muttered. "Maybe I should get in on this billionaire supervillain thing."

"Eh, I gave all my money to my sister," I said, pointing over to her billboard. "Kerri is much better at managing all the vast fortunes I've stolen. I'm now on a strictly regimented allowance of mere millions."

"Oh, you poor baby. I barely make ends meet thanks to my wife being a model."

"You complaining?" I asked.

"No." I could see the grin under his mask despite it being

completely opaque. "You should probably head back to your family, Gary."

"I will," I said, nodding. "It's good working with you, Splotch."

"Thanks. It's been a while since I've had a partner. I used to do a lot of team-ups with Gabrielle, but she hasn't visited the city in a long while."

"She's been...busy."

Truth be told, a part of me suspected Gabrielle didn't want to return to Atlas City. It was her father's city and while she'd been raised in it, there was nothing but memories of her long-dead family here. It bothered me that her living family was living here, though, and that wasn't enough to bring her back. She visited all the time but deliberately avoided spending more than a day at a time and always prevented the locals from knowing she was here. In a city dying for lack of heroes to inspire them, it was a conspicuous absence.

"I bet," Splotch said, sounding sad. "Well, if you see her again, tell her we miss her in the Big Orange."

"That's Tampa," I replied.

"So, they claim," Splotch said, taking off into the night. I hoped he got back to his home safely and that he was met by a family every bit as loving as the wall-springer deserved.

Turning around, I went floating through the air of Old Town and thought about what I'd done today. It was strange how Splotch had made me realize a few things that I'd somehow forgotten along the way to trying to be a superhero. Specifically, that this was never supposed to be about the fame. It was supposed to be about revenge. Then it was about the people. I'd achieved my revenge against Shoot-Em-Up and countless others who'd wronged me. Maybe it was time to start working on the other thing.

Protecting people.

Which made Splotch's death all the more gross and unfair. Six months after our first team up, the Super-Duper Splotch Man got killed trying to talk down a mentally ill man the police were going to shoot due to feeling threatened. It hadn't even been the mentally ill man who'd done it, no, it had been the police being twitchy and over-armed with military surplus from the Foundation for World Harmony. I'd attended his funeral, met his family, and watched his young biracial son take on the mantle. Before my deal, he would have ended up alive as a clone or resurrected by a cosmic entity or brought back via time travel. Now he was just dead, and the world was a worse place for it.

It wasn't right.

I deserved to be in the ground instead.

Maybe that was justice.

Lies, a voice spoke in my mind. *Death is not a punishment. It is a transition. You of all people should know that?*

Death? I asked, speaking into a featureless white void. I was now immaterial, lacking even a body, and surrounded by nothing. *Is that you?*

I hadn't seen Death since the tournament. I'd honestly felt abandoned by my former master and it had only added to my sense that I'd made a mistake. I'd made Death the ruler of the Primals until the next tournament was hosted in a thousand years, but I hadn't really thought through the consequences. A part of me had felt used.

I'm always with you, Gary, Death replied. *I'm with everyone at every moment of every second. The beginning and the end.*

Well, that's not creepy, I thought back, sarcastically. *I'm not sure what I'm supposed to do.*

Whatever you want, Death replied. *That is my gift to you. This universe is yours now.*

What? I asked.

You are the one who made the wish, Death replied. *You are the only one who can undo it. I crowned you the God of Death for this universe, just as I crowned many others in other dimensions. The good, the bad, and the damned are determined by you. If you wish to bring back the dead, then it is within your power now. Ironic, when you spent years seeking a way to bring back your wife, you only gain the power when you know she wished to move on.*

Why tell me this? I asked, feeling like she'd punched me in the gut. *When it's too late.*

Oh Gary, you're not dead, Death said. *You're far too stubborn for that.*

With that I woke up to a vampire's fangs in my neck.

Chapter Thirteen

Camp Blood on Beautiful Slaughter Lake

There was a slight difference between the vampires of my world and the vampires of Jane's Earth. On Jane's Earth, vampires were sex symbols and their bites induced mind-blowing orgasmic bliss akin to heroin mixed with a *Star Wars* sequel that didn't suck. Normally, on my world, vampire bites hurt like hell and usually ended with you dead on the floor.

Vampires could hypnotize you into feeling pleasure but that was not really the same thing. It was part of the reason that they'd remained feared monsters on my world rather than become a *Twilight*-esque phenomenon. Well, you know, outside of *Twilight*. The one-time Mandy had bitten me, it had hurt like a mothersucker.

This was not like that.

No, instead, this was much more like I'd wanted the prequels and sequels to be like. The phrase "better than sex" gets thrown around a lot and really depends on who you're with as well as how talented you are at it but even with a skilled partner you like, this was definitely better than sex. I suddenly understood why Jane kept complaining about how vampires had effectively taken over her world via social media and good marketing. If this was what the undead could do, no wonder people were signing up to be bled dry. Hell, paying for it. I bet the first nibble was free too.

As someone who had more self-control and willpower than you'd probably imagine from looking at me, I wasn't about to just about to lie there and be bled dry. I was no man's Capri Sun and I managed to summon the willpower to reach around the neck of whoever was biting me and give their hair an enormous tug. Not the most elegant of martial arts move but there was a reason most superheroines kept their hair short unless they were indestructible.

"Ow!" an awfully familiar female voice spoke after her fangs broke free from my skin. "What the hell, Gary?!"

"Mandy?" I asked, leaking out of my neck.

Random aside, but there's something about vampire saliva that serves as an anti-coagulant. Seriously, if vampires didn't slow down the flow of blood then biting an artery would result in a geyser akin to *Dracula: Dead and Loving* it as well as immediate death. It'd also be like drinking from a fire hose. I bring that up because otherwise I'd be dead, and this would be a book narrated by my ghost. Which was possible but not how this story was going to end, at least here.

I was lying on top of a bed in the middle of a log cabin underneath a window letting in the moon's light onto my face. The cabin was full of junk and looked like it had been recently used for storage. It wasn't very large and maybe had two rooms. Straddling me, wearing her catsuit and trench coat, was my wife (ex-wife? We never really divorced but she died?) Mandy. Mandy's hair had changed from raven black to stark white and she was wearing a domino mask. It was a slight change to her costume but was still a noticeable one.

Standing just to the side of the bed, looking embarrassed, was Jane. Jane had changed out of her normal clothes to a pair of shorts, boots, and a white t-shirt that said, COUNSELOR. She was holding a freshly carved wooden staff in her hand and it looked like she'd burned some crude runes into the side.

"Okay, what the hell is going on?" I asked, not feeling like getting up. Mandy's bite had left me paralyzed, or maybe I was just suffering massive blood loss. Then again, that was a remarkable improvement over death.

"*Cure Serious Wounds!*" Jane shouted, waving her staff over me. "*Cure Serious Wounds! Cure Serious Wounds!*"

I felt an immediate sense of relief as well as a return of my previous energy. So much so, I was able to relax. I could also feel my own magic had returned without Sheriff Injustice there to drain it, which was a relief. It almost made up for the fact that I woke up being Mandy's Capri Sun juice bag.

Mandy spit to the side. "I've been sucking out the alien poison in your blood for the past half hour while Jane kept you from dying."

"I tried *Neutralize Poison* but apparently that's not a high enough level spell for an alien redneck parasite thingy," Jane replied.

"You're lucky I'm a spitter rather than a swallower, but you knew that," Mandy replied.

I rolled my eyes. "Yeah."

My flashback to Splotch's death and nasty beating at Sheriff Injustice's hands left me in no mood for jokes, which was a sign of the apocalypse according to some religions. There was also the fact I had no idea how to react to Mandy. When last we'd talked, I'd sucked out the ghost possessing her and banished it to Hell.

I was sure Mandy blamed me for her being possessed in the first place, though. Never mind that she had been psychotically murdering supervillains and criminals throughout Falconcrest City before she'd been possessed too. That was part of the reason I'd been so desperate to get her soul back.

Vampirism in my world differed from the kind in Jane's world in more ways than just how much of a full mast you were sporting after being bitten (or how gushy you were as a lady I presumed). No, it also differed on a metaphysical level too. On Jane's world, vampires were still fundamentally the same people they were while alive. They were undead, cursed with an inhuman hunger, and tainted with demonic magic. Pretty bad things but they were the people you knew in life for the most part.

On my world, the souls of someone transformed into a vampire were split like a wishbone. Everything that was good and pure about them ascended off to their afterlife while the negative traits they'd had in life formed into a newborn demon that inhabited the body. Imagine your best self and your worst self then have them get a divorce with the latter getting the house. It was just enough to torment the loved ones of the recently turned to maximize their pain and suffering, which was exactly what the Great Beasts intended when they made vampires.

Mandy surprised me by sliding off the bed and offering me her hand. "Are you going to be alright?"

"Uh, yeah," I said, taking it and pulling myself up. "Where the hell am I? How the hell did you get here? Oh, and thanks."

"Welcome to beautiful Camp Blood on Slaughter Lake," Jane replied. "You should use that as a name of a chapter in your next book."

"Sure," I replied, not up to thinking about another volume in my memoirs right now. "Wait, the place where all those teenagers were murdered in the Eighties?"

Satan's Hollow had a bad reputation even ignoring its crooked sheriff. The place had once been home to a bunch of undead cannibals called the Clan. Note, that's clan with a C rather than a K. Though they were probably members of that too. The Clan had stalked, murdered and ate travelers throughout the area until the Nightwalker had finally put them down. He'd done it despite Sheriff Injustice's interference and multiple attempts to reopen the summer camp by landowners who really had no concept of good taste.

"Yep," Jane said. "I'd comment on how your world is apparently ripping off horror movies now but that would be grossly hypocritical."

"Yes, yes it would," I replied. "That explains where I am and being treated for my ass-beating explains why, but it still doesn't say how."

"Cindy and I are running this place," Mandy said, crossing her arms. "William and Nancy just sort of wandered in one day. We've been using them to help fight off the ghouls, cultists, demons, and ghosts in the swamp."

I pinched the bridge of my nose as I felt a headache coming on. "Why in the world would you guys re-open up a haunted summer camp? Here of all places?"

I wanted to wrap my arms around Mandy and kiss her. Vampire or not, I'd missed her so much and didn't care if she was a demon or evil. I felt guilty about that since I'd tried—and failed—to accept Mandy's death. Her ghost had appeared to me twice to reassure me that she didn't blame me for her death. Nevertheless, I wanted to be with her and love her even as a shadow. It felt like cheating since I'd forged relationships with Cindy and Gabrielle both, which Mandy wouldn't have approved of. Still, all I could think of when I saw her was how much I missed her. I was close to tears and hoped they'd mistake it as a result of the pounding I'd taken.

"Let me show you," Mandy said, sounding nothing at all like the angry predator she'd been before her possession by Spellbinder.

Confused but owing her my life, I got up off the bed and followed her. Jane trailed up behind me and handed me her staff to help me walk. I was still weak despite her magic that helped me recover, but every second made me feel stronger. There was something about this place that had the opposite effect of Sheriff Injustice and his daughter.

I could feel the Primal Orbs again but there was something strange about them. They were reacting with a kind of manic energy that I could feel even without actively using them. There was also a lot of magical energy in this place, buried beneath the floorboards as well as swirling around in the mud below. Camp Blood was a very magical place and possibly a natural reservoir for crossed ley lines. Beyond that, and this was just me speculating, there was another one of the Primal Orbs nearby. Like, really, really close. Possibly within the confines of the camp itself. That was going to make my job much easier (and I'd probably just jinxed it).

Nevertheless, stepping out through the front door of the cabin, I was confronted by a most unusual sight. Camp Blood was in full swing despite it being past sunset and the activities going on were less s'mores or singing than Super boot camp. I saw teenagers throwing fireballs, turning into various shifters, and at least a few of them flying around. Nancy was teaching a variety of teenage girls how to use enchanted bows and arrows.

William, by contrast, was pointing to the various parts on a dummy with a curved knife. I saw some other familiar faces present here like the Trench Coat Magician, Swash! the Pirate Thief, and a surprisingly subdued Bloodscream the Retributive. There was even Splotchgirl, the daughter of my old friend, who had gotten cheated out of the legacy just because she was not a dude. Over in one fenced-off area, I saw they were conjuring illusions of giant Exterminator robots to blast.

'What in the world?" I asked, blinking at the sight.

"Camp Blood is a summer camp for Super children," Mandy replied. "Cindy and I are running it for people who can't make it to Texas Guardians institute or just don't want to be subject to all the scrutiny of the government."

"Or deal with the Evo-Lutionaries racist BS.," I replied. As bad as it was having the government trying to take away my children, the superhero side of things was almost as bad. Mindblaster and Earth Goddess had shown up at my house one day and argued it was better for my daughters to be raised in an environment among their own kind.

I'd taken that poorly.

"How the hell did you get so many?" I asked, wondering how Cindy had kept this from me. More to the point, I wondered *why* she'd hidden it.

Mandy grimaced. "I'm not going to say we launched raids on the internment camps for juvenile Super offenders, undocumented immigrants, and unregistered Supers. But we launched raids on the internment camps for them."

"Your world became like a thousand times less cool when I found out it was a place where you could be arrested for being alive," Jane said. "I'm surprised you weren't burning the places to the ground."

"I was tempted to," I replied, telling the truth. "Gabrielle convinced me it was better to try to find a legal solution. I've been funding like fifty different legal teams to try to oppose President Trust on the issue. Kerri was also working with Super Representative and former President Android John to draw attention to it."

Honestly, it felt like a weak defense to me. I'd wanted to start burning the places to the ground from the very beginning. Unfortunately, I feared making things worse for everyone. Being a superhero meant I had to be responsible for the results of my actions both good and bad. I'd straight up murdered President Omega and "saved" the day, but undoing his legacy had proven a lot bigger deal. He'd cultivated hatred and fear against Supers for eight years, and that wasn't easy to remove.

"Yeah," Mandy said. "We've been substituting surplus Foundation replidroids androids one at a time. The government has figured it out, but they'd rather pretend everything is fine rather than admit that they've lost five hundred children."

I nodded. "That's brilliant. Why here, though? I mean, Sheriff Injustice is right here."

"This place is a sorcery vortex," Mindy said, confirming my suspicions. "All the runoff from Falconcrest City's occult buildings and sorcery gathers here. No one can sense us here. As for the Sheriff, we also have rocket launchers."

"That is one way to keep the cops away," Jane said. "The *Resident Evil* solution."

"I wish I could have helped," I said.

"I wish you could have too," Mandy said.

I could sense the disapproval in her voice, though. They'd clearly been doing this under my nose and probably had been for the better part of a year. Cindy robbing the various rich jackasses of their wealth had probably been to get the seed money for this. So, being the tactless fool that I was, I decided to put the kibosh (such a great Jewish word) on this whole line of dialogue.

"So why aren't I?" I asked, dryly.

Mandy frowned. "You're too close to Gabrielle."

I blinked. I had not expected that answer. "Gabrielle? *Ultragoddess* Gabrielle?"

"Gabrielle is not who you think she is, Gary," Mandy said, sighing. "You are not going to have the relationship you want."

I narrowed my eyes. "Gabrielle is a hero. We're *engaged* now."

Mandy looked sad rather than angry or surprised. "Is that because Cindy won't marry you and I'm undead?"

I blinked. "What?"

"You know, it's statically more probable for widowed happily married men to get married quickly after rather than staying unmarried?" Mandy asked, switching topics. "They jump into new relationships because they can't live without the love they felt."

I rolled my eyes. "That's... not what happened, at all."

"Sure," Mandy said. "Like you haven't been chasing down every superheroine or villainess on Whore Island to fill the void in your life."

"Consenting Adult Sex Island," I replied. "Whore Island makes it sound nasty. Also, it's a joke on *Archer* even though it's a real place. We just call it Ibiza."

Mandy rolled her eyes. "You're not going to find happiness with Gabrielle."

"I can love more than once in my lifetime," I said. "She's someone I cared for a lot and she's open to the polyamory we had."

"Because she doesn't care about you, Gary," Mandy replied. "She's using you as a convenience. You and her other boyfriends. The only reason you're a hero is because it's easier on her to have you as a good guy rather than a villain. Worse, you're going along with her."

I narrowed my eyes. "You don't know her."

"I know she brainwashed you to cover up her secret identity, she's executed dozens of supervillains over the years, and runs a secret black ops team of ex-supervillains that overthrows governments hostile to the Society of Superheroes. Oh, and she made a pass at you while we were married. On the moon no less."

I blinked. That did sound terrible, but it was not the Gabrielle I knew. "Okay, you're putting a very negative spin on all this."

"Worse, she's trying to make you into one of her minions," Mandy said, crossing her arms. "Which is not you."

"I am not a minion!" I snapped.

"No, you aren't. You don't even keep minions," Mandy said. "You helped encourage Cindy to reach her supervillain potential and pulled Diabloman out of a rut. You supported me becoming a superhero. Gabrielle keeps everyone under her superpowered thumb. Gary, she's an antihero."

"She is *not* an antihero," I snapped.

"If she knew about this then she'd attempt to take it over and use it as a weapon," Mandy said. "I know that for a fact."

"How?" I asked.

Mandy pulled out a Primal Orb, the Primal Orb of Order, from her utility belt. I mean, her outfit did not leave room for pockets. "Because she had this after the Eternity Tournament. She had it and had been using it. Gabrielle never told you about this, though. Who knows what she's been using it for and who she's been using it on."

I stared at the object. "How did you get it?"

"I stole it," Mandy said. "I'd rather be Robin Hood than the Sheriff of Nottingham."

"We already have a Robin Hood," I replied. "He and Maid Marian are the protectors of Sherwood City in Washington."

Mandy rolled her eyes. "Not the point, Gary."

I sucked in my breath, trusting Gabrielle to have a reason for hiding this from me. Mandy had never liked Gabrielle and still blamed her for breaking my heart. There was something to her words, but I did my best to ignore it. Instead, I had another question. One that would possibly change the entire nature of our conversation.

"I believe you," I replied, sucking in my breath. "I do need to know one thing before we

continue, though."

"Yeah?" Mandy asked.

"Why are you not evil anymore?" I asked.

Chapter Fourteen

The Complicated Nature of Superhero Metaphysics

"Excuse me?" Mandy asked, as if she didn't understand the question.

I took a deep breath. "Not to make any sort of judgements, but when you were a vampire, you were like, 'I shall kill all the evil-doers and live forever, bwhahaha.' When you were possessed by Spellbinder, you were a bit more relaxed but that was not you and didn't count. Now you're, well, you-ish."

"I'm pretty me-ish, yes," Mandy said, looking confused and off-put. "Also, you should probably release Spellbinder from hell. Maria doesn't deserve that."

Jane blinked raised a finger as if to interject.

I cut her off. "Maria lied to me and impersonated you for years, possibly centuries depending how we're dealing with time travel—"

"Let's not deal with time travel and say we did," Mandy said.

"Smart move," I replied. "Sexual assault via deception is not something I'm inclined to forgive. So, yes, I sent Maria to hell."

"We were more a fusion," Mandy said. "I was there throughout all of it. Alternate futures and everything. I was the reason she fell in love with you and there was no action she could do without me. It was a bit like you and Cloak. I remind you that he was there whenever we had sex for more than a few years."

"I did my best to send him to the coffee room in the back

of my head whenever that happened," I said. "He was a good sport about that despite however long he had to go without getting any."

Jane looked like she was getting a headache. "Okay, sorry, I need to interrupt. *Gary can remove people from Hell?*"

"He's the Grim Reaper of this reality," Mandy explained without explaining. "It comes with certain perks."

"Yeah, all gods of this universe answer to the Primals," I replied. "They dictate who gets what sort of powers over the universe. Hades, Arawn, Shao Khan, and so on all have their own afterlife realms but they derive their power from Death. Demeter, Aphrodite, and Idun get their power from Life. It's all very Discworld. Personally, I try not to think about it."

Mercury Takahashi, a potent witch in her own right, had stated that my long exposure to the Reaper's Cloak and Death's power had resulted in me becoming a god. Just a really-really tiny, almost pitifully small god. Given gods were more like spiritual bureaucrats rather than omnipotent incarnations of reality like the Primals, it was more impressive sounding than the reality. Hell, I'd killed multiple gods by this point in my career so that just further illustrated I had a cool title and nothing more.

"Gary is a god," Jane muttered. "Oh my Goddess, so much about the universe makes sense now."

"Oh, like you haven't met insane loser gods yourself," I replied. "Mythology is just one long reality TV show."

"You're not a loser, Gary," Mandy said. "I never would have married you if you were. Still, if you won't release her from Hell for me then do it for Diabloman. You broke him with what you did. That's why he betrayed you."

"He broke me with his betrayal," I said, sighing. "But I'll never deny you anything. Good, bad, or vampy."

Mandy frowned.

I conjured the Reaper's Scythe in one hand and banged it on the ground. "There. Sentenced commuted."

Mandy blinked. "That's it?"

I was sure since I had a cosmic sense regarding the disposition of souls. Don't ask me to explain it. "Maria's off to Heaven or wherever her celestial caseworker wills it. I sentenced her to the first circle of Hell anyway. It's heck adjacent with people like Aristotle and Augustus Caesar. You know, all the people the pagans thought were righteous but were still kind of slaving assholes. It was the nicest part of Hell I could send her to. Really, I could have left her in Sheol but I'm not that kind of guy."

"The first circle of Hell is real?" Jane looked ready to have a mental breakdown. "Dante's *Inferno* is how Hell operates here?"

"Yep," I said.

"How does that square with you being Jewish?" Jane asked.

"The same way my knowing Odin does, I suppose," I said. "You just learn to roll with the ecumenist nature of the multiverse. You still haven't answered my question, Mandy. You're...so, you."

Mandy frowned. "I don't know."

I blinked. "You *don't know*?"

Of all the possible answers she might have given ranging from cosmic realignment to divine intervention, I hadn't expected that one.

"That is deeply unsatisfying storytelling," Jane said. "Maybe it's in the middle of the trade paperback and we'll get it later."

"What is she talking about?" Mandy asked.

"Jane thinks we're in a comic book," I replied. "Which is ridiculous."

"Does she know she has a book series and a CW show in this reality?" Mandy asked.

"No," I replied. "I was waiting to show all the fanfic people have done of her. The weirdest is the G/ Jane shippers because those are actually canonical."

Jane stared in horror.

As much as I wanted to continue this line of teasing, I was more interested in Mandy's situation. "So, I just sucked out Spellbinder's soul and you were fine?"

Mandy shook her head. "No, it was more complicated than that but even then, I've lived about two hundred years as a vampire thanks to time wackiness. It's just that was two hundred years in a post-apocalyptic Earth where you were John Connor and Cindy was Sarah."

For perhaps the first time in my life, I longed for the days when a sentence like that wouldn't make sense.

"That would make her my mother," I replied.

Mandy blinked. "Not what I was going for, Gary."

"Okay," I said.

"I learned to master my hunger and I've since got it under control with a serum that Cindy created," Mandy replied.

"Because doctors can create super-potions in this world," Jane replied, sarcastically. "I bet your local electrician can build power armor. I wish super-science was a thing in my world. We can't even get people to get vaccinations. My local general practitioner is suspicious of vaccines and is a creationist, which I know isn't true because I have an angel in my gun. He says it's nonsense."

"This is kind of an important conversation for me, Jane," I replied, surprisingly unwilling to debate politics. "Could you, I dunno, go graze or something?"

Jane glared. "I would call that comment racist but there is a nice patch of mushrooms nearby."

She walked off.

"Even with my hunger for blood under control, I was lacking something essential," Mandy replied. "I felt betrayed, even hated you a little, for taking away that part of me that was human. Worse, you did it after putting it in me in the first place."

"Technically, Merciful was the one—" I started to say.

"Don't interrupt," Mandy said. "You never bothered to ask whether I wanted my soul back. Whether it was possible to make me who I was again or even if you should. You wanted your wife back and that meant destroying what I'd become. Even though that being still loved you. Even though the mortal Mandy left that part of her behind when she ascended to Heaven."

I never understood why the good part of Mandy left behind our love. Was Eurasian Wiccan Heaven only for people who abandoned their earthly attachments? Had they adopted Buddhism, Jediism, Vulcan logic? It was a real kick in the pants to know that your love was considered a character flaw by the powers that be.

"I don't care about that now," I said, my mouth dry and voice cracking.

"Sure," Mandy said, looking down. "I wandered around, trying to figure out what I was supposed to do with my life. I couldn't be a superhero because the Society of Superheroes was playing ball with the Trust administration. Even those risking their lives to fight against the system were attached to Gabrielle and you know my opinion on her. I didn't want to be a supervillain. You had your family now and I wasn't a part of that."

"You left me, Mandy, I didn't leave you," I said.

"You made it clear I wasn't the person you wanted," Mandy said.

I stared at her. "No, I didn't. You will always be part of my family, Mandy. Horrifying undead abomination or not."

Mandy opened her mouth, closed it, then laughed. "Goddammit, Gary."

"I try," I replied. "So, somehow you ended up hooked up with Cindy."

"Yeah," Mandy said. "If I was going to be a bad guy then I wanted to be the best bad guy I could be. So I ditched the Nighthuntress label and have been working as a thief. I haven't really settled on a name, though I was thinking Kumiho or Calico."

"Animal based cat burglars are played out," I replied, surprised she was changing her name. That was a big deal among superheroes and villains. Your brand was everything. "So you just woke up one day and felt like not eating people?"

Mandy stared. "I don't know, Gary, it's weird. My powers have been changing and I feel less... vicious."

"Your bite is also different," I replied. "It's possible the merging of worlds is resulting in an alteration of magical principles. The vampires of our world becoming more like the vampires of Jane's world."

"Really?" Mandy asked. "Where the hell did you get that idea?"

"Honestly, I just made that up because I wanted to sound smart," I replied. "But time-compression and other weird facts of reality are something I'm trying to fix on behalf of my daughters."

"What?" Mandy asked.

I explained.

Mandy stared and then handed over the Primal Orb of Order. "Okay. Well, I guess you need this more than I do."

"Really, you're just giving this to me?" I asked, taking it. Immediately, I felt the orbs in my possession increase their power as they all had a synergistic effect on one another. They were now well beyond my power to control and I would have to be extra-careful using them.

"Gary, you're the one person in the world I trust with omnipotence," Mandy said.

"Why in the world would you do such an incredibly silly thing?" I asked, avoiding the word dumb or stupid despite the fact I wouldn't trust myself with any of the hundreds of supernatural artifacts or powers I'd gained over the years.

"You and Cindy both responded to getting Primal Orbs by deciding to use them to empower people rather than keep all the power yourself," Mandy said. "Yeah, I know about your deranged open-source magic system. That is a terrible idea, but it shows exactly what sort of person you are. Power to the people versus trickle down sorcery. A rising wind lifts all flying broomsticks."

"Wait, Cindy has a Primal Orb too?" I asked, wondering where the hell she'd gotten that. It's not like they could be picked up at the local UltraMart.

Mandy grimaced, clearly having said too much. "Maybe?"

Wow, this was turning into the easiest epic quest ever. This was like Frodo and Sam getting the Eagles to take them to Mount Doom like every fourteen-year-old reader suggested. Mind you, that would just mean Sauron would get it that much faster since it was unlikely that he'd miss them with his all-seeing eye, but that was a whole other argument. Four Primal Orbs were within my possession or in the hands of allies. Just four to go.

"In any case," I took a deep breath. "It's good to see you, Mandy. Please come back home."

"You don't want me around your kids, Gary," Mandy said, flatly.

"Of course I do," I replied.

Mandy and I had only one subject that we'd ever disagreed on, which was the subject of children. I'd wanted them, she didn't. Only later in life had I discovered that was because Mandy had a daughter back when her father was a Foundation for World Harmony agent attached to the Londonium embassy. It had been a teenage pregnancy and she'd given her daughter up for adoption. It had left a profound scar on her soul and, furthermore, had compounded when time travel had wiped her child from existence. Mandy had never wanted to go through that experience again and still was cagey around children.

Mandy sunk her shoulders. "Gary, we've both changed. You're engaged. You love Cindy. Would you really choose to give all that up for me?"

"I do love Cindy and we have changed," I said, taking a deep breath. "Maybe you're the demon soul of Mandy. Maybe I'm a psychotic supervillain with delusions of grandeur. But I think you know that it was always you. It will always be you."

Wow, that was something I could not walk back. I didn't want to, either.

"Gary..." Mandy trailed off.

"Yeah, that's my name," I said, not sure what this meant for any of us.

"Screw it," Mandy said, grabbing me by the shoulders and kissing me.

I kissed back and we fell back into the cabin. Mandy and I made love on the same bed where she'd fed on me, but I was more responsive this time around. She nibbled on my neck but didn't fully bite, perhaps because feeding on someone twice in one day was likely to kill them. I was feeling significantly more recovered, but I was glad she didn't risk it. Instead, I was more interested in kissing her all over and holding her in my arms after what had seemed like a lifetime. Her mouth tasted of blood and while that wasn't exactly a turn on, I didn't care.

I didn't know how long we spent there but it was at least a two-rounder and I enjoyed holding her in my arms between sessions. I'd missed my wife so much and a part of me couldn't help but wonder if this was yet another trick by one of my enemies. Was Destruction screwing with me from outside the universe? Would it end up being a Mandy replidroid? Had I just conjured her with the Primal Orbs?

I didn't care.

This was going to be a big twist in my life. I'd confessed that I loved Mandy more than Gabrielle and always would. It was like cheating and I hated myself for it. Gabrielle deserved better than to be anyone's second pick. Hell, so did Cindy, though our relationship had always been different than mine with Mandy (or Gabrielle). She was my best friend and family in the same inseverable way. Yet, Cindy had lied to me and kept this entire enterprise secret. I needed to talk to her with that. I needed to talk with Gabrielle. To set things right.

I had no idea how this was going to go, or what would happen when I fixed the universe with the Primal Orbs, but I had this moment now. As I lay there, both of us naked under the sheets, I realized that it didn't matter whether I was a supervillain or a superhero. All that mattered was that I protected and cared for those I loved. Everything else was secondary. The world could look after itself.

That was when an enormous bear-sized red wolf jumped onto the bed.

"Gah!"

Chapter Fifteen

Where I Finally Start Getting
Some Answers

An enormous red wolf, about the size of the wargs in *The Lord of the Rings*, plopped itself on top of both me and Mandy. The bed collapsed beneath us and we were trapped beneath its enormous paws as well as slavering jaws. The beast's fur was bright red, even brighter than the kind found in the woods, and her eyes were an enormous yellow. That was when it opened its mouth, its breath reeking of fresh blood, and stuck out its massive tongue. That was when it licked me and Mandy both.

"Ah! Dog lick!" I said, covering my face.

That was when the enormous red wolf transformed into Cindy. She was noticeably not wearing any clothes and it was something that immediately caused me to become conscious of my own lack of attire as well as Mandy's. It was also noticeably affected when Cindy planted a big old wet kiss on Mandy, who returned it.

"Really, Gary?" Jane said—thankfully dressed—at the front door. "You just have to be a guy about these things, don't you?"

"Oh like you don't write all manner of guy-on-guy fanfiction," I replied. "I bet you have a huge collection of *Supernatural* and *Vampire Diaries* stories."

Jane's eyes widened. "How the hell did you know that?"

"Just guessing," I replied, smiling. "Why do you have supernatural dramas on your world when the supernatural is real?"

Jane narrowed her eyes. "I dunno, why do we have cop shows on both our worlds?"

She had a point there. "Hey Cindy."

"Hi Gary. Sorry for jumping on you while you were in bed. Canine instincts. I'm also required to sleep on top of you and push you of the bed simultaneously." Cindy got up and waved her hand, before shouting. "Costume! Costume! Costume!"

This resulted in her getting her magical outfit.

"You're really password protecting this omnipotent magical power network you've built," Jane replied.

"I should probably change the invocation for *Wish* spells from password," I replied, smiling before getting out of the bed myself. I snapped my fingers and once more was dressed in the Reaper's Cloak. I also smelled like my favorite shampoo and was completely clean. Which was important after physical exertion and nearly getting killed.

Mandy pulled up her covers and smiled. "Hello, Cindy. I probably should have told you Gary was awake."

"Ya think?" Cindy asked. "It seems you two are reconciling despite all the murder attempts, possession, and necromancy between you."

"That's just marriage," Mandy said before immediately stopping. A pained look passed on her face and it was echoed in mine.

Yeah, marriage. Our marriage had ended with the "till death do you part" section of our wedding vows. It had been years since Mandy had considered me her husband and I'd considered her my wife. There'd even been confusion over our status when we were living together, and she was possessed. Mind you, that had included a prison stay in an underground fortress and Cindy living with us, but my life was weird like that. Mandy technically remembered being married to my future self for about two hundred years, which put another weird spin on our relationship. Why couldn't we be a normal couple like reincarnating Eagle people or President Android John and his bride from the future? Yes, that was sarcasm.

"So, this is your secret," I replied. "You've been running a secret paramilitary training camp for future horror movie protagonists."

"Yep," Cindy said. "I didn't want to tell you because I knew you'd go running right to Gabrielle."

"I would not have," I said, hoping to talk to her about the fact that Dracula was somewhere nearby. Also, we'd killed Sheriff Injustice's daughter. As cowardly as the alien redneck had been in abandoning Missy in her hour of greatest need, I suspected he'd take that personally.

"Would so," Cindy said. "I know you, Gary. You don't operate well without people around you. As much as you love us, you've been on a kick of being the good guy for the past two years. It's alienated all of your friends and left you isolated."

"Clearly, you're in denial of reality." I shook my head, disregarding her armchair psychology. "This is like that time in high school you insisted you were Deborah Harry's daughter that she gave up to hide from ninjas."

Cindy narrowed her eyes. "There's no way you can prove that's not true."

I stared at her. "The fact that you're ninety-nine-point-ninety-nine percent conclusively your mother's daughter according to the DNA tests you keep doing every month."

Cindy looked to one side as if I'd told her there was no Jewish Santa. "DNA can be altered. Clearly, Blondie's frontwoman is doing her best to deny our relationship."

I sighed. "This is why we have restraining orders from half of Hollywood."

Cindy snorted. "I'm sorry, this from the guy who claimed he was dating a time-traveling teenage Pat Benatar at age sixteen."

"That was true," I said. "She left our galaxy via her mutant teleportation powers."

Jane stared at us both. "You know the worst part? I know each and every issue you're referencing. The celebrity crossover issues of Amazing! comics were pretty awful. Wait, does this mean the Back Street Boys vs. Insync issues in the Nineties are canon?"

Cindy said, "Space Christ Timberlake could beat all of the others up with his superpowers."

Jane blinked. "You know, I believe that. What can Britney do?"

"Anything she wants as Galaxy Empress," I replied. "In any

case, I'm glad you two have reunited and are doing a team-up."

I pulled out my cellphone and turned on Lzzy Hale's "Daughters of Darkness" as background music.

"The thing is," I continued. "I'm kind of on a mission here to save the multiverse for our daughters."

"*Your* daughters," Mandy muttered.

"Our *family*," I corrected, wondering how Gabrielle was going to react to all this. Being someone literally powered by the Sun and cosmic energy, she hated vampires. I also didn't think she was going to accept my wanting to renew what I'd had with Mandy. That was assuming Mandy wanted to. I had to break things off with Gabrielle and that was going to be hard on Mindy. I wondered if Mandy knew that I'd named my daughter with Gabrielle after her and Cindy.

"Yeah," Cindy said, pointing to a raven sitting above the doorway to the cabin. "Heckle and Jekyll here told us all about it. You're also supposed to rescue the president's daughter so he can be famous again. You know, even though President Trust got beaten by Nathaniel Hawthorne in the election."

"Hawthorne's only president-elect," David said, sitting up there. "I don't care what your politics are, rescuing a princess or First Daughter is still a way to get back into the superhero game. The Nightwalker and I rescued Lyndon Johnson's daughters like five times. Man, did PHANTOM really not like that guy."

I looked up at the bird. "You weren't watching the whole time, were you?"

David raised his beak in the air. "As if I would want to watch your disgusting mammalian perversions."

He then conjured a tiny bag of popcorn from seemingly nowhere and used his beak to put a piece in his mouth.

"Right," I replied. I was really going to have to have words with that bird.

"Dracula has conjured his castle in the middle of Satan's Swamp in order to take full advantage of the magical energies around here," Cindy said. "I don't know what he's doing, and I wasn't about to endanger the camp by launching a full-scale assault, but there's apparently a small army of Infamy cultists as well as alternate universe baddies gathered around the place.

I had to fight Franken-Cindy a few days back."

"Franken-Cindy?" I asked.

"Yeah, patchwork golem me with bolts in her neck," Cindy said. "I took her down, though."

"Aw, but what if she was a poor and misunderstood golem that just needed love?" I asked. "Maybe not realizing some guys and gals are into scars!"

"Don't make this weirder with your fetishes, Gary," Cindy said. "*I'm* the one assembling the weird harem of cute monster lovers."

"I think technically all of us are," I replied. "We've got a werewolf, vampire, and grim reaper. Now all we need is a mummy and ghost to do our own Halloween cereal line. I need to text Kerri and see if she'd be up for that."

"Excuse me, Dracula *conjured* his castle?" Jane asked.

"Dracula carries around his castle with him," I replied, trying to figure out how to best explain it. "He used to rule the country of High Carpathia, but the Aeon Society eventually drove him out of it and brought the liberating joys of democracy to the nation. As I understand it, they're on their sixth civil war since. Dracula just keeps his castle in an alternate dimension until he needs it then pops it out wherever, complete with undead horde and ghostly followers. I understand the castle can also move between time and space on its own."

"It's a little between *Castlevania* and *Count Duckula*," Mandy said from the bed. "I tried joining the guy when I was evil, but it turns out a guy from the fourteenth century doesn't have the most enlightened views about women. You're either a bride or a problem to him."

I was surprised that Mandy had ever tried to associate with a dedicated supervillain like Dracula, especially since her evil side had been of the antihero "I want to kill and eat criminals" type. That was part of what made her accusation against Gabrielle so strange. Still, this was good information as it helped clarify where we were on finding the remaining Primal Orbs. "Call me crazy but by the Law of Narrative Convenience, I'm pretty sure that Dracula has to have the remaining four Primal Orbs as well as the president's daughter."

"Four orbs?" Cindy asked, looking at Mandy. "Has someone been sharing state secrets during pillow talk?"

Mandy looked abashed. I didn't know vampires could blush. It was also a reminder that Cindy was hiding things from me.

"You need to attack the castle directly!" David said, sounding pleading. "Who knows what's happening to that poor, beautiful, blonde girl who is our meal ticket to who knows how many interviews! If we rescue her, my comeback is secured. I'm talking *Dancing with the Stars* and book deals!"

"You're a bird, you only dance during mating," I said. "Cindy, I need to talk with you in private."

"Please tell me you're not stepping out to have sex," Jane muttered.

"Oh please, Jane, I wouldn't leave if I wanted to have sex," Cindy said. "The benefit of being a polyamorous, bisexual werewolf—"

"Lalalala," Jane said, covering her ears. We really had established that brother-sister dynamic which transcended time and space.

I gestured to the door and walked out with Cindy. The two of us then headed behind the cabin where there was, thankfully, no one to listen in. "Yes, Mandy told me about you having the Life Orb. Also, that you've been keeping me out because you're afraid of Gabrielle."

"You are just too loyal—" Cindy started to say.

"Bullcrap," I interrupted.

Cindy blinked. "Gary—"

"I'm sorry, you've clearly forgotten that I only pretend to be an idiot on TV," I said. "I'm actually quite shrewd."

"No one thinks you're an idiot, Gary," Cindy said.

"If that were true then Entropicus would rule the multiverse," I said. "Being underestimated is about the only reason I've survived as long as I have. Nevertheless, I would like to think you could be honest with your live-in partner who you won't marry."

Cindy rolled her eyes. "Gary, if I married you then I'd be lying to you more than any other person. Marriage is a free license to abuse your partner."

Yeah, Cindy had some issues with the institution of marriage. Could you tell. "What's really going on?"

Cindy was still clinging to her cover story. "Why do you think—"

"Because you love Gabrielle," I replied. "She's your best friend. Mandy *hates* Gabrielle, so I'm certain she believes the reason you told her to keep me out of this. Mandy never forgave Gabrielle for brainwashing me in college and breaking my heart even if it led to our relationship. She always felt Ultragoddess loomed over us despite the fact I loved her, Mandy, with all my heart. You, however, pledged your undying devotion to Gabby at the Eternity Tournament."

Cindy sighed. "Stupid love confession. Who knew completely straight superheroes existed?"

"Certainly not me," I replied. "But we agreed not to talk about my love of Ewan McGregor. Besides, that's only if we somehow become cellmates in the future."

Cindy snorted. "Okay, maybe the reason I kept you out of this isn't because I'm afraid Gabrielle is secretly evil."

"No kidding," I said.

"But she *is* an antihero," Cindy said. "Which you have problems with but most of us don't care about."

I narrowed my eyes. "Cindy, tell the truth."

Cindy threw up her arms. "Fine, Gary. You want to know why I kept this from you? I wanted something for me! I've been called your sidekick, your henchwoman—"

"Henchwench," I added.

"Henchperson!" Cindy said. "They think I'm just your girlfriend and baby mama. I'm more! I'm a doctor, not a prostitute, goddammit! I need to have my own career as a supervillain! One that will shake the heavens and show just how far I can go. I am going to break the glass ceiling for supervillains everywhere. There's never been a woman archvillain and I will be the first!"

"There's been like a dozen: Morgan Le Fey, Circe, Baba Yaga, Tiamat-Abaddon, the Nightmistress, Doctor Madness, like all of Guinevere's rogues in fact—"

"That's not the point, Gary!" Cindy said. "This is all about me. I wanted to show what I could do. These kids are our future!

Supervillains and superheroes that will look to me as someone who helped them. I am laying the groundwork for the next generation! I can do that without you!"

I nodded. "So, what's the real reason?"

Cindy sighed. "Really?"

"I'd vote for you for the Oscar but it's like you don't think we've known each other for two thirds of our lives," I said.

"Really? That long?" Cindy asked.

"'Fraid so," I replied. "That's not including time compression either."

Cindy blinked and sighed, reaching into her pocket and pulling out the Life Orb. "Yeah, I kind of have this. I thought you'd get a bit upset when you found out I had it."

"Why would I care?" I asked, suspecting I was going to hate this.

"I use this Life Orb for good, Gary," Cindy said. "I don't just liberate the Supers from the camps. I've been giving powers to people who have been abused, kicked around, and otherwise torn to shreds by society. Minorities and persecuted peoples around the globe are getting a boost because of me. Victimized women, former slaves—"

"Cindy—" I interrupted.

"I've been depowering the government's goon squads as well. Johnny Rebel and the Klansman are now just a pair of ugly white dudes. So is the Incel, Psychoslinger II, Slaughterbug, Commie Commando, and the Nationalist. Oh, and Becky Thompson who had the power to convince people of anything through television signals but just used it to sell infomercial products. Remember her? Bitch never cut me in despite it being my idea."

"Cindy!" I snapped. "Where did you get it?"

Cindy blinked. "Merciful. Your doppelganger. He gave it to me. He's alive."

Well, shit.

Chapter Sixteen

What the Hell, Cindy?

It was a rare situation when I went completely silent. This was one of those circumstances. I just stared at Cindy then blinked once.

"Really, Gary? The silent treatment?" Cindy asked. "Who are you, my father? Which I really hope is not the case because, eww, but is theoretically possible if you slept with Deborah Harry in 1981 via time travel. That would be gross, though."

"Extremely," I replied. "I also know you're trying to distract me from the horrifying betrayal you just confessed to."

"Who me?" Cindy asked, blinking innocently. "No!"

"Why would you do this?" I asked, holding out my hands, though. "How could you? Merciful!"

The fact Merciful was alive was less surprising than it should have been. I'd "killed" him before I'd instituted the ban on resurrection in our world (and I never even made the wish directly—the Primals just felt my grief over my passing loved ones and made the wish for me). He was also the Chosen One of Life, so I'd always thought he'd gone down a bit too easy. By the time I'd decided to chop his body into pieces and bury it in concrete a few days later, it had already vanished. I'd tried several times to sense where his soul had gone post-mortem but all I'd gotten was a weird buzzing sensation. But I'd wanted him to be dead and had allowed myself to believe that yes, maybe this time, he was really gone. More superheroes and villains fall into that trap than should. Blame human nature.

"I had my reasons," Cindy said, defensively.

"No," I said, interrupting her. "Merciful is evil."

"Don't get judgmental," Cindy said. "Just because you're a superhero now—"

"No, this isn't about that," I said, taking several deep breaths. "Merciful kidnapped me and Mandy before putting us in an underground Fifties playset for years."

"Months due to time compression," Cindy pointed out.

"Don't," I replied. "He tried to kill my sister. He tried to kidnap our daughter. He *murdered Ultragod*."

"Gary—" Cindy started to say.

"Moses was my friend," I said, on the verge of tears. "Someone who was worth looking up to. I don't know what's going to happen with me and Gabrielle, but he was family. Just as much as Cloak was. Merciful locked away Gabrielle for years to serve as a goddamned reactor for his free energy plan and he killed billions via President Omega."

"They got better!" Cindy said, as if that was a defense.

"President Omega was his ally, a freaking Nazi!" I said, as if this whole thing couldn't get any more insane.

"Only so he could betray him!" Cindy said.

I closed my eyes. I sucked in my breath and gave a desperate response, *"Why?"*

Merciful was, to make a long story short (too late), my doppelganger from a previous universe. The Big Ass Time Disaster destroyed the previous Silver Age universe where heroes were good, villains bad, and the former always beat the latter with minimal casualties. He was the sole survivor of his reality and woke up in our crappy universe in the Nineties after his was destroyed.

Our universe was a place where good guys were emotionally tortured, bad guys won as often as they lost, and it wasn't always easy to tell the difference between the two. That would have been traumatizing enough if not for the fact that I existed and was living a worse life than his previous one. In his reality, he'd been married with kids and was one of the most beloved superheroes, if not top tier in respect. He was the Society of Superheroes' healer and the Champion of Life instead of Death.

Merciful held on for about a decade but finally broke bad

when President Omega was elected. The country electing an actual goddamned supervillain caused him to lose faith in democracy and instilled in him a belief in authoritarianism. He decided he was going to bring back his universe, bring order to this reality at the point of a wand, and kill anyone who stood in his way. Merciful planned to bring back everyone innocent he killed, too, which was an extra layer to his crazy.

The thing was Merciful was competent. Really-really competent. Like, one of those super-genius bad guys who knew what the hell they were doing and was waiting for everyone else to catch up. He ran rings around me right up until the point that Cloak and me had double-teamed him in magic. Together, we'd finished the spell he'd planned to bring back his universe to restore his Earth (a lot easier than an entire reality). Then, being in a particularly foul mood, I'd let him look at his family one last time before blowing his brains out. Yeah, not the worst thing I'd ever done but pretty damn close.

"Because he was you, Gary," Cindy said. "During your last fight with Merciful, when Cloak died, I followed you to his world."

"How?" I asked.

"Mandy gave me a lift," Cindy said. "Mind you, in retrospect, her having teleportation magic should have perhaps tipped me off that she was possessed by a witch. Anyway, I found Merciful dying from being shot in the head."

"Yes, I know, because *I was the one who shot him*," I said, trying to keep my temper. Cindy and I had been known to fight but I attempted to apply Jedi principles during that time. It didn't ever work but it was the one area that neither of us ever even contemplated violence.

I was contemplating never wanting to see her again, though.

"He should have been dead," Cindy said. "However, he was still alive, and I ended up treating him for the better part of a week while you hung out on Earth-B."

"It's a nice place," I replied. "I should know, I made it."

"Other Gary recovered and gave me the Life Orb before leaving," Cindy said. "I used it to give myself werewolf powers. It was a chance to make myself a big leaguer."

"That at least explains your inexplicable powers. I feel like we're getting a lot of explanations for seemingly random stuff in our world like time-compression and all the crazy retcons. I wonder if our writers were getting complaints from fans."

"Don't you start," Cindy said. "In any case, I don't regret what I did."

"He's a monster," I said, staring at her. "You unleashed a psychopath—who killed people we knew—onto the world."

Cindy closed her eyes. "He's you, Gary. Just… insane with grief. I saw what happened to you after Mandy died. Imagine that happening but a thousand times worse. What would you have me do?"

"Kill me because I didn't deserve to live," I said, truthfully. "I'd rather be dead than hurt the people I love."

"He has his home world back," Cindy said. "Let him have his happily ever after."

"There's no going back after what he did," I said. "Certainly, Ultragod is still dead and so are all the other people President Omega killed. Merciful is the guy who kept that guy in power when he would have been gunning down the White House Press core after a week. Merciful cannot return to the people he knew and loved. He's changed too much."

"Has he?" Cindy asked.

"There's no Anakin and Padme reunion in Force Heaven," I replied, thinking of myself and Mandy. "I'm sure they got Force divorced as soon as he showed up. Maybe she's hooked up with Obi-Wan or Sabe now."

"It saddens me you know the name of her chief handmaiden," Cindy said. "Even if she was played by Keira Knightley."

I sighed. "I'll just put it on my list."

"What?" Cindy asked.

"Killing him," I replied. "After this, I'm going to go to Earth-B and put him in the ground forever."

"Don't," Cindy said. "Just leave him alone."

"I can't do that," I said. "He's a threat to us."

"He'll kill you," Cindy said. "You got lucky last time."

I took a deep breath. "Yeah, well, I suppose that's one

reason why he's beaten me so badly. The only person who doesn't underestimate me is myself."

"Well, that and the crazy redneck Sheriff," Cindy said. "He beats you because you're a one-trick pony. Take away your magic and you're screwed."

I didn't have an answer for that. "Cindy, we're not okay right now. I love what you've done here, and I love *you*. You're entitled to your secrets and if you wanted to tell me things then you'd do so. I'm not the guy who thinks he's entitled to know every little detail of your life. However, Merciful is a monster."

"I don't believe that," Cindy said.

"He went after Leia," I said, simply. "For that, no hell is deep enough toss him."

Cindy sighed. "Go get yourself a drink from the staff quarters, Gary, and we'll take about this later. We can figure out what we're going to do next after you rescue the princess and gain omnipotence. Which is the strangest juxtaposition I've ever heard."

"Not if you've played the *Legend of Zelda*," I said. "Also, you have drinking at your summer camp?"

"I couldn't get through an hour of teaching these brats without Jack Daniels," Cindy replied. "That's with the help of our psycho killer friends. You're the one who likes kids, Gary. You're welcome to help. Maybe you can teach Supervillainy 101."

"Ah," I said, nodding. I didn't comment on the fact that even my best friend, baby mama, and partner still thought of me as a supervillain rather than a hero. "Before I go get utterly sloshed, I do have a question."

"You're going to ask about Mandy, aren't you?" Cindy asked.

"How did you know?" I asked.

Cindy rolled her eyes. "Because I think that after a decade of supervillainy, two kids, sleeping around with multiple superheroines as well as supervillains—"

"Like three others than you and Gabby," I replied. "Two of them you were dating."

They were Nightshade and Splotch Woman by the way. The third we don't speak about.

"That you still only think about her," Cindy said.

I lowered my head.

"It's the only thing that Mandy had in common with you anymore," Cindy replied. "It's the one topic I can't get her to shut up about."

I gave a half-smile.

"I'm not sure you're good for each other, though," Cindy replied. "It seems all you two ever do anymore is cause each other pain. You were a fantastic couple when you were mundanes but terrible for each other as superhumans. I'm just cursed with the fact that I love you both more than anyone else in my life. Gabrielle included."

"Except your child, our daughter," I said.

"Oh, yeah, her," Cindy said. "Did you leave her with someone? Do we have a replacement policy if we lose her?"

"I know you love her," I said.

"I do," Cindy said. "Even if she came out gross, helpless, and a pain in the stomach."

Cindy tossed me the Life Orb. "I want this back. I'm not going to go back to being a side character."

"You'll get your own series someday, I promise." I smirked and walked away. I should have kissed her then, but I was still too furious. I knew that I was being a hypocrite. Diabloman had done even worse things than Merciful. Hell, Diabloman was arguably the worst person to ever live in any timeline ever in terms of sheer body-count. However, I'd forgiven him and done my best to clear his karmic debt. Yet, I hadn't been willing to extend the same courtesy to Merciful that Cindy had.

Indeed, I kept trying to find excuses for hating her for it. The funny thing was that I was pretty sure Ultragod would tell me to forgive her and Merciful both because he was that kind of Rabbi Joshua ben Joseph sort of guy. I, however, was more of the Old Testament "eye for an eye" thing. I was all for Biblical plagues, Sodom and Gomorrah, plus the Ark of the Covenant melting Nazis. Maybe it made me a hypocrite—certainly it made me a hypocrite—but that was just the way I was wired. Vengeance is mine, so sayeth Merciless. Hell, it was in my frigging codename.

I wandered through Camp Blood, taking in the sights and

taking a moment to get my bearings. Cindy really had set up something spectacular here, but maybe it was just because I was easily impressed by anyone who wanted to give the downtrodden a hand up. I thought I saw Jun and Ken Masterson among the counselors but did not go their way. Those two teenage heroes were the kind of people who deserved to be living normal lives rather than getting caught up in the stupidity of adults' problems.

Mind you, I was a first year Millennial and almost forty, so the definition of adult had gotten a bit longer. Who knew that my generation of Omegaphones and widespread internet would one day be the people looking at people too young to be entering adulthood? We were supposed to be the future, but the same people who had been in control when I was born were the same people in control as I entered middle age.

Man, I needed a drink.

Heading into the counselor's cabin, I swiftly headed to the kitchen and managed to find Cindy's liquor supply in the cabinets. In every cabinet in fact. Honestly, it looked like she had enough alcohol to get a small army sloshed. I double checked behind the refrigerator and noticed she'd also hidden a package of weed large enough to get the same drunk army high as a kite. A pattern was starting to form here.

"Dare I have sex, get drunk, and smoke pot?" I asked to no one in particular. "I feel like that's tempting fate in a place called Camp Blood."

"I believe that only applies to teenagers, virgins, and twenty-somethings pretending to be both," the deep Darth Vader-esque voice of William England spoke.

I turned around, a bottle of Merciless brand vodka in hand. William was standing there, still wearing his same outfit from before and looming over me like the well-dressed Terminator he resembled.

"You've got some serious stealth skills there, Accountant," I said. "Michael Myers could learn a thing or two from you."

"No, he couldn't," William said, "because Nancy and I killed him in my world. The serial killer he was based on, at least. In my world, all supernatural serial killers are based on real-life figures. Jane probably didn't mention that."

"No," I said. "She keeps trying to depict her world as a kind of supernatural utopia where humans and monsters get along. Just with idiots for leaders. My impression is the place sounds like Eighties Horror World with a dash of *True Blood.*"

"Both accurate and misleading," William said. "Do you always relay complicated concepts through the vernacular of pop culture?"

"You have no idea," I said, offering him alcohol.

"I do not drink... alcohol," William said.

"What do you drink?" I asked.

"Soda," William said, going to the fridge and getting an Ultracola. Personally, I preferred Omegapsi.

I blinked and shrugged before taking a swig straight out of the bottle. "So, uh, did you want something?"

"Yes," William said. "I wanted to tell you that you're being deceived. You have been lured into this swamp for a reason and I believe it relates to undoing the changes you made to the multiverse."

Chapter Seventeen

What the Hell Is Going on, Really?

I took a second, much longer swig. It tasted like swamp water and lighter fluid, which was probably what it was composed of. It was, however, just what I needed right now. "It's never asking me to move my car or helping make s'mores."

"Wait," I said, lifting my hand to stop William before he spoke. I took a second, long swig of the locally produced Merciless-brand vodka. "Ah, that was the good stuff as only cannibal hillbilly redneck moonshiners can produce."

"Must be my relatives," William said. "Or at least this universe's counterpart to them."

I put the bottle to one side and crossed my arms. "Okay, what do you mean you think this is a trap?"

"I believe you were lured here to this haunted swamp in order to steal the Primal Orbs," William replied.

"Uh huh," I said, not believing it but not disbelieving it yet. I owed this guy and his wife my life, but I didn't know them from Adam either. The only reason I was giving him the time of day was because I was always looking for a double (or triple) cross and Jane vouched for them. "How do you even know about the Primal Orbs, William? You don't even come from a universe where people know about them."

"My master told me," William said. "The Spirit of Murder."

"Does she know Death?" I asked, half-kidding.

William paused as if listening to an invisible friend beside him. I knew that feeling. "She says yes."

"Ah," I said, believing him. "So, you think David is working for Dracula?"

I hoped not. That little bird had successfully rescued me from my longstanding funk, and I wasn't about to turn on him. Mind you, if he'd set me up to steal the Primal Orbs, I'd fallen for it hook, line, and sinker. It also meant that he had intimate knowledge about how my mind worked since it required a fake Mindy, Jane, and Society of Superheroes Dark. God, that was a stupid name for a team.

"I think Dracula is dead," William said. "Permanently."

That was a claim that gave me pause. As much as the deaths of heroes was leaving me nonplussed, a lot of supervillains had died in the past couple of years as well. They weren't coming back either. Tom Terror was the biggest name on that list, killed by yours truly, and his absence had resulted in a bunch of infighting among PHANTOM's goon squads. Given they were Nazis, I couldn't help but feel schadenfreude. Which was German for happiness at the misfortune of others, a concept I heartily endorsed when the others were fascists.

"He's come back before," I pointed out. "Bela Lugosi, Christopher Lee, Frank Langella, and Gary Oldman. Dude is like a Time Lord."

That was not the nerdiest statement I'd ever made but probably in the top ten.

"Yes, but you made a magical ban on this universe that altered the fundamental rules of its metaphysics," William said, completely ignoring my jokes. "Resurrection magic, divine or otherwise, no longer works. Undead can't be created in this world anymore and if they are destroyed, they stay destroyed. There are no more ghosts created either."

I blinked. "No wonder I've been so lacking in business lately. It's like that crappy decision to make the Ghostbusters drive themselves out of business in the second movie. This is why *The Real Ghostbusters* cartoon is the true sequel."

William didn't even blink. Wow, this guy obviously didn't know pop culture at all. "I'll have to take your word for it."

"Still, Dracula could have been revived from his last defeat before the ban went into effect," I suggested. "I mean Mandy's still alive-ish."

"Nancy and I slew your universe's Dracula a week after

coming here," William said. "He was attempting to seduce teenage girls into marrying him with Young Adult fiction."

"The cad!" I said, faking shocked. "So, what, is the Dracula here an alternate version? Assuming you really did kill ours and not an imposter. I mean, I've met vampires who have claimed to be Lestat, as well as Gary imposters. It happens."

Honestly, given William and Nancy had torn through Sheriff Injustice and his gang, I didn't doubt they could deal with Dracula for a minute.

Dracula may have been one of the A-listers among supervillains, the guy who put the A in archvillain, but he'd also suffered countless defeats over the years. The only reason he'd remained a threat was because he always came back from Hell within a few months at best. He was the Dread Pirate LeChuck of vampires, or well, the Dracula. I didn't need to reach for another example there. My bad.

"It is possible, but I doubt it," William said. "I believe the imposter is possibly far more dangerous than Dracula, though. Our realities are merging, and I can sense how the ley lines are intersecting. This world is being overlaid with multiple other realities to circumvent the ban you placed. The worlds being merged are ones with strong necromantic energies to them, which implies to me they are trying to brute force their way past your enchantment."

"Speak English, Doc," I said.

"Someone wants to raise the dead in this reality and are willing to smash universes together to do it," William said.

"Huh." I blinked, processing that. "Sounds like Merciful."

"Your doppelganger," William said.

"Yes," I said. "But it could also be Dracula. If anyone knew how to escape the rules of final death, it would be the original grandmaster of it. Maybe it's an alternate universe Dracula. These things happen."

Rarely, even in my world, but they did happen. Mr. Chaos had been the nastiest and most evil enemy of the Nightwalker for decades, a serial killer with a twisted sense of humor and the ability to inflict horrifying bad luck on anyone he met as long as it was funny. We'd never fought. He'd ended up gunned down by a gun-toting grandmother while trying to launch a bank into space. The next week, his doppelganger from Earth-B had shown up and started raising hell in an identical manner. Because, really, we just can't have nice things.

William was not easily distracted, though. He remained laser focused on our current situation. "Either way, it seems to me that bringing the Primal Orbs to him is an astoundingly bad idea. It is very probable that this world merging is the result of him having the other four as well as magic or technology enough to harness their power."

He had a point. My world often didn't seem like it, but it did have its own internal form of logic. "Well, thanks for the warning. I suppose this is time that I call in the Society of Superheroes. Which I note a lot of people have been advising me not to."

"Yes," William said. "They are also suspiciously busy."

"What?" I asked, looking up.

William pulled out his Omegaphone—though it was apparently made by some company called Apple—and showed me a wireless feed of the Society of Superheroes battling hordes of zombified superheroes. The Texas Guardians were there, the Society of Superheroes Dark, the Shadow Seventeen, and the Evo-Lutionaries too. The zombified heroes looked a lot like the Nightwalker that had attacked me, which told me that there was a whole Lich-Wight invasion going on.

"Those sons of bitches," I said, staring at the phone. "They're having a multi-team crossover without me!"

I was getting distracted again—blame my undiagnosed ADD from childhood—but this could not go unchallenged! When there was a big universe-spanning crossover event, you invited everyone! That was the rule. That was the whole point! Whether it was an alien invasion, Great Beast, zombie attack, time getting rewritten, or supervillain mass team-up, you brought all hands on deck! I was being snubbed!

"My condolences," William said. "It must be hard not to be important enough to be invited."

"Strong e-mails will be sent," I said. "I fully intend to podcast about this. They've done this to me before, ya know! Like when they had a big secret invasion by a bunch of Venusians that caused a civil war on multiple Earths, you know who got left on monitor duty? Me! It's like they're ashamed of me."

"Probably because they are," William said, proving that showing tact was not his strong suit.

"I didn't even get an invite to the Christmas Party at the Island of Hot Druidesses that Guinevere comes from! Mr. Inventor got invited to that one and he's married!" I said. "Cindy still is ticked that I didn't bring her."

"Your world is a very silly place," William said, his expression remaining somewhere between stone faced and lifeless. "What are you going to do?"

"I honestly don't know," I admitted. "I've only known the feathery jerk a little while, but I'd rather not think David is leading me into a trap."

"I looked up his Superpedia page," William said. "The Nightflier was a creation by the Filmation company for their short-lived Nightwalker and Sunlight cartoon. It aired in 1968 and the Nightflier was voiced by Casey Kasem."

I blinked. "I thought he sounded familiar. Still, the fact the Nightflier is fictional doesn't necessarily mean he's not real."

"That is literally what it means," William replied.

"Then explain Mercirat!" I said, frowning. "My furry cartoonish friend from animation world!"

"I understand you've only seen this figure when you've been concussed or when fighting LSD Man and Marijuana Girl," I said.

"Ah yes, Lawrence Sylvester Dodds and Mary Jane Pottsman," I said. "Good times."

"I repeat, your world is a very silly place," William said.

"Thanks," I replied.

"It wasn't a compliment," William said. "Either way, I know something about what people are willing to do in order to bring back their loved ones. They are willing to shake heaven and Earth to do so. Nothing stands in their way and all evils become justifiable in the name of restoring what they have lost."

"I know what that's like," I replied, sighing. "But you can't go home again."

I couldn't help but think of myself as toxic and a danger to those I cared for most. Cindy was my best friend, Mandy was the love of my life, and Gabrielle was somewhere between.

"Perhaps home is where the heart is," William said. "I know I keep the beating heart of my worst enemy there so I can always make sure it's not regenerating into a full resurrection."

I stared at him.

"That was a joke," William said. "I keep it in a locked box in an underground vault."

"I really need to get back Diabloman," I replied. "The substitutes I've been using just aren't working out."

"I must return to training the young men and women of this camp how to survive," William said. "Education is not to fill a hole but light a fire. The next generation of your world's heroes must be prepared."

That was a weird sentiment coming from a guy who was one skull mask away from being the villain of a Blumhouse movie. Still, I wasn't about to let him go just yet. "Do you really think there is a Big Ass Time Disaster going on?"

William blinked. "I don't know. Your reality seems to be pretty twisted. Jane tried explaining to me that you had two eight-year-old daughters born years apart and who you both raised as well as didn't raise."

"Yes," I said. "Time compression."

"Perhaps something is going on," William said. "But would you change time so it moved only forward?"

I blinked. "I dunno. I can't exactly talk about wanting to undo reality because I love having my kids. If not for all these shenanigans, I wouldn't have either Leia or Mindy. But I also don't want them to be eight years old for the next ten years then suddenly become adults like we're watching *Days of Our Lives*."

"Is that show still on in your reality?" William asked. "In ours, it was cancelled for a vampire orientated soap opera. They felt it was a missing daytime television demographic."

I tried to wrap my head around that. "Why would you make daytime television for vampires?"

William blinked. "That is a good question. Someone clearly dropped the ball at the network."

My discovery that William did have a sense of humor was interrupted by the sound of an explosion just outside of the cabin, which caused me to cover my ears. It shattered glass and left the windows of the cabin broken in pieces on the ground. My ears were ringing, and I needed to steady myself since it turned out that explosions were not things you could power walk away from, unless you were invulnerable or a Michael Bay character.

Looking up, I asked, "Any chance that is one of your students?"

"No," William said, frowning. "We must go protect them."

I sighed. "Well, another chance to kill bad people. I'm in."

The two of us headed out the door of the counselor's cabin and found ourselves in the middle of a battlefield. The summer camp was under attack by a horde of Lich-Wights and I had flashbacks to the invasion of Falconcrest City by the Brotherhood of Infamy's zombies. These particular monsters were a lot nastier and uglier looking than those zombies too, being deformed seven- and eight-foot-tall mounds of muscle wearing burlap sacks or hockey-masks. They were ogres, one and all, with a variety of farm equipment as weapons. Some had pitchforks, shot guns, chainsaws, and others had machetes. At least one of them was a depraved looking giant Daisy Duke sort of girl with razor teeth who was driving a tractor that had been outfitted with buzzsaws.

It was the Clan.

I hadn't entirely been kidding when I'd said that there were mutant cannibal hillbillies in Satan's Hollow. The Clan was a bunch of Scottish Satanists who had been driven out of their home country in the sixteenth century. Unfortunately, they'd ended up in the New World seeking religious freedom to continue eating people for the Devil. The Nightwalker had supposedly defeated all of them, but it turned out there was a fairly large number of the extended *Hills Have Eyes*-rejects and they'd come back numerous times for revenge.

This looked like someone had managed to successfully bring the entirety of the horde back at once and it wasn't just Scottish Baba Yaga's descendants here either. There were also the remains of the Brotherhood of Infamy, dressed in pointed black hoods and robes that made them look like discount Death Eaters. Hell, that wasn't even a joke so much as an observation as a few wielded wands that were blasting away at the campers. A few were even riding around like Satanic Sabrina the Teenage Witches.

Wait, that was a thing now.

"Early graduation day, it seems," I muttered.

"I must protect my students," William said, grabbing an ax buried in a tree stump and running into the battle.

"I have to admire a teacher who takes his job seriously," I said, throwing a fireball at the tractor before it ran over a pair of frightened blue-skinned eleven-year-olds. They were among the children not being trained in combat because, well, eleven-year-olds. The tractor exploded and Mandy scooped up both kids and spirited them away.

I levitated six feet off the ground and turned insubstantial, hurling fireballs one after another into the attacker. This was something I knew how to do and would allow me to be an actual hero. Almost as soon as I froze a guy waving around his chainsaw in a particularly phallic way, I fell back to the ground and landed in a pile of mud. I also felt all my magic fade away.

Uh oh.

That was when I was grabbed by the base of my cloak and dragged into the air, upside down, before the face of Sheriff Injustice. He was staring at me with red eyes and a face that contained all the hatred in the universe.

"You killed mah daughter," Nordbert said, breathing hot air into my face that reeked of the same cheap whiskey that I sold for way too much in pharmacies.

"Well, crap," I said.

Chapter Eighteen

Where I Get My Ass Kicked (Again)

"You killed mah daughter!" Sheriff Injustice shouted again, glaring at me with pure fury in his eyes as he held be suspended in front of his face by my cape.

"And my mother insists she looks like Barbara Streisand in *Funny Girl*. Neither of which is remotely true," I said.

Truth be told, I was of a mixed opinion of how I should respond to Sheriff Injustice's accusation. The fact was that his daughter was dead and that was peripherally related to me, even if I wasn't the guy who finished Missy off. A part of me, the dad part that suspiciously sounded like my own dearly departed abba, sympathized with him over it in a universal non-individualist manner. The rest of me knew that he was the one who'd abandoned her to die and brought her to murder us in the first place. I didn't get a chance to find out which part would have won their hypothetical debate because Sheriff Injustice started banging me around against the ground one bash after another.

Honestly, if not for the fact that I was on a heavy concentration of magic that seemingly disrupted Sheriff Injustice's powers—at least that's what I assumed was happening—I would have been dead right then and there. Even then I could feel my supernatural powers slipping away again and if he could properly digest this haunted campsite's magical wellspring then we were in serious goddamn trouble. Now a sane person would have fled like a jack rabbit and called William or Nancy down here to deal with Yosemite Sam the same way that they'd done earlier. I, however, was anything but sane.

"This is because I had sex in a haunted summer camp, isn't it? That and the drinking plus wanting to smoke weed? I'm cursed now. Those are the rules," I said, spitting up blood in the muddy pit I was currently laying in. At least, I hoped it was mud. I could hear pigs squealing and noticed that I'd been thrown through a damaged fence into what had formerly been the petting zoo. Either that or Cindy's personal pigsty. She'd never been kosher and had become even less so inclined after turning herself into a werewolf. Sweet, sweet pork, how you tempt even the most Maccabean soul.

"Imbecile!" Sheriff Injustice said, pulling me back by my cape. "You think you're Bugs Bunny but I'm gonna skin ya alive."

I reached into my utility belt and pulled out the Kangaroo Hunter's boomerang. "You think it's an insult to compare me to Bugs Bunny, I consider it a compliment. Also, that would make you Elmer Fudd. Which is weird because I already mentally compared you to Yosemite Sam. You're really messing with my references here, man."

Sheriff Injustice seemed honestly impressed at my gumption or maybe he was just savoring that last bit of tension before the kill. Maybe he just really loved Looney Toons and was giving me props for making a reference to ninety-year-old cartoons. "You ain't gonna hurt me with that thing there, boy. Do you even know how to throw a boomerang?"

Once more hanging upside down in front of his face, I shook my head no. "Not in the slightest. No, it's mostly this is a grenade and a knife as well as a boomerang."

"What?" Sheriff Injustice asked right before I stabbed him through the eye with the orichalcum alloy weapon. The weapon passed through his flesh like it wasn't as hard as Ultragod's and burned against the anti-magic properties of the metal. He promptly dropped me, and I rolled away from him, holding the boomerang's detonator in my hand. It was almost a shame to detonate it, but I did so, taking off the alien's head.

"Huh," I said, impressed by the Kangaroo Hunter's weapon's effect. "I really should have used this first."

That was when I saw Sheriff Injustice turn into the horrifying humanoid alien thing his daughter had become earlier, growing multiple tentacles that cracked with alien energy. I belatedly recalled that decapitation was not enough to deal with him.

"Ah crap," I said. "This is gonna suck."

"You ain't just whistling Dixie," Sheriff Injustice said, his voice a horrifying distortion of his traditional Southern accent.

"You are really committing to this Southern redneck thing," I said, dancing around his tentacle blows, mentally thanking Mr. Inventor for giving me the basics of combat training.

"An adopted son of the South is no less a Southerner!" Sheriff Injustice said cheerfully. It showed that any grief he had for his dead daughter was purely an illusion.

"And yet you're against immigration I bet. You want to kick the ladder out from under you after climbing it," I said, pulling out my Nightwalker Shark Repellent. It was useless here, but Nordbert didn't know that. Also, why did the Nightwalker have such a specific weapon? Even more so, why had I picked it up? "Back off, man! This is Corbomite Spray! It has the power to blow up an entire football field!"

"Corbomite is a reference to *Star Trek: The Original Series*," Sheriff Injustice said, pausing in his attacks to rebuke me. "Captain Kirk used it to threaten aliens in two episodes and it was a bluff both times."

I stared at him. "It saddens me to know you're a fellow Trekkie."

"Well, I *am* an alien," Sheriff Injustice said, successfully grabbing me with all his tentacles at once. "Say goodnight, fool."

Feeling my bones crack under the pressure of Sheriff Injustice's assault, I look him right in the eyes. All three hundred or so of them. "Goodnight, fool."

Sheriff Injustice paused then let out a hearty laugh. It was apparently something he considered to be funny and gave me a second more of life. That was when all the tentacles were severed by a katana that caused him to pull back.

"Mothersucker!" Sheriff Injustice shouted and he proved to be correct because the katana was in the hands of my former (?) wife, Mandy. Standing next to her was Cindy in her pre-wolf form, which was basically her normal one except six-feet-tall and looking like she was half-feral. Oh and built like she could toss around MMA fighters. I'm not saying it played into any of my personal fetishes but, yeah, let's be honest. It did. I was a perverted, perverted man.

"Come on, a vampire with a katana?" I asked, stepping away from the pieces of Sheriff Injustice slithering on the ground. "What is this, the Nineties?"

"You're welcome!" Mandy shouted.

"Oh, and thank you," I replied.

"You magic fools just make me stronger!" Sheriff Injustice said, growling. "I can feel myself growing fat on your camp's energy every second!"

"Actually, I'm a magically changed Super that, nevertheless, has science-based lycanthropic genes," Cindy said.

"What?" Sheriff Injustice said, confused.

"It means kiss your ass goodbye," Cindy said, transforming into her full wolfwoman form with a long set of canine claws that she used to tear into Sheriff Injustice. It was a bit like watching a rotten banana being thrown into a blender.

I ducked under each of the flying pieces of Sheriff Injustice and watched several move toward me. I used my Nightwalker Shark Repellent on each of them and they shriveled up like slugs with salt poured on them. Refusing to ignore my good fortune, I managed to destroy at least half of the monster's body before the rest slithered away.

"I think we got him!" I shouted, cheerfully.

"We?" Mandy asked, lifting her katana. "Gary, you're really not doing well as a superhero. Maybe you should rethink your present life goals and go back to being a bank robber."

"I like to think of myself as a classy cat burglar," I said, putting my hand over my heart. I could feel my powers returning but I needed a few more minutes before I was able to go back to helping defend the camp. "Except I'm not really that classy. I'm more like Bruce Willis' Hudson Hawk or Japan's Lupin the Third."

"Any other weird random facts you want to share?" Mandy asked, cutting down a trio of zombified cultists that had risen from the dead after being struck down. I had no idea where

Mandy had learned to be a samurai. It was like she hadn't been content to be a Eurasian vampire assassin but now just wanted to go full anime character. No wait, she was a fully grown adult woman, so anime wasn't an appropriate comparison. I felt bad for the Red Schoolgirl who leaned heavily into that motif. She was a thirty-year-old woman and still dressed in a schoolgirl's uniform. Not that most men and some women were inclined to complain.

Oh right, Mandy was expecting an answer to her question. "In college, I was part of a heavy metal band. Our gimmick was that we dressed as badass warrior pandas. We were called Pandamonium."

Mandy facepalmed. "Oh Goddess."

"If I were to time travel back to then, I'd advise my younger self to go with Mage against the Machine," I said. "Of course, unlike you, I couldn't sing or play an instrument, but that was never going to stop me. Why I ended up a member of the Black-Eyed Peas."

"What did the Viking Battle Boars think?" Jane asked, coming up from behind me and shooting her magical pistol into a buzzsaw wielding Lich-Wight with a tanned pig's head as a mask.

"I don't think they were a band," I said. "Which is a shame as that would be a hard gimmick to beat."

"Gary, do you have a concussion?" Jane asked, concerned.

I blinked. "I believe I do, yes."

The Pig Man lifted his sickle to decapitate me, which he had plenty of room to do since he was about eight feet tall and built like a brick wall.

"Powers back," I said, before blasting him with a fireball so powerful that it blew off the upper half of his torso, leaving only his waist and legs. They wobbled a bit before falling over. "I call that one *Power Word: Rocket Launcher.*"

"You didn't say *any* magic words," Jane said, looking at me funny. "Gary, have you been holding out on me?"

I shrugged. "Never create a system you can't game."

"Could you two focus on defending the campers?" Mandy shouted, turning into mist and moving with inhuman speed across the battlefield. She would turn into a bloody cloud, disappear, appear behind a baddie, cut off their head, and then move on. "We're losing this battle!"

Mandy wasn't wrong. Despite the fact that I didn't see any of the campers killed and all of their defenders were still alive, the monsters had pushed everyone into the center of a circle that was eventually going to break. I was pretty sure I could make it out of this alive and so could just about everyone else here among the fighters.

The fighters weren't the people I was worried about, though. This was a refuge for kids and that was the target of the attackers, I realized. This wasn't about going after the superheroes here (such as they were) but the children. The next generation of superheroes, perhaps, or maybe just to deal a psychological blow to the current one.

After all, nothing would break Cindy worse than trying to rescue teenagers stuck in the same sort of situation she'd been growing up only to lead them to their deaths. Well, that or losing her credit cards. Ouch! I can feel her psychically pissed at me for that comment. She does love her Omega Corp Black Card, though.

"I can tell!" I said, trying to figure out a possible way to deal with this situation. "I think I have an idea."

Cindy lopped back in her warg form, spitting out a severed tentacle before resuming her human form. "It'd better be a good one, Gary. We depend on you for plans stupid enough to work."

"I am both insulted and relieved," I replied. "Get back to the children and hope that Death is still favorably disposed to me. I'm about to invoke my God of the Dead powers!"

Cindy blinked. "You have God of the Dead powers? I thought it was just a stupid but blasphemous title you gave yourself."

"That too!" I said, conjuring my scythe and drawing on the power of the Primal Orb of Death to supplement my own natural abilities. The grass around me started to die as the bugs in the air began to drop.

Cindy blinked. "Yeah, probably a good idea to run away now."

"I hate when comic books keep introducing new powers to

characters," Jane muttered as she fired shots into more of the Lich-Wights coming our way. "This is how Superman got the power of Super-Hypnosis and Super-Basket Weaving. Which is only slightly more egregious than the fact you're a werewolf now, Cindy. I consider that cultural appropriation."

"Jane, to quote you, shut the buck up," Cindy replied, turning into a wolf and mauling away a Lich-Wight before it bit a camper on the arm.

William and Nancy were barely managing to hold off a half-dozen of the enemy Lich-Wights as well as the horde of zombified cultists that had been created from the rest. The campers, to their credit, were not planning on going down without a fight themselves. One of them could generate shields and had created a large bubble over the others. Another had eyebeams that she was using to blast the attacking monsters one after the other. A third? A third was blasting them with flower petals that, well, weren't doing much, but points for trying.

As I felt my power reach the limit my body was capable of handling, David proceeded to land on my hand. "Yo, what's up?"

"Not the time, David!" I shouted, feeling like I was about to explode. "Also, I know you were leading me into a trap. Not cool, dude!"

"Ah, what's a little betrayal between friends?" David asked, not even bothering to deny it. "The important thing is that I get what I want. Which is you to confront Dracula."

"Why?" I asked, confused and angry.

"That would be telling," David said, his voice devoid of humor.

Growling, I held tight to my scythe and shouted to heavens. "I command you, in the name of Death, to return to your graves. I, as the psychopomp for this dimension and Lord of the Dead, compel you to die."

One of the hillbilly cannibal zombies hurled a pitchfork at my head that I instinctively ducked under. The rest had the gall to laugh as if I'd just spoken the funniest thing the cursed horde had heard all year. It appeared that I didn't have any special power over these particular undead. It could be because they were from another dimension or just my plan was stupid from the beginning.

"It didn't work," David replied.

"I know," I said, watching the horde ignore me and descend on the children. Cindy, Mandy, Nancy, and William had made a wall out of the attackers, but I noticed they were all getting up after being destroyed. Severed hands, severed limbs, and more moved of their own accord to merge together into new horrifying abominations that seemed to get more terrifying with each attack.

"Gary!" Cindy shouted. "Do something! I stopped your guy, the least you could do is stop mine!"

One of Sheriff Injustice's tentacles went for my face, only to be grabbed by David's claws before he flew over the lake to toss it in. That gave me and idea and I sucked in my breath before slamming down my scythe. "GO BACK TO HELL!"

That was when I opened a portal to Hell.

That was a good idea, right?

Chapter Nineteen

Where My Plan Completely Backfires

Sometimes I just do things.

This is going to what they write on my tombstone if there's enough left of me to bury. I am the poster boy for Chaotic Neutral, which isn't even an alignment in the modern edition of *Dungeons and Dragons* as I understand it. I have almost zero impulse control and I swear, getting older and becoming a father has only made it worse. Like, for example, when confronted with an unkillable horde of Lich-Wights, why did I think for a second that opening a gateway to Hell was a good idea? Seriously? That was my solution and I'm not even sure that qualifies as one.

As mentioned, I've been to Hell a few times in my life and it's never been a pleasant experience. The Underworld has a wide variety of places to visit and plenty of interesting people but you're never going to have a good time in even the nicer sections because, again, Hell. They will somehow manage to make a four-course meal of the best food you've ever tasted an experience that you won't want to recall. I remember when I managed to get the world's greatest BBQ as a meal and after finishing, they led in my rabbi in order to make sure I felt guilty for violating kosher. So damned good, though. Literally.

Wait, where was I? Oh yes, I'd opened a gateway to Hell because I figured that if you had a bunch of monsters that were unkillable abominations against God then the only thing to do was take them off the board—literally. Hell *is* the place you put unkillable abominations against God, after all. I assumed. It's not like I actually bothered to take a census down there about whether Kronos and the Titans plus Azazel were the only guys imprisoned in the fiery pits. Really, this is why I preferred Jewish Hell because a really dark empty place was less theatrical but no less effective for an afterlife. Oh dammit, I keep getting distracted. Why was that? Oh yes, I'd stupidly opened a gateway to Hell!

The idea that I'd made a terrible mistake was instantly understood as a swirling vortex appeared underneath the majority of the Lich-Wights. Most of them didn't have a chance to react other than to scream in shock or surprise as they suddenly started to fall into the demonic red light that blasted forth an unnatural heat. This was the fire and brimstone Hell that was not the place I'd visited. The flames belched forth and consumed many of the Lich-Wights that had been already falling to their doom. So far, so good. If I had closed the portal then, I would have saved the day.

Unfortunately, I couldn't. I reached out to start closing the portal I'd conjured—or at least try to slow its expansion—but it turned out that I was unable to do either. Instead, inch-by-inch, the vortex to the second most feared place in the Multiverse (the first being Oblivion) started to grow. Worse, I could already some unearthly howls of unholy abominations coming to escape through the hole I'd poked into their prison. Things I could sense were powerful and terrifying enough to make the Lich-Wights look like a set of rowdy toddlers. Yeah, that was not good.

"Gary, you idiot!" David shouted, flying around my head. I noticed he didn't actually fly so much as levitate, which made me start to wonder if the whole bird thing was just an affectation on his part. Mind you, most birds I knew didn't talk either.

"I didn't know this would happen!" I shouted, trying to figure out some way to fix the situation.

"You opened a gateway to Hell!" David shouted. "That is by definition a bad idea!"

"Details, details!" I snapped. "If you're not going to help me solve this, then flock off!"

"You mean bork off," David said.

"I mean fuck off!" I snapped.

"Listen," David said, ignoring my curse. "You need to absorb the Hell energy into yourself!"

"That sounds bad!"

"Do not try to argue with me about this!" David said. "I am way better at magic than you!"

"Just who are you?" I snapped, deciding to follow the bird's advice as I saw something start to emerge from the Hell gate I'd opened. It looked very large, red-skinned, and horned in a way that made me realize that at least some depictions of the Devil might be accurate. Either that or the demon emerging liked to play to stereotypes.

"I will devour your soul!" the booming voice of the giant, skyscraper-sized, red demon said, its enormous hand reaching up through the top of the gateway.

"Yes, because quoting the *Evil Dead 2* makes you cooler, not lamer," I muttered, concentrating on the power within the gateway as well as attempting to link the power of the Primal Orbs with the Reaper's Cloak. "Real fans quote *Army of Darkness!*"

"I think that's the reverse," David said.

"Shut up!" I said. "Bruce Campbell is a god and that's all that matters."

David didn't argue the point, probably because it was self-evidently true.

"Absorb and close the gate! Absorb and close the gate! Absorb and close the date!" I shouted, making up a new spell on the fly in the silliest way possible. Well, not quite the silliest way possible, there were no rubber chickens, but if I'd had Fozzie Bear there then everything would have worked out fine.

What followed was a tidal wave of negative energy pouring through every cell in my body. If I wasn't someone that Death had been subtlety manipulating the bloodline of for millennia—assuming you believed the Queen of the Underworld—then I probably would have been shredded in an instant. Instead, I was just washed over with more Hell energy than the protagonist of *Doom*.

I was hit by the usual standbys of regrets and horrors that I had experienced over the past thirty years of my life.

The death of my brother, Keith.

The failure to save Mandy.

The failure to save Falconcrest City.

Cloak's death.

Diabloman's betrayal.

The fact that I read Cindy and my fanfiction from junior high to our kids when they were barely old enough to understand English. I mean, I don't know if the fact reading *My Immortal* at story time qualified as child abuse, but it probably should.

That time I won the Grammy Award for Best Single when I absolutely cheated using sorcery and it belonged to the K-Pop superhero team Alt-Language. Kayne and Taylor Swift were right to call me out for that.

"Focus, Gary!" David said. "Also, have you considered that your crimes are less actual crimes than mischief?"

"I am not mischief! I am a serious supervillain, I mean superhero, goddammit!" I snapped, feeling a thousand burns across my body as red lightning poured from the portal like the Emperor's Force lightning being reflected by Mace Windu. I felt agonizing pain but that increased my ability to channel sorcery.

Strangely, I felt another presence helping me draw in the Hell energy expanding before us. It was a much more powerful wizard's presence that managed to drain away many times more than what I was accomplishing. It made me realize that if I was being suckered by the little raven then I was being suckered by an archmage of considerable power.

Nevertheless, I coordinated our efforts and they had a synergetic effect. Whatever was on the other side of the Hell gate—I mentally decided just to think it was Beelzebub because why not—was pushing against the opposite side of the door we were trying to push closed.

Normally, that would have had the same effect as a ninety-five-pound cheerleader trying to hold the door against Jason Voorhees, but we managed to keep the door wedged with the monster's nightmarish head, as well as its arm sticking up through the hole like a building.

The thing really was the whole Halloween Devil with goat

horns, shark teeth, brimstone-colored eyes, and a mouth full of hellfire. I was offended on behalf of all the pagans who'd had the image of Pan modified into a symbol of evil.

Beelzebub snarled at me. "You may have destroyed Gog and Magog, Merciless, but you cannot destroy me! I will burn your world to ashes!"

"Wow, that was like way back in the first novel of my biography! I was a newbie supervillain then!" I said.

Beelzebub pulled back his mouth as if he was going to belch a dragon's breath full of hellfire—and probably was—which I couldn't guard against because I was trying to prevent an archdemon from entering reality. He gathered a massive vortex of flame within the back of his mouth and I saw it was going to blast us with the power of a volcano. Unfortunately, I couldn't turn insubstantial to avoid it either since magical fire could still affect intangible beings. Those were the rules you know.

"Whelp," I muttered. "This sucks."

"I want you to know before we die," David muttered. "I always hated you the most."

"Would mean a lot more if I knew who you were," I replied.

"I am—" David started to admit.

That was when Nancy jumped on top of its head and jabbed down a fishing harpoon, something I had no idea as to why a summer camp had, through the top of Beelzebub's head. The monster screamed, howled, and then slowly crumbled to dust before the gate sealed under him. The ashen remains collapsed into an enormous pile of outdoor barbeque clean-up with Nancy standing triumphant over it.

"Huh," I said, staring. "That was anticlimactic."

"Artemises are made to kill demons," Nancy said. "I'm the best of them. No matter what reality."

I gave a golf clap. "Since he died here, he won't be regenerating anytime soon. That should probably lower the divorce rate, car crashes, and depression across this reality. Demons don't make people do bad things but they sure as hell don't help. No pun intended."

That was when David started pecking my head and

beating me with his wings. "You moron! You complete and utter moron!"

"Ow! Ow!" I said, trying to protect myself with my hands. I wasn't doing a very good job.

"If you get a bunch of rats, you do not get a bunch of cats, then a bunch of dogs to get rid of the cats," David shouted.

"Why would I want to use cats to get rid of rats? Cats eat mice. There's numerous dog breeds designed to hunt rats," I said.

David paused, mid-attack, looking confused. "What?"

"It's why pit bull and bull terrier breeds exist," I said. "People keep forgetting I'm a dog man. I sponsor like fifteen different rescues and kennels. People who think pit bulls are violent should also note that's entirely on the owner. You'll be grateful if one of those disease carrying Mercirats comes—"

David resumed attacking me during my speech.

"Ow! Ow!" I repeated. "You know you have to tell me who you are now! It's dramatically appropriate!"

That was when David flew off.

"Oh come on!" I snapped, watching him fly away.

Mandy, Jane, and Cindy arrived soon after. Nancy and William hung back, finishing off a few straggling Lich-Wights that strangely crumbled to dust when they killed them. It seemed that both serial killer killers possessed an ability to make dead things stay dead that the rest of us didn't. I personally believed that was cheap since, as the psychopomp of this dimension, I should be able to kill anything. Like the Raid can of the undead. Still, ninety-nine-point-ninety-nine percent of the army attacking Camp Blood was destroyed, so a win was a win. Right?

"Gary, what the hell was that?" Mandy asked.

"Either utter genius or utter madness," I said, replying. "Surely not just plain incompetence."

"I think it was anything but plain in its incompetence," Jane said. "And don't call me Shirley."

"Damn, I was going to make the *Airplane* reference," Cindy muttered. "This was Dracula's revenge for setting up on his turf, even though we were here first."

"Someone is using us as chess pieces," Mandy said. "Probably to get the Primal Orbs."

"Yeah, well," I said, taking a deep breath. "Now it's time to have fun storming the castle. I'm going to go Belmont on his ass. Anyone got a whip."

"I do," Cindy said. "But it's for funsies not killing vampires."

Jane looked at Cindy.

"What?" Cindy asked.

"We have a spy in Dracula's castle," Mandy said. "It was extremely hard to get him in and he clearly didn't have a chance to warn us so he could be compromised. Still, I think that gives us an opportunity if you can put aside quoting Monty Python and the Holy Grail or whatever for a few minutes."

"Oh God," Cindy said, muttering. "Now you've done it."

Jane looked at Mandy. "You just had to dare him. Didn't you?"

"What?" Mandy said.

"There's a castle in the swamp!" Jane said. "They said I was daft to build it!"

"The first castle sank, so did the second castle!" Cindy said. "The third burned down, fell over, and then sank in the swamp. The fourth one, though, that stayed up!"

I stared at them. "I should point out that you're the ones who did that bit, not me. Also, of course the fourth one stayed up, it was built on a foundation of three sunken castles."

"Can we do the bit about the terrifying bunny?" Jane asked.

"No we cannot!" Mandy snapped. "I swear, it's like dealing with children."

"Who is more the fool, the fool or the fool who follows him?" I asked, crossing my arms and doing my best Alec Guinness impression.

"You would be the fool in that analogy, Gary," Cindy pointed out. "I also regularly question why we hang around you when you're always doing things like opening gateways to Hell that almost end the world."

"Almost!" I pointed out. "The key word is almost!"

"Don't do that again," Cindy said.

"Say please," I said, smiling.

Cindy gave me a dope slap to the back of the head. "Never!"

"Right!" I said. "I promise to never again open any portals to Hell unless I really-really need to."

Cindy sighed. "Listen, will you go along with our plan or not?"

I took a deep breath. "You guys have graduated to become the Charlie's Angels of supervillains. I'm so proud of all three of you. I trust you all to have some truly dastardly plan that will bring about the fall of our opponent and our ultimate victory."

"We're going to turn you over to Dracula," Mandy said. "That will get us inside Dracula's castle."

"Literally the plot from *Star Wars* and *Return of the Jedi* with me as Chewbacca," I replied. "Yet I am the immature pop culture quoting one."

"Yep," Mandy said. "This is gonna hurt."

"What's gonna—"

That was when Mandy slugged me in the face, and I hit the ground. It was like being hit with a small car.

"Sorry," Mandy said.

"I'm still conscious!" I snapped.

"Oh, crap," Mandy said, lifting her foot to stomp on me.

"You know, we could drug him," Cindy pointed out.

"Or use magic," Jane said. "I know 'Sleep'! Just he may be too high level to affect."

"Think this through before hitting me!" I snapped, lying on the ground.

We finally figured it out about an hour later.

Chapter Twenty

It's Like a Family Reunion

Yes, today was a day for getting my ass beaten. Sometimes it was by redneck alien sheriffs, other times it was at the hands of my so-called allies. Jane, Mandy, and Cindy had come up with the plan to use me as bait to get me inside Dracula's hidden fortress. By the way, *Hidden Fortress* was the Akira Kurosawa movie that *Star Wars* was based on. I learned that in college film studies. Really, it should be required viewing along with other classic Western and samurai movies for anyone who wants to make a *Star Wars* movie. Seriously Disney, hire me as a consultant. You'll only regret it, like, weeks after you hire me.

Okay, where was I? Oh yes. I was waking up from getting my ass beaten by my allies to do a somewhat stupid plan that would probably get me killed. There used to be a rule of supervillainy that you didn't kill superheroes that fell into your clutches. Yes, I said fell into your clutches. Spare me your criticism, I think I had a concussion.

I woke up in a dingy cell made of Medieval construction with a set of bars in front of me. It was, in fact, a literal dungeon and there was a skeleton chained to the wall. Honestly, it felt a little Disney-esque, as if someone had put some poor bastard up against the wall and let him starve to death in order to complete the ambiance. Then again, thinking about that, it actually made the whole thing a lot less Disney. There were the bones of rats on the ground as well as several loose bricks to complete the effect. All the other prison cells were empty as the moonlight trailed in through our windows.

166 C. T. Phipps

"Sorry, fella," I said to the skeleton. "I guess you got sentenced to life."

"And death!" the skeleton said.

I blinked. "Oh, wow, you're one of those talking skeletons."

"Yep!" the skeleton replied. "I had my soul damned to be in my body as it rotted away. Now I'm imprisoned here until I can feast upon the flesh of the living in order to rejuvenate myself!"

"Harsh," I said, looking at him. "What was your crime?"

"Eh, kids," the skeleton said. "I love 'em."

I blinked then snapped my fingers to see if I still had my powers. Nope. Apparently, something about these cells—or Castle Dracula in particular—suppressed my powers. With that, I picked up a brick from the ground and smashed the skeleton's head to pieces before doing the same to rest of him. I didn't stop until the skeleton was completely shattered and whatever spirit inside it was released to the Hell it deserved.

I paused. "In retrospect, I hope he didn't mean he loved kids and refused to hurt them on Dracula's behalf."

"No, he was a pervert," A female voice spoke at the end of the hall.

I turned around and saw two figures approaching my cell. The first was Leslie Trust, who had traded out her business suit dress and blonde hair for a tight leather outfit with green highlights. She looked like she was copying Mandy's style and it was kind of ridiculous. Standing beside her, in a business suit with a grinning Japanese oni mask, was a figure I didn't recognize. He was, however, holding an advanced super-technology pistol equipped with a laser silencer that looked like it had been built in the future. Given the amount of time traveling I'd done, I'd say circa 2040 or so. Really, they looked like someone had gone to central casting for "Bond villainess and henchman."

I looked at Leslie. "It would appear you are not actually a prisoner at Chateau De Count von Count."

Leslie sneered. "As if!"

I blinked. "Wow, you really need to work on your accent. Alicia Silverstone circa *Clueless* is not going to take you very far in supervillainy."

"I am the Countess von Cobress!" Leslie said. "Enemy of Merciless and Supreme Executive Leader of Neo-PHANTOM!"

I blinked. "First of all, I think that title is going to get you sued by Hasbro. Second, weren't you satisfied being the president's daughter? I mean, you had your own crappy clothing line and everything. Third, Neo-PHANTOM is not a thing. This is not a video game. You kill the boss of an organization, like Tom Terror, and the group collapses."

"That is exactly how a video game works!" Leslie snarled. "You can't kill an idea!"

"Yes, you can," I said. "You can kill every single person who holds an idea. That does wonders for killing it. They were also Nazis and Nazis are bad."

I was really hoping Leslie Trust was brainwashed because if she actually had gone and become a supervillain then this whole thing was for nothing.

"They're not Nazis!" Leslie said. "I know because I founded them."

"You founded a group that's the new version of a Nazi group," I said. "What does this have to do with Dracula?"

Leslie chuckled. "Dracula is the first recruit to my new organization! We shall make America great—"

"Don't please," I said. "That was overused years ago."

The man in the oni mask chuckled. Clearly, he had a superior sense of humor since he was laughing at my jokes.

Leslie stared. "I would kill you now if not for the fact that you are needed, Merciless."

"I am needed, really?" I asked, smiling. "It's nice to be needed."

Leslie hissed. "You have the missing Primal Orbs but even they cannot be used to overturn the resurrection ban until you will it. I intend to make sure you're tortured until you do so."

I blinked. "How the hell does...wait, is that what this is all about? You guys lured me here to get the Primal Orbs and have me overturn my tournament wish? That's it?"

"That's it?" Leslie snapped. "Do you realize what you did?"

"Stopped the revolving door of death?" I said.

"Yes!" Leslie said. "So many supervillains used to be able

to raise as much hell as they wanted! Tom Terror, President Omega, the Death's Head—"

"All Nazis," I said. "I'm noticing a theme."

Leslie shook a fist in front of me. "They could get killed but our necromancers and clone masters would have them up and running within months—sometimes days—after their deaths. Nothing would stand in our way but heroes and while they could come back too, our eventual triumph was guaranteed! Now heroes and villains both die while peasants live."

I blinked. "I've got to say, maybe it wasn't the best thing to put President Omega's former VP in charge. I am so glad I voted for the other guy."

"Can you even vote as a felon?" The guy asked. There was something very familiar about his voice, no matter how muffled it was by his oni mask.

"No," I said. "However, if I did vote, it would be for the other guy. I figure I made my feelings unambiguously clear when I killed the time traveling Nazi who brainwashed everyone into voting for him."

"I don't think that's a real political position," the man in the oni mask said.

"Says you," I said. "Make America Nazi free again! Not invoking Godwin's law, not calling my opponents Nazis, just actually against Third Reich supporting jerks. If that's a wrong position, I don't want to be right."

"Give me the cattle prod," Leslie said, holding her hand out to the man. He proceeded to give her an electrified prod that looked like it, too, came from the future. "I am going to make you pay for killing President Omega. When you beg for a chance to undo your wish, I will torture you some more. Then after we resurrect him, I will give him the privilege of being the one to take your life, Merciless."

"Yeah, I don't think you're really giving me much reason to cooperate, toots," I said, leaning back against the wall of the cell.

"We have ways of making you talk," Leslie said, adopting a fake German accent.

"Bork off, lady," I said, staring.

I had the plan of dodging past her when she tried to torture me. Leslie was a deranged First Daughter who had spent most of her life selling clothing made in economically underdeveloped countries and playing off her family name. I didn't expect her to be particularly difficult to fight. Magic or no magic on my part. The unknown quality was the man in the oni mask. I had no idea if he was tough or not but there was something about him that said he was the Oddjob in this particular Bond movie. Oddjob, racist caricature aside, beat the living hell out of Sean Connery. Not many villains could say that.

Leslie opened the door and I proceeded to jump her with my cat-like reflexes. So, it was much to my surprise when she caught me in mid-air by the throat. Then proceeded to jab me with the futuristic cattle prod. It was the week of getting my ass kicked it seemed, and I managed to hold off from screaming for a good thirty seconds before succumbing. I wondered if this ever happened to the Nightwalker. If you find that to be a non sequitur even by my standards, take note my brain was truly scrambled.

"What do you have to say for yourself?" Leslie said, putting her boot on my chest. It was, of course, a high heeled one. Leslie had apparently gotten her ideas of how supervillainesses acted from dominatrixes. Which, honestly, is not my scene.

I coughed, smelling my own burning flesh. "I actually am one of the few musicians on Earth who know how to properly use a keytar."

"A keytar is just a keyboard shaped like a guitar on a strap," Leslie said, jabbing me with the prod again. "It's also a really stupid instrument. Tell me what I really want to hear. Tell me how to bring an end to the resurrection ban."

I grimaced, forcing down my next scream. "Even if I knew how, I wouldn't tell you."

She jabbed me again. "Talk!"

"I'm really fond of William Shatner's *TekWar* series from the Nineties! I intend to review it after I finish my *Murder, She Wrote* retrospective!"

"No one was fond of that show!" Leslie shouted, jabbing me again. "Now, I shall begin work on your genitals!"

"Usually that's a good sign with women," I said.

Leslie moved to jab me between the legs only to stop, the sound of three tiny gunshots going off. Leslie looked shocked and fell forward, landing face first on the ground. The man in the oni mask was holding his futuristic pistol behind her. He'd gunned her down while she was distracted with me.

Instead of expressing my confusion or gratitude, I looked up at him. "You couldn't have done that before the electric torture?"

The man in the oni mask removed his disguise and revealed Case Gordon, aka Agent G. Case was a man of somewhat indistinct features but was a white-passing man that had hints of other ethnicities in a way that couldn't quite be identified. As I understood, his mother was black/ Hispanic and his father Caucasian. Except he was a robot based on the guy he resembled and said guy was a psychopathic cyborg. Yeah, the sad fact was that this was normal among backstories of people I knew.

"No," Case said. "I couldn't. Because you frigging banished me from your dimension without so much as a by your leave."

"We're already full on our Monty Python quotes," I said, trying to get up and failing. "Ow. I take it you're Mandy and Cindy's spy in Castle Dracula."

"What gave it away?" Case asked. "The fact I'm a spy or the fact that we're in Castle Dracula?"

Case was like Jane in that he was every bit as much of a smartass as me. I'd never realized how annoying that was until I'd met them both. "In any case, you just killed the president's daughter and that's going to get you some flack."

Case gestured down with his head and I saw that the body of Leslie Trust was sparking where she'd been shot. "She's a human replacement droid or HRD. Programmed by President Omega to secretly support his agenda while he was gone."

"What happened to the real one?" I asked, surprised.

"I don't think there is one," Case replied. "President Trust is probably also another one of his minions."

I stared. "You know, that's why I only pretend to vote. That and I'm legally prevented from doing so."

If President Trust was a robot duplicate, then that went a long way to explaining why he was still carrying out the anti-Super crusade that his master had instituted in previous years. It also explained why he was hesitant to do anything too overt. With the exception of fully sentient machines like Case, most androids and gynoids didn't work very well outside of their programming. I wasn't sure what had triggered Leslie going full Baroness from *G.I. Joe* but maybe she'd had that in her code all along. Really, that said something about President Omega in itself. Guy couldn't even recruit his own perky female minions, he had to build them.

"I'm more curious why you can't tell if a president is a robot or not," Case said. "Aren't you guys supposed to be more technologically advanced than my world? Which has AI and robots too. I mean, we have a thing on my world called an x-ray."

"Ah, so you don't have the subsonic phase inducer that puts up a fake set of vital signs?" I asked.

Case narrowed his eyes. "How the hell would that even work?"

"Very well, thank you," I replied. "In any case, it's wonderful to see you."

Case banged me on the top of my head with the butt of his pistol. He didn't hit me as hard as he could have, especially as Case was the world's chattiest Terminator, but it was enough to let me feel it.

"What the hell was that for?" I snapped.

"You separating me from Jane," Case said. "Sending me back to my world was equivalent to exiling me to Hell—"

"You have no idea," I interrupted.

"But breaking up Jane and me was unforgivable," Case said. "I am seriously pissed at you, Gary."

I held back a few things that would have been needlessly nasty. That Jane was in a new relationship. That Case should have realized he couldn't just run away from his problems by skipping worlds. That I'd probably saved Case's life since an android assassin was pretty small potatoes in a world where we had people who could move the moon out of orbit. Instead, I said something that probably made matters worse but was as kind as I could think of. "Jane is here now. Apparently, someone has been using my family and friends to try to lure me in."

Case kicked the dead body of Leslie. "How did they lure you in?"

"My children," I said, frowning. "They said I had to save the Multiverse."

Case snorted. "You?"

"I know! I should have guessed it was really pandering to my ego. They also sent a talking bird to lure me in."

Case stared. "Uh huh."

I frowned. "Talking birds are cool."

"So, did Jane ask about me?" Case asked.

I took a deep breath. "Not the time here. I need to know how they managed to fool me with a fake version of my daughter. Whoever managed to get me here knew me intimately and secrets about my family that I shared with perhaps a half-dozen people in the world. Did you sell me out?"

Case stared at me like I was an idiot, a look that I'd gotten a lot over the years and was only sometimes justified. "Gary, why the hell would I rescue you if I sold you out?"

"Because you are devilishly clever!" I said, pointing at him.

Case rolled his eyes. "I know who sold you out, Gary. This is all one large complicated psy-op to gaslight you into assisting in the resurrection plot."

"Psy-ops mean something different in my world. That's when you use psychic powers to control someone into doing your bidding," I said.

"I mean someone is messing with your head," Case said. "There's a bunch of superhero human replacement droids in a closet nearby. One of them was a heavily beaten-up version of your daughter, Mindy. I even saw them growing zombie-looking clones in a lab of things, like the Nightwalker. They were made of nanites that made them all but indestructible."

I blinked. "So, all this sorcery stuff is just super-science? Is Dracula even here? Who the hell is helping him screw with me?"

"Dracula is not here," Diabloman said, standing twenty feet away at the door to the dungeon. The old luchador was standing there in a lab coat of all things, still wearing his mask but looking like a mad scientist themed wrestler as much as his old self. David was sitting on his shoulder, looking guilty.

I stared at my former friend. "Well, shit."

Chapter Twenty-One

Bittersweet Reunions

I stared at Diabloman.

Diabloman stared at me.

Case looked bored and looked away from us both. "Go ahead."

"What?" I asked.

"Do a *Star Wars* quote," Case said. "Make light of the situation. Your old friend is behind this and gave the enemy all the information he needed to manipulate you."

"Really?" I asked, looking at Case. "You'd think I'd do that? Diabloman was my friend. I don't even know how to parse this kind of betrayal. I'm certainly not going to demean events by making jokes."

"Oh, sorry," Case said. "I guess I wasn't thinking."

I turned to Diabloman. "I've been waiting for you, D. We meet again, at last. The circle is now complete. When I left you, I was but the learner, but now I am the master."

"Goddammit, Gary," Case muttered under his breath.

"Do robots believe in God?" I asked.

"Yes, Gary," Case said. "The creator of everything."

"I can't get you to say, 'Thank the Maker'?" I asked. "We can get you a foul-mouthed R2 unit and you can be our etiquette and protocol assassination unit pair."

"I will pistol whip you, Gary," Case said, raising his gun again. "Properly this time."

"I have missed these discussions," Diabloman said. "They are memories of a simpler time. A time when I thought redemption was possible and peace was not a lie."

"Yeah, before you sided with your sister who raped me," I said, devoid of all humor. I hated Spellbinder and would have kept her in Hell, highest circle or not, if not for the fact that I'd been asked to show mercy.

It turned out my name had been another lie which I'd told myself on my road to being a supervillain. I wasn't particularly merciless, and I wasn't a particularly good supervillain either. Because, honestly, a real supervillain would have just incinerated Diabloman right now. I had the power and unless he had the other Primal Stones, nothing was stopping me from doing so. Instead, I just felt sick and tired of the whole thing and miserable that events had come between us.

"If you have to blame someone for what Maria did, it would be better to blame me," Diabloman said. "The cult that raised us made her the Chosen One and me as the man meant to be her bodyguard. Instead, she rebelled, and I made her life a living hell. I stalked her across seven continents and ruined any normal life she sought to build for herself. I killed her loved ones and tried to corrupt her at every turn. In the end, I took her life and trapped her in a space between both this world and the next."

I stared at him. "She made her own decisions, Diabloman."

"Did she?" Diabloman said. "It was your alternate self, the one known as Merciful, who offered her a chance at new life. Merciful gave her a second chance at life, love, and happiness. All she had to do was wear the soulless body of a monster."

"Yes, my wife," I said. "Maria just had to lie to me every night and torture me by thinking my wife was alive rather than gone."

"To Heaven," Diabloman said. "Instead of letting her go, you wanted to selfishly bring her back."

"The difference between you and me, Diabloman?" I stared at him, coldly. "I don't care. I own my actions and decisions. I don't attempt to blame the victim for their assault. For being lied to. You did horrible things to her. You probably don't deserve her forgiveness. However, she gave you it. You got a universal pardon for destroying the frigging universe. That was my wish, not a ban on resurrection, and you tossed it away to side against me. To side with her."

Diabloman didn't respond. "You truly hate her, don't you? Even though her influence helped change the monster back into something resembling her old self."

"She's rescued from Hell," I replied. "Mandy, vampire or not, asked me to release Maria, so I did it. But if you still want to throw down, I'm game. I've lost any and all respect for you as a villain. You're not my mentor anymore, you're not my friend, and I'm sure as shit not afraid of you. I'm prepared to put you down and there's not a damned thing you can do to stop me."

Case interrupted me. "Gary—"

"Don't Gary me," I snapped. "You don't know what it's like to be betrayed."

Case looked down at me.

"Except for all the times it's happened to you," I replied. "Okay, point taken."

Case sighed. "I think you should listen to him."

"There's not a damn thing he could possibly say to me that I want to hear," I replied, fully prepared to fight.

"I'm sorry," Diabloman said. "If you wish to kill me, my life is yours."

I blinked. "Excuse me?"

"Ooo, an apology!" David said, on Diabloman's shoulder. "Didn't see that coming."

I threw a fireball at David, who managed to dodge out of the way.

"Dammit," I muttered. "It looks so damn easy when Mario does it."

Diabloman stared. "I did arrange the trap that was meant to lure you in. I did it on behalf of my master—"

"Your master?" I asked, incredulously. "What the hell have you gotten yourself into?"

"I did many terrible things that have almost assuredly thrown away the redemption you warped the nature of the universe to give me," Diabloman said. "I did so because you sent my sister to Hell and I hated you for it. I intended to force you into releasing her. To undo the ban on resurrection so she could live again. Now you tell me you released her from damnation."

"Yeah, I'm not you," I said. "My hate has limits."

"So literally this entire plan has been for nothing," Diabloman said, sounding more broken and defeated than he was when I first found him working as muscle for the Typewriter.

"What plan?" I asked. "Who are you working for?"

"It doesn't matter," Diabloman said, sighing. "It occurs to me now that I could have just asked you to release her the entire time. I left my wife and daughter, the two people I cared for most, to concoct an elaborate revenge plan. The faked Society of Superheroes Dark, the temporal crisis—"

"You mean the Big Ass Time Disaster?" I asked.

"We're not calling it that," Diabloman said before continuing. "I even drew Case and Jane from their respective realities. It took some doing and I summoned the wrong people a few times, but it was the perfect bait. I even hired some monsters and created other ones in the lab to lead you in."

"Where does the bird fit in?" I asked.

"I'm Diabloman's master," David said, cheerfully.

I rolled my eyes. "Then you, what, got in touch with Dracula to put his lair in my backyard next to Cindy and Mandy?"

"Not quite," Diabloman said. "The real Dracula is dead. I have gathered supervillains from all over the multiverse in hopes of using them to force you to obey. To gather the Primal Orbs together so we can fix the world."

"All to save your sister," I said. "Which I did without you."

Diabloman stared. "You would do no less."

I stared at him. "I'm trying to wrap my head around this insane revenge plot. Why not just kill me?"

"It's not about revenge," Diabloman said. "I needed you to surrender the Primal Orbs to me. Voluntarily. But yes, it may have gotten overly complex. I actually teleported Dracula's castle here so I could use Sheriff Injustice against you. Cindy and Mandy's camp being nearby was a complete coincidence. Apparently, the real estate market prices are insane in this area. You have to build your hidden base in a swamp. It worked out, though, because they were people that David told me had their own Primal Orbs."

David somehow smiled despite not having a mouth, only a beak. It made me think his claim to being Diabloman's master wasn't entirely false.

"You attacked a camp full of children with Lich-Wights!" I shouted. "Children!"

"What's a Lich-Wight?" Diabloman asked.

"It doesn't matter!" David said, landing on Diabloman's head. "The thing is you're here now and we can proceed with Plan B!"

"Plan B?" I asked. "Why do I have the feeling this is like one of those comic book crossovers where the writer quits halfway through the story then another picks it up and completely rewrites it? Oh God, we're in *The Last Jedi*!"

"I thought *The Rise of Skywalker* was worse," Case said. "I didn't like *The Last Jedi* but I understood its themes. I felt The *Rise of Skywalker* was just silly."

I narrowed my eyes. "Just because I can make Star Wars references in dramatic moments doesn't mean everyone can, Case."

"Whatever," Case said. "So, you got what you wanted without having to kill anyone."

Diabloman didn't respond to that, making me think he'd killed anyone. "Unfortunately, it is not that simple. I had to call in every favor I owed and make elaborate promises of power, revenge, and wealth to get all the people I wanted involved. It is one of the rules of supervillainy that you must always pay your debts."

"Like the Lannisters," I said, still too furious at Diabloman to think straight. "So, all that bullshit about being sorry was just that."

"Not quite," Diabloman said. "If you want to kill me now, I meant it. I will not resist. There is nothing left for me now. It's just I want to warn you that this castle is full of supervillains that have been waiting three or four days for your arrival so they can all get their wishes granted by the Primal Orbs."

I stared at him. "This sounds like a terrible plan from top to bottom."

Diabloman frowned. "I confess, I am somewhat out of

practice in evil scheming. David has also been adding to it left and right."

David gave me a wave with his left wing. "His original plan was just to kidnap you and steal the Primal Orbs himself. I said, 'why not involve Dracula's castle and the president's daughter?' Then I said, 'Why not build a castle in a swamp?' He said I was daft to build a castle in a swamp—"

"No more Python!" I snapped. "What's next? Quoting the movie version of *Clue*? To make a long story short—"

"Too late," Case muttered.

"—we've got a bunch of supervillains upstairs who you assembled to kick my ass," I said. "All so they can do what Princess Reich down there—"

"Contessa de Cobress," Diabloman corrected.

"I like mine better," I said. "All so they can do what Princess Reich promised to do in torture me into removing the resurrection, which I don't even know if I can do, and grant wishes with the Primal Orbs. Of which I now have four."

"And they have the other four," Diabloman said. "I sort of helped them steal them."

I stared at Diabloman. "So, they're really this close to omnipotence."

Diabloman had the decency to look guilty. "To be fair, this is usually the part where the Society of Superheroes shows up and starts beating everyone up. They're distracted with the army of Lich-Wights, as you call them, though. I really didn't expect that plan to work. It never would have distracted them this long in my heyday."

"Was this when Ultragod and the Nightwalker were still alive?" I asked.

Diabloman didn't answer.

"Merciful Moses," I said, taking a deep breath. "I take back every good thing I said about you as an archvillain."

"Which is good because I was awful," Diabloman said.

"Even when you succeed you screw up!" I snapped. "Now I know how everyone feels like when they're dealing with me!"

Diabloman looked startled by that comparison. "I do believe that is the most hurtful thing anyone has ever said to me."

"Case, can you sneak me out of here?" I asked.

"I'm pretty sure that can be arranged," Case said. "It turns out if you put on a scary mask and are a killer android, people tend to assume you're a supervillain."

"Can't imagine why," I muttered. "We'll get the Primal Orbs away from this place and come back with an army to take the others."

"Pfft!" David made a raspberry, which was another thing that he shouldn't be able to do as a bird. "You haven't heard Plan B yet."

"You're one of the bad guys!" I snapped. "You lured me here to ambushed!"

"Only so I could betray Diabloman!" David said.

"What?" Diabloman said.

"It's all part of the plan!" David said. "The plan that can successfully turn this all around."

"What?" I asked, more confused than ever.

"All of it!" David said.

I had no idea what my fine feathered frenemy meant. "What the hell are you even talking about?"

"Gary, don't listen to the bird," Case said, warning me with sensible advice I was bound to ignore. "I can just shoot him now. It'll be like *Duck Hunt*."

"*Duck Hunt*?" I asked. "How old do you think I am?"

"Honestly, I'm not sure," Case said. "What with the time compression thing that is a real thing in your world."

"Yeah, we can fix that too," David said. "The Big Ass Time Disaster may be fake but that doesn't mean you getting the Primal Orbs isn't a worthwhile goal by itself. It's why I arranged all this."

"Wait, you weren't kidding about the bird being your master?" I asked Diabloman.

"It's complicated," Diabloman said. "He is actually—"

"Shh!" David said. "Spoilers!"

"Yes, master," Diabloman said.

"Gary, this is your Rocky moment!" David said.

"Where I lose but win the public's approval?" I asked.

"This is your *Rocky 2* moment!" David corrected.

"Where I'm an unnecessary sequel made for more money," I said. "Technically, I think we may be *Rocky IV* if we're counting my biographies. Those ran out of steam awhile back. Really, we should have stopped with *The Science of Supervillainy*."

"Hush, they're still entertaining," Case reassured me. "Besides, *The Tournament of Supervillainy* is when I show up."

"Exactly. Nah, I'm just kidding. I've always had plans for at least twelve books," I said, turning back to David. "I'm listening, Corvidhead."

"Weak insult," David said. "You've been trying to be a superhero for a long time, Gary. You've failed miserably because you need a big win. Something so uncontestably great that no one will ever doubt you again."

"I've saved the universe," I replied, listening more closely than was probably healthy. "Twice."

"Who hasn't?" David asked. "I think Mr. Tiny and Gorilla Steve have saved the universe. Imagine, however, you are getting all the Primal Orbs in a castle filled with all the archvillains. Diabloman has gotten some truly heavy hitters upstairs. The real world-beaters. Imagine if you can make them all disappear with a snap."

"This is totally a rip off of *Avengers: Endgame* and *Spider-Man: Far from Home*," Case muttered.

"I really need to see those movies," I said, sighing.

David pointed at me with his wing. "The Age of Superheroes will end with a bang not a whimper. No more world-threats, just petty criminals and a better, safer world for your children. You will go down in history as the greatest hero who ever lived. Even bigger than Ultragod and the Nightwalker combined. Maybe you can cure cancer or end world hunger as an encore. The possibilities are endless."

I stared at him, examining all the angles. Diabloman didn't respond but just stood there, showing he really was under David's control. How the mighty had fallen. Maybe he just wasn't comfortable making his own decisions anymore.

"Gary—" Case started to speak.

"Okay," I said. "I'm in."

I was terrible at this superhero thing.

Chapter Twenty-Two

Exploring Castle Dracula's Mini-Map

I hummed the Stonecutters theme from *The Simpsons* while walking down the halls with Diabloman and Case. David flew above my head and I kept a watch out for the bird crapping on me since I was stupidly following his lead for reasons I didn't entirely understand. He just had a way of making the surreal sound sensible. I wondered if that was how people reacted to me.

"I'm still weirded out you have that show on this world," Case muttered. "Not even a volcanic eruption could get it canceled on my world."

"Yes, but is Bartman a superhero on your world?" I asked. "He was a great inspiration for my supervillainous persona."

Case stared at me. "My God, it explains so much."

"Don't have a cow man," I replied.

"You have a wonderful way of making mundane things horrifying," Case said.

"Thank you," I replied.

The interior of Dracula's castle was less impressive than I'd expected, and kind of disappointing overall. I was hoping for something akin to full-on *Castlevania: Symphony of the Night* with an upside-down castle resting on top of the regular castle as well as every sort of monster imaginable. Instead, the place kind of felt like an upper-class Romanian hotel.

The place was heavily carpeted with the expected reds and blacks. The walls were covered in lots of portraits of old generals and vampires. We passed a werewolf French maid who was vacuuming the place with pointed ears and cute fangs. It was such an incongruous image, I actually chuckled to myself.

"Are you really sure this is a good idea, Gary?" Case asked.

"Absolutely not," I replied. "In fact, I am fairly sure this is a terrible idea. However, if I don't get the other Primal Orbs back from these guys then we're going to end up with villains that are going to unleash their power on our third rock from the sun. If any of these baddies are an actual wizard and not a complete chucklehead like me—"

"They are," Diabloman interrupted.

"Then who knows what they've already been able to do," I replied. "I've created an entire alternate magical system."

"That was you?" Diabloman asked. "You know that nerds across the world are unleashing lightning bolts and mind-controlled orcs on their enemies."

"Orcs that they mind-controlled or conjured magical constructs?" I asked.

"Magical constructs," Diabloman said. "Why does it matter?"

"Yeah, I don't support mind control," I said. "I refused to make *Charm Person* spells or *Suggestion* real. Because we know what the worst kind of nerds would use those for. Fanboys and girls would be keeping their celebrity slaves everywhere."

"Well, that got dark quickly," Case muttered. "So, you trust them with the power to throw fireballs but not control minds?"

"Yes," I said. "Just say no to mind control. Not even once. Death magic is fine, though."

Case looked like he was getting a headache. "The sad fact is, I actually understand the basics of that moral system."

"Thanks," I said. "Just for that, when you die, I'm going to upload you into the Merciless Mobile and we can fight crime like *Knight Rider*."

"Wait what?" Case asked.

"Sorry, just seeing if you were paying attention," I said. "Though I totally would have you as my crime-fighting car. Wait, is that bigoted against robots? Roboticist?"

Case stared at me. "You're a sick man, Gary."

"Thank you, times two," I said. "So, Diabloman, where do we stand?"

"I'm sorry, what?" Diabloman asked. "I was attempting to tune out your inane patter."

"That's an exercise in futility," David said. "One of the qualities I admire and despise both in Merciless is his being a human word salad. Imagine if instead of Merciless, he'd gone with the name Nonsequitor or Pop Culture Reference."

"That would be both more accurate and a heavy theme to play into," I replied. "I'd probably need powers related to referencing things versus just making quips like Splotch. But you didn't answer my question, D."

"Are you suggesting that we put aside the fact I tried to kill you and you sent my sister to Hell?" Diabloman asked.

"Yes," I said.

"No," Diabloman said. "Not because I hate you, though a part of me still does, but because I know that I am a monster who has no place in the lives of a family. You have forged a family around yourself and that is something I cannot be a part of."

"Your wife and child love you," I said. "I know both of them. Your daughter's a little weird but—"

"My wife divorced me," Diabloman said. "When I told her my plans of revenge, she said that I was insane and betraying someone who had shown me compassion when no one else would. I told her that she could choose you or me. She chose to leave with our child and used santeria to bind it so I could find neither of them."

"Ouch," I said. "That would make me more determined to kill me. Wait, you. Okay, I've lost the pronoun somewhere."

"*Si*," Diabloman said, sighing. "It was the end of a long period of rebuilding. She had become accustomed to me trying to be a better person. Backsliding, it turned out, was worse than the lowest point."

"I'll talk to her," I said.

Diabloman stopped and clenched his fists. "It is not your place to clean up after my mistakes."

I stared at him. "No. I thought you were my brother, though. That you are my family. I'm willing to forgive and forget but take that swing and you will regret it."

Diabloman did. He blinked and found himself covered in bright yellow sharpie doodles of Hello Kitty. I avoided drawing genitalia because I wasn't fourteen anymore. I was at least fifteen at heart. Diabloman stared as I was a foot away from his fist. "How?"

Honestly, I had no idea. Whether I'd given myself super-speed, magically transformed Diabloman's outfit, or stopped time was something my conscious brain was unaware of. One of the funny things about speedsters is they're not actually that good at what they do. The human brain can only function at the speed of thought so plenty of them get taken over by their powers or slow time down so they can do everything at a regular pace for themselves. In this case, I'd used my cosmic abilities for the equivalent of a freshman college prank. No regrets!

"Okay, that was impressive," David said. "Where the hell did you learn that?"

"Chaos Orb," I said, simply. "As long as I have it and the others, I'm pretty awesome."

"Which is why I'm going to steal them," David said.

"What?" I asked.

"Sorry, huh?" David asked. "I didn't hear you."

"No, I heard you say you were going to steal them," I said, staring at the bird. "I just wondered why you would admit that aloud."

"Drama," David replied. "Also, Diabloman, you look adorable."

Diabloman proceeded to throw up his hands and release a torrent of curses in Spanish which were, honestly, mostly the same ones used in English. It was just done in a Spanish sort of way. You had to hear him to understand. Still, I'd clearly gotten on his last neve. I was good at that.

"Is it wise to taunt him like this?" Case asked.

"It's not wise to taunt any supervillain but plenty of people do it," I replied. "Besides, Splotch is gone so someone has to pick up the pace."

"You are no Splotch," David said, sounding surprisingly serious.

"No, no I'm not," I said, looking up. "Which is another reason I'm doing this."

It was another spectacularly bad idea I was having but I wanted to see how these archvillains were progressing in trying to get around the ban on people staying dead. I was the Chosen of Death and I'd understood Mandy as well as Lancel's arguments that the fallen should be allowed to rest in peace. However, the simple fact was that I regretted every single day since I'd made that decision. If the bad guys wanted to put an end the ban, then I was willing to hear them out.

Was it selfish? Hell yes. Did it potentially contradict all my progress as a so-called superhero? Probably. However, this world benefited more from having Ultragod and the Nightwalker than it did to suffer from all the evils that I'd extinguished over the years. I'd gladly trade a return of the Ice Scream Man, Typewriter, and even frigging Tom Terror if it meant one of them would come back. I could always kill them again after all.

How much of this was due to my encounter with the seemingly restored Mandy back at Camp Blood? Probably a lot, to be honest. She seemed close enough to my memories of her that it was like having her back. A little more antihero-ish but not a psychotic monster either. The smarter part of my brain noted that probably meant it was a trick of some kind.

Walking down the hallways, we passed the laboratories Case had mentioned earlier. There were all the clones of superheroes and villains inside, ready to be released on the Society if they defeated the current bunch. There were more Nightwalkers, Ultragods, Tom Terrors, and other horrors floating in green fluid while lab coated mad scientists worked on them. I recognized a few of them like Doctor Yes' daughter Doctor Maybe, Professor Bedlam, the Clonemaster, the Electrician, and Shiro Roboto who was more someone you called mister before thanking. Yes, that was a Styx reference and I know Austin Powers already did that joke. None of them were top tier but all of them had respectable careers perverting natural philosophy to their own ends. There was also another supervillain I recognized among their ranks that I found myself disappointed to see among the baddies here.

Nicky Tesla waved at me from behind one of the control panels. "Hi, Gary!"

Nicky Tesla was an above-average looking, dark haired woman with large glasses, brown hair, and a perpetual lab coat on over regular work attire. She also sported a bunch of metal tentacles coming out of her back that had briefly given her the name Professor Hydra. She was a former henchman of mine and the first of the "cracks" in the resurrection rule. She'd been murdered by Merciful during the early days of President Omega's plans to kill all Supers.

Nicky hadn't come back from the dead, not really, but had taken advantage of the Diet Coke of immortality in brain uploading. The original Nicky was still dead, but her successor was walking around in an android body that had all the same memories as well as personality.

Nicky hadn't hesitated to add some "improvements" to her body as we all would if we could but I wasn't about to bring attention to them. The only former employee of mine that I sexualized was Cindy and I swear that sounded less creepy before I thought it out completely.

I hadn't seen her in a year, and it was quite shocking to see her doing evil science for the bad guys. She was only supposed to be doing evil science for me. Which, admittedly, I no longer had much need for since I'd joined the side of angels.

I pointed at her. "This is not cool!"

"You weren't hiring since you became a superhero!" Nicky defended herself.

I paused. "Good point."

"Is it?" Case asked. "Is it really?"

"Agent G!" Nicky said, flirtatiously. "If you let me take you apart, I'll show you my special attachments."

Case looked at her sideways. "I'll pass."

"Really? You don't know what you're missing," Nicky said. "I have the hour-long orgasm program for both male and female androids."

Case opened his mouth then closed it, clearly not sure how to respond.

"This is why the end of humanity will not come with the bang of nuclear warfare but the whimper of the holodeck's invention," I replied. "Humanity will go inside and never come out."

"That's actually how *Rossom's Universal Robots* ends," Case said, referring to the first story about robots from 1921. "Humanity stops breeding because they all have sexbots."

"And here I thought that was a parable about communism," I replied.

"Don't worry, Gary," Nicky said. "When the Robot Uprising happens, you will be among those spared and allowed to live out your days in peace as we exterminate the other biologicals."

"Not unless you can kill John Connor," I replied, fairly sure she was kidding.

"Skynet is a moron," Nicky said. "Kill him when you know when and where he is. Then again, who am I to judge? He's pretty badass for a computer made in the Eighties. The guy is making complex world domination schemes on floppy disc and magnetic tape."

"Can we get back to the meeting?" Diabloman asked. "Please return to your work, Doctor Tesla."

"Just so you know, these things are fully capable of killing the Society of Superheroes. Are you sure actually want to make more of them?" Niki asked.

Diabloman stared at me. "It doesn't matter anymore."

"Weren't you the guy who said that it was a terrible idea to kill superheroes?" Niki asked.

Diabloman didn't respond for a moment. "It doesn't matter anymore."

"This isn't one of those midlife villain suicide things is it?" I asked.

Diabloman looked at me sideways. "I have longed to ask you this, Merciless. Do you have undiagnosed ADHD or are you simply easily amused?"

"Who says its undiagnosed?" I asked.

"See ya, Nikki," I said, turning around. "Don't cross any lines you can't uncross."

"You mean like preventing me from resurrecting the dead?"

Nikki asked. "I used to have a thriving business in that!"

"Everyone remembers that!" I said, walking off. "What about my other accomplishments?"

"What other accomplishments?" Nikki called behind me.

I gave her the bird without looking back. "I swear, abandon your henchmen for a year and they get all up in your business."

"Shame," Case said.

We also passed another scientific monstrosity that made me take back everything I said about this place resembling a hotel. It was an automated robot factory that was manufacturing duplicates of the Society of Superheroes Dark. I saw, indeed, Mindy and the other members flopped over like dolls tossed in a corner.

It was a horrifying image in a way that couldn't be put into words to see my daughter lying lifeless there, even knowing it was just a robot that had been programmed to act like her. The fake Mindy had been so lifelike and played me like a fiddle, even if it was just, "Go to this swamp where you nearly die before carrying your incredibly important magical artifacts that the villains want to steal." The one thing that confused me was why they had it as a backup plan since I was already going there with David. Were there multiple villains at work here or was I just overthinking things? Honestly, this plot felt too confusing as is.

Still, I had to ask, "Is Jane actually real? Is Case?"

"Hey!" Case said. "Not cool."

"You think I'd replace a robot man with another robot?" Diabloman asked.

"I wouldn't think you'd have a bizarre plan to gaslight me," I replied. "Yet here we are."

"Eh, these big epic crossovers always have twists and turns in them," David said. "I said we just had to pay you in Nazi gold."

"You cheated," Diabloman said. "My plan would have worked."

"Any plan would have worked with Gary," Case replied. "Including leaving a trail of Snickers Minis to the castle."

"That probably wouldn't work!" I snapped. "Mostly because

the chocolate would have been on the floor. Even if it's still in its wrapping, its unappetizing. Okay, I'm lying. It totally would have worked."

I didn't ask the real question that was bugging me: whether the Mandy I'd slept with back at the camp was another one of Diabloman's robot duplicates. I wasn't worried about sleeping with a robot, I wasn't robophobic, but I didn't think I could get back a semblance of my wife only to have it proved to be a cruel trick.

In that case, I would kill Diabloman. I'd do it with my bare hands if not for the fact he'd tear me limb from limb. I could do it with magic, though, and would. That would be the cruelest act of them all, but I couldn't figure out a reason why Mandy had changed otherwise. The bird might know but there was no reason to trust anything that came out of his lying beak.

With that, we arrived at the main dining hall of Castle Dracula. There, waiting for me on the other side, was a sight that stunned me. I stared, open-mouthed at the gathering of villains, and realized just how borked I was. I had stood up to Great Beasts, the president of the United States, Entropicus, and multiple archdemons. This? This was more than I could handle.

"I think we're going to need a bigger boat," I muttered.

Chapter Twenty-Three

Where I Join the League of Archvillains

The gathering of the villains was beyond impressive. The closest thing I'd ever come to seeing something similar was when I was a captive of the Society of Superheroes on New Avalon in the archvillains wing. I'd been misidentified, to say the least, as a much bigger supervillain than I was and shoved in with the most dangerous people on the planet. To say that this group of people made that look like a preschool would be an exaggeration, mostly because a lot of those people were here tonight, but they were the baddest of the bad and then *worse*.

The dining room was arranged in a large semicircle with a podium at the end, inhabited by Dracula himself as the chairman of this little get together. The walls had enormous banners behind each of the guests, all customized to their personal heraldry. Everyone was dining on gold plates and goblets, which made me think that Maleficent wound find herself at home among the group. Each of the baddies before me was sitting down and looking at me as if they'd been expecting me, which they probably were.

There was the blue-hooded General Venom, the head of the Scorpion terrorist organization and defender of posthuman democracy (to paraphrase Terry Pratchett: "One man, one vote, General Venom being the one man who casts the vote."). He had different politics than PHANTOM and had picked up the slack since that organization had mostly collapsed.

I saw Helios the Sun King, the aged light-bending Polish Super Supremacist who had the excuse of being a Nazi prisoner to justify exterminating regular humanity. My grandmother had weirdly been a defender of the guy due to sharing, uh, living conditions during WW2. Yeah, there's nothing funny there.

Professor Skeleton was present, being a top-hat-wearing black man with a skull tattoo on his face who was part-man/ part god. He was not the first Voodoo themed villain I'd faced but significantly more powerful than The Left-Handed Bokor who had been one of his many bastard children. The guy probably wasn't a fan of me for killing Lefty. I could have really used the help of Mother Brigid or Doctor Houngan right now.

Morgana Le Fey was there, I doubted she needed any introduction. She was Guinevere's mother and looked like Elizabeth Hurley's hotter sister. It wasn't a necessity for superheroines and supervillainesses to both be ridiculously hot, but they tended to be. Only a handful of people on both sides didn't look like Greek gods but that was mostly cantrips at work.

Contrasting her was the Crone, who was the inspiration for Baba Yaga and every Wicked Witch throughout history. The Crone was the mother of the Hag race and the enemy of all good witches in the world. If you wanted to blame people for the persecution of magic-users, it was ninety percent old sexist dudes, but the remaining ten percent was all her.

The King of Crime was present, being a rotund black man who wore a custom-tailored suit for his egg-like appearance, but actually was more Mark Henry than Biggie Smalls. He wore his literal crown on his head and puffed on a cigar while smiling diamond-studded teeth. He'd outlived Splotch and his father, which was an injustice that bothered me to no end. Many of these villains had personally killed thousands of people but the King of Crime had done much worse for making the lives of the poor worse since the Seventies. He was a New Amsterdam gangster who had forced the drug cartels, camora, and Russian syndicates to answer to him.

Sovi-Ape was far more terrifying as a hyper-evolved ape-man than his name should allow. His brain was several times larger than a normal simian's, and he'd had multiple cybernetic enhancements added onto it since the days when he was Stalin's scientific advisor. Sovi-Ape had sprung the dictator from the League of Nations after Ultragod captured him and later was the one to disintegrate Stalin for betraying the Revolution.

I could go on, but you're starting to get the idea of the two-dozen guests here. It was a collection of history's greatest monsters and it bothered me that Diabloman had supposedly gathered them from other dimensions and realities. The Society of Superheroes had gone to a lot of effort to seal these people in the Annihilation Zone and the Prison Dimension, barren dead realities where they could do no harm, as well as the Underworld. I'm not sure how putting someone in the latter was different from death but some heroes had a real hang up about killing people.

Obviously, our host for the evening was Dracula and I feel the need to clarify which version we're talking about. This is not the Bela Lugosi, Christopher Lee, or even Gary Oldman versions. He was probably closest to the latter in appearance, but this was the bodybuilder version of Oldman that had a practiced habit of spearing people then lifting them up over his head to watch them die.

He was an incredibly powerful wizard, I could feel it from across the room even among the already luminary collection of magicians present. But he was sealed in a suit of dragon scale armor (yes, that was a thing) that had been bound with demonic runes. His sword was also singing with incredible killing strength, begging to be unleashed upon the innocent. In short, this wasn't so much Dracula as Dracula by way of Darth Vader. *A New Hope* and *Empire Strikes Back* version, *Return of the Jedi* and prequels need not apply. Maybe *Rogue One*'s hallway scene. Honestly, as impressive as I found William and Nancy, I had a hard time believing they'd managed to kill my world's Dracula.

"Welcome, Merciless," Dracula said, his voice booming through the room like he was on speaker, "to the League of Archvillains."

"Uh hey," I said, waving. "Nice to be here."

It was weird to think I might have matured, God forbid, but

it occurred to me that I would have been all over this at the start of my career. I'd been so obsessed with becoming a supervillain that I'd pretty much ignored the fact that most of them were godawful people. Yeah, I know, it's in the name super*villain* but the simple fact was I'd had a very skewered philosophy about how the world worked. Now? Now I was just sick of all these people and their plans to make the world a worse place so they could make themselves better. Who knew evil was actually bad? I guess most people.

"The League of Archvillains was established in the nineteenth century when I came to the British Empire and slowly began taking it over from the inside," Dracula said. "I turned the richest of society while recruiting ancient magicians, criminal masterminds, mad scientists, and exiled alien warlords. Soon, I was master of an invisible empire stretching itself throughout Europe and eventually the world!"

Morgana rolled her eyes. "*One* of the masters, Prince Dracula."

"Of course," Dracula said, continuing to pontificate. "It was I who brought low ancient kingdoms and peoples to set up a new human race, the engines of commerce and technology as my new tools to reign supreme!"

Dracula droning on and on about how he helped invent colonialism was a sign that the guy didn't know me very well. Then again, what did you expect from a guy who was most famous for the fact he stalked two teenage girls in Whitby before being killed by a cowboy? Dracula had managed to improve his circumstances in the past hundred years, getting his own country and routinely menacing the world's supervillains but I wasn't nearly as impressed as I suspected this gathering was meant to be. I had no chance in hell of beating any of these guys alone—well, maybe Sovi-Ape but this wasn't my jam. The Illuminati would have to do without my membership. I was pretty sure Jews were banned from that particular heretical offshoot of Freemasonry anyway.

I looked up at the King of Vampires and spoke. "Yes, it's all very impressive. However, I'm going to have to ask why you think it's a good idea to invite me now?"

"Ah, he's being humble," Sovi-Ape said. "A good quality in a Jew. Much like Karl Marx himself."

Oh yeah, this was going to be a politically incorrect band of supervillains too. Just great. I should mention that my family ended up fleeing Poland after the Nazis were defeated due to the fact that the Soviet Union had put a bounty on my grandfather's head. He was a resistance fighter against all tyrants. So I was the rare left-leaning wacko who was also a die-hard not-fan of Marxism. Anarchy meant no rulers and while I sometimes flirted with the idea that I could do a better job than these knuckleheads, I was pretty good at avoiding ruling the world. Yes, that was totally the reason I hadn't taken it over yet. Honest.

"You have distinguished yourself these last few years, Merciless," Dracula said. "Your killing of the Extreme, your takeover of Omega Corporation, your killing of the U.S. president, and role in the death of Ultragod."

I grimaced before forcing a smile. "Yeah, that was me alright."

Dracula chortled. "That last one would have gotten you membership by itself, but it is tradition that our numbers remain no more and no less than thirty. As such, it was not until you killed Tom Terror that an opening on our illustrious council was made."

I looked over at Sovi-Ape then Dracula and bit down my tongue about the fact they had a Nazi mad scientist and a Soviet mad scientist on the same team. I also had to wonder why Helios the Sun King hadn't incinerated both. I was tempted to ask him. Instead, I just said, "Wow, that's great news! Here, I thought I was a prisoner! What with waking up in a dungeon and all."

"I also agreed to sponsor you," Diabloman replied.

David chuckled. "He shouldn't have. I mean, he really shouldn't have."

"I agree," I said, looking around a bit more. "So this isn't about the Primal Orbs?"

"Oh yes," Dracula said. "It is. You are going to remove the ban on resurrection in this reality. We have all lost beloved slaves, pets, minions, concubines, and allies over these past few years. It took Diabloman to free us and gather us together for the first time in a decade to realize how badly things had gotten to."

"Yes," Diabloman said, sounding ashamed. "I fell back on many old alliances for this plan."

"He had an elaborate plan with his familiar to destroy you mentally and physically," Dracula said.

"Sweet," I replied. "I take it we're not doing that now?"

"Oh no," Dracula said. "Not at all. It is said that the worst plans of supervillains are made when you have multiple masterminds in charge. When you were brought here as a prisoner, I knew that there was a better opportunity than just trying to torture the Primal Orbs out from you—the late Countess de Cobress aside."

"I really do think that is violating copyright," I said.

"No, I want to simply offer you the world," Dracula said.

"The world?" I asked. "I thought you all would want that."

Dracula snorted. "No, I could never share the rulership of the world with you or any other archvillain. Which is why this is so perfect."

Dracula pointed at me. "Once we have all the Primal Orbs in our possession and you are bound to make the proper wishes, we shall have no limits to our ability to achieve our ends. Why not start with dominion over the multiverse!"

I was now confused. "You'll have to excuse me. I'm still suffering a concussion at the hands of my wife. What now?"

"Banded together from remote galaxies are thirteen of the most sinister villains of all time: the Legion of Doom," Case whispered. "Dedicated to a single objective: the conquest of the universe."

"I think only a couple of them are not from Earth," I replied, softly. "Also, the universe is pretty ridiculous to conquer. A single galaxy should keep you occupied for eternity. Keeps your ambitions realistic is what I always say. I don't know what these people are thinking wanting to take over the multiverse."

"Each one of us shall have his or her own world!" Dracula said. "You inspired us by recreating Merciful's homeworld and putting it in counter-position to the Earth across the sun. We can forge a new cluster of solar systems with the domination of living beings all dictated to our tastes. A world of vampires for me, an eternal Mordred-ruled Camelot for Morgana Le Fey, a Stalinist Soviet Earth for our simian associate, and so on."

"And you want me to do this?" I asked.

"Absolutely," Dracula said. "Our original plan would have been to break you mentally and emotionally, but you seem remarkably resistant to that. I was most disappointed we couldn't bring you here after witnessing the death of your loved ones at the hands of our undead horde. Sheriff Injustice and his daughter are dead as well?"

"As a doornail," I said. "Not understanding how that phrase came to exist."

Dracula narrowed his cold dead eyes. "A pity. Not because you succeeded in destroying him, but I had a wager he would win."

"What a shame," I replied.

The Crone cackled. She then narrowed her eyes and spoke, her voice raspy and not too dissimilar to the Wicked Witch of the West's. "You are all fools. You pretend to think you are fooling him with this banquet and offer of knighthood, but he is not nearly as stupid as he appears."

"No one could be," Helios the Sun King said.

"But you have all forgotten the old heroes. You have all become so used to fighting demigods and kings that you don't remember older archetypes. Merciless is a clever peasant boy."

"I object to the term boy, Grandmother," I said, strangely feeling the need to call her that. Something about my actual grandmother's tales that you should always be respectful to the fae, even if you were fairly sure they planned to eat you. Especially if they intended to eat you.

"The Jew, the Golem, and the Strongman are not ones who will match you fist to fist but with cunning," the Crone said, getting up. "You have let doom in through the front door and acknowledged him as a guest. If you'd been smarter, Little Vlad, you would have crushed his head in with a rock the moment they brought him. However, I suppose we all have our roles to play."

The Crone transformed into a dragon right in the middle of the dining hall before disappearing in a ball of green fire. I half expected "Night on Bald Mountain" or Maleficent's theme from *Sleeping Beauty* to start playing. This despite the fact the Crone was no Angelina Jolie.

I had to admit that managed to rattle my cage. I'd been to alien worlds, with archdemons, and met with the Lady of the Underworld on a regular basis. However, there was something about the Crone that terrified me. I was rapidly realizing that there were people out there who could brute force their way past all my magic and others who managed to see right through my idiot-hero disguise. Well, as much as it was a disguise and not just being way over my head.

"Well, she had to mess things up, didn't she?" David muttered.

That was when it occurred to me that everyone was looking uneasily at me. I suppose that when an old witch spouts prophecy that you're a danger and they've severely underestimated you, most archvillains are inclined to believe her. I suspected in the next few seconds that I was about to blasted to pieces, turned into a toad, or turned into a toad then blasted to pieces.

Dracula looked down at me, a bored expression on his face. "What an interesting display. Tell me, Merciless, do you intend to betray us all? Is it a better idea to kill you before you manage to pull off some miracle that allows you to defeat the greatest alliance of evil in the world?"

Wow, the dude described himself as evil. Somehow, despite being born in 1496, the guy was a full-on edge count. Everyone looked at me, including Case and Diabloman, with the implication that my next words would decide our fate. The only one who didn't look concerned was David and that's because he seemed to actually know what the hell was going on.

"Well?" Dracula asked.

I sucked in my breath. "Of course, I intend to betray you. I'm a villain. Obviously, I'm going to look for any possible advantage I can that will propel me to the top. Loyalty is enforced solely by personal charisma and power. Anything else is just for the feebleminded. Why would I be here if I wanted to share power?"

A long moment of silence passed. Every archvillain then burst out laughing, including Dracula. I had no idea if that was a good or bad thing, so I just laughed along. It was like high school all over again.

Dracula then pressed the tips of his fingers together, resting his elbows on his podium in a move that would have made Mr. Burns proud. "Now, Merciless, I suppose it's time to raise the dead."

With that, a hole opened in the ground and a pedestal containing the other Primal Orbs rose from it. They were all were bound in a magical circle dedicated to the other Primals and called to me. Whoever could unite them all would be omnipotent. The problem was, they had to know this just like I did.

So, what was the catch?

Chapter Twenty-Four

I Have the Power
to Be Master of the Universe

The Primal Orbs are the most powerful magical artifacts in the universe. Unlike a certain other series that Jane and Case were always comparing them to, they didn't have any power on their own. If you somehow managed to gather all eight of them and snap your fingers, you couldn't wipe out half the universe or bring them back from the dead. Yes, I was making a comparison to the titular objects from *Dragonball Z*. Which was what I assumed they were referring to when they were talking about fictional objects to compare them too. What did you think I meant?

Anyway, the Primal Orbs were more like eight versions of the One Ring. They were objects that the Primals—as close to real gods as existed in the universe other than God himself—poured their essence in order to link them to the Multiverse. That energy needed a basis in the user to be wielded and was proportional to the strength of the person holding them. I didn't understand the details, being the equivalent to the puny god of lint rollers in terms of celestial hierarchy, but basically the orbs are the objects that enhance parts of the wielder rather than grant power by themselves.

If that didn't make sense, a simpler version was that someone like me could wield them and do pretty awesome things like make their own magic system and turn a crappy hedge wizard into a pretty powerful archmage. For someone who was already an incredibly powerful wizard, it would strengthen them into a god. For a god? Well, you got the general gist of things. The thing was that the Primal Orbs exerted their own influence on their wielders.

You want to know how you got Gollum? Well, you had someone like Smeagol try to use a Primal Orb too much against the kind of gods that it was set up to serve. I had gotten by through using the Death and Chaos Orbs because, well, I was Death's Chosen and a pretty chaotic guy. Cindy had access to the Life Orb and was a doctor. Mandy? Well, I didn't know if her access to the Order Orb had also changed her but that might explain a few things.

Right now, though, there were eight orbs that each radiated out the kind of power that threatened to overwhelm me. I hadn't used the Order Orb because, well, I couldn't think of something more antithetical to my personality. I felt the same for the Life Orb, just because of its association with Merciful. The remaining Primal Orbs were Creation, Destruction, Fate, and Destiny. In the Infinity Tournament, seven of them had been up for grabs with Destruction's absent, but now there were all eight present. It was Smaug's horde for Goldfinger and a chocolate feast for a chocoholic, except the chocolate was power. Okay, yeah, I totally lost the metaphor, there didn't I?

"Where the hell did you get these?" I asked, suddenly remembering I was with some of the worst villains in the universe.

These asshats were probably just waiting for me to bring out my Primal Orbs so they could have all eight in their possession. There was also little I could do against all of them. Yet, David had suggested that I could just destroy them all with the orbs' combined power. I wasn't sure if he was underestimating them or overestimating me, but the possibility was there. I'd wanted to be the world's greatest hero and now was a chance to make a significant effort toward that goal. If I didn't get myself eradicated by the power I was going to harness. The encounter with Beelzebub earlier showed I couldn't control the power I'd called up.

"It was difficult," Dracula said. "After the Infinity Tournament, the Primal Orbs split across the cosmos to various guardians. Heroes, gods, legends. Diabloman helped us hunt down them all."

"Great job, D," I muttered.

Diabloman did not answer.

David, however, chuckled. "Any champion of one of the orbs can find all of the other orbs if they trust their gut. The orbs want to be reunited."

"I suppose if you've got the balls, you can do anything," I said, doing my best Scarface impression.

"He never said that in the movie," David said.

"I've been running low on material this entire adventure," I said, looking at the display. "So, you guys just want me to reverse the death ban?"

Dracula nodded. "For now. I wish my beloved Elizabeta to join me once more. You of all people, I suspect, will understand the elaborate lengths I will go to regain a loved one. Morgana wishes her son back—"

I grimaced. I really didn't want to humanize any of these people, which was an irony coming from a guy who had lost his brother to a guy who considered him just another supervillain. I didn't want to become another Shoot-Em-Up. "How are you going to make sure I do what you want? Because no way are you relying on trust after all the attempts to force me here."

Dracula showed a fanged smile. "You are, indeed, the only person we do trust with the orbs because you are the weakest person here. Even the King of Crime, who has no powers, has a far greater will than you who simply stumbled onto his powers."

I'd like to think that Dracula was underestimating me, and that I had the Crone backing me up there. But reminding him of that probably wasn't a good idea. "So you think I can overturn the rule I created but not much else?"

"Yes," Dracula said. "Also, the fact is that we have a satellite weapon aimed at your mother's house."

I stared at him, looking for any sign that he was joking. "Really? You'd think the United States government would keep a better handle on those things."

"President Trust proved remarkably easy to bribe with his leaving office in two weeks," Dracula replied. "Mind you, he might regret his daughter's death. Then again, I suppose that depends on his programming."

"You've had robot presidents?" Case asked me.

"Oh yeah, since the Nineties," I said.

Case shook his head. "This world, man."

I sucked in my breath. "So, if I do what you want then you'll get back your loved ones and then we'll work on getting all the worlds you want to rule. However, if I don't do what you want, you'll kill my mother and kids who are with her right now."

"Yes," Dracula said, simply. "Consider it an incentive on your good behavior."

I glared at Diabloman. "And you were part of this?"

"No," Diabloman said. "I would torture you but never endanger your family."

"And yet you did," I replied.

It was an extremely high-risk gambit that Dracula was taking but I couldn't say they were wrong. Even if I managed to wipe out everyone here with the orbs—which was a big if—they undoubtedly had weapons that could be used against my family. If I used the orbs to protect my family, well I was surrounded by a bunch of archvillains who could obliterate me in a single moment.

"The clock is ticking, Merciless," Dracula said. "Perhaps you would like us to eliminate one of your associates to spur you along?"

Yeah, this membership in the supervillain Illuminati was starting off crap. I hadn't even gotten the key to the executive bathroom or access to the evil buffet. The cake was a lie and yes, I was aware that meme was overdone in 2007. "You think that I would care if you eliminated Diabloman?"

"Yes, yes I do," Dracula said. "So does Diabloman. Which is part of why you have ruined him.

"Si," Diabloman said.

"Do it now," Dracula said. "Or we shall return to the torture part of our plan. I can also launch another attack against your foolish band of campers lying outside this castle, believing they have a chance against our forces."

"Yes, this battle station is quite operational," I replied. "The rebel fleet is flying into a trap."

"Indeed," Dracula said.

Too bad Dracula didn't remember how that movie ended. "Alright then. Time to boogie."

As last words went, they weren't my finest, but I said them right before moving my hands over the remaining four orbs and absorbing them into the Reaper's Cloak. With that, all eight of them linked together and I became one with the universe. Or the universe became one with me. Either way, it was an experience that I lacked the words to properly convey the immensity of.

Actually, no, on second thought, I did have a sentence to describe: I became more powerful than they could possibly imagine. Yep, no bad prequel or sequel will ever get those movies out of my brain. I also liked *Solo* and *Rogue One*. Even *The Force Awakens* to a certain extent. Plus, we have *The Mandalorian* now!

Either way, I felt my entire body undulate with power. More power than I could possibly imagine and yes, I know I'm repeating myself. There was a *lot* of power. Life, space, reality, and time folded upon one another while my consciousness expanded to be able to understand it all. I understood the number forty-two in all its permutations and why there was fundamentally something screwed up in the universe.

Unfortunately, he whoever said knowledge was power didn't know what the hell he was talking about. My brief moment of cosmic enlightenment might have also gotten me points if I was a Zen Sunni Buddhist like on Arrakis but didn't do much for me right then. I knew for absolute certainty that if I harmed the League of Archvillains with the orbs that my family would be killed. I also knew that if I cooperated, Dracula would kill me, steal the Primal Orbs, and then kill my family. Which, to be honest, was just dickish.

As I felt my spirit transcend its physical form and become one with everything. Yes, even Spokane, Washington, I did find it being called somewhere else. I couldn't resist this strange call and resented that it drew me away from various plans to find a way out of my current predicament. I wasn't nearly as cornered as Dracula thought, my new magical system making me an archwizard of a kind, but I needed to very carefully word any *Wish* spells cast with the orbs backing them up.

Instead, I found myself sitting at a table before the Council of Archvillains' table. The kid's table, so to speak, except the people sitting before me weren't the ones threatening my family. Instead, I saw Death sitting at the podium where Dracula had stood and seven other figures that radiated omnipotent power. She looked like Mandy with, and I don't mean to be insulting, a sluttier wardrobe (but in a good way!).

There was the overweight geek Destruction, a bearded Moses-looking Creation, a slightly overweight but still hot Cindy-looking Life, a Nightwalker-esque looking Order, a Chaos who honestly looked a lot like me, a Fate that resembled the late Tom Terror, and a Destiny that looked like Ultragod. These weren't the Primals' actual forms but even in my ascended state, I couldn't take in their full power.

If you wanted to know who really ruled the universe then it was these eight beings, the disconnected fragments of God (whatever your religious beliefs) that were everyone and everything. They feuded over reality, constantly tugging us all in multiple contradictory directions. Which, yes, says that the will of everything is crazy pants. Explains a lot about reality doesn't it?

"Hey guys," I said, wondering if this would end up in some religion's Torah some days. I sincerely hoped they spruced up the dialogue. Mind you, mine had such odd entries as Isaac getting in a fist fight with God and constantly arguing him down on murdering the populations of gross cities. Plus the whole whale incident with Jonah.

"Hello, Gary," Death said. "You certainly always find yourself in the thick of things don't you."

"As I said in college," I said, taking a deep breath. "I like 'em thicc."

Death actually rolled her eyes. "Never change, Gary."

"That would require self-awareness," I replied. "But yes, I assume I am here because I have united the Maguffins to bring about the thingamabob that immanentize the eschaton. If this were an anime, then church music would be playing over people becoming orange goo."

"No, Gary," Death said.

"Oh," I replied. "So, what is this?"

"Your trial," Death said.

"Oh," I said, again. "Well, that's not good."

Creation, who sounded exactly like Ian McKellen's Gandalf, spoke, "It was decided long ago that everyone who would wield the power of all the Primal Orbs should have to be judged on their worthiness by our spirits."

"Well, I'm borked," I muttered.

"Why would you say that?" Chaos said. "You were judged as worthy of having two Primal Orbs early on."

"And that was probably a mistake on your part," I said. "I'm absolutely unworthy of any sort of power. In fact, I clearly should not be trusted to do people's laundry. Letting me have access to the Primal Orbs I did have was bound to mess up the universe. But all *eight*? Oh man, it might be better to let Dracula have them. Except you know, all the good people should have them above him. Also, less evil people. Actually, no, let's keep Dracula from them altogether."

"That is why you are worthy," Destiny spoke, now looking like Guinevere instead of Ultragod. "Because you do not believe you are worthy, you are worthy."

I stared at her. "Really, we're going with the Socrates thing? The reason he's the wisest man on Earth is because he's the guy who knows he knows nothing?"

"Nice of you to quote something other than Star Wars for once," Life said, now looking like Aeris from *Final Fantasy VII*. Really, the fact that I perceived the godhead as looking like this was another argument for why no one should let me anywhere near power.

"I also note that Nietzsche would be appalled at the idea that seeking power should disqualify you from having it," I replied. "Mind you, that guy got seriously misunderstood and I totally blame his Nazi sister for rewriting his stuff."

"The problem is, Gary, that you're not the only Gary being judged here," Death replied.

I blinked. "Excuse me?"

Death pulled out an hourglass and it looked like it was made of plastic before being put in a microwave, melted as well as distorted so that it wasn't really dripping sand anywhere coherent. It reminded me of Rincewind's from Discworld where their version of Death had no idea when he was going to die or if. "Your timeline is utterly confused due to the rebooting of the universe. Other Gary, aka Merciful, and you are two incarnations of the same soul, shared between two beings and fragmented across parallel realities. Who you were meant to be and who you are aren't remotely comparable."

"Not necessarily worse but not really better," Destiny said.

"Oh, absolutely worse," Fate replied, looking a great deal like the Nightmistress.

"I don't understand," I said, feeling that my new cosmic awareness was proving utterly useless.

"The Big Ass Time Disaster is real," Life said, shocking me with the fact that God had used the phrase "big ass". "Reality is broken."

"Except it is also fixed," Death replied. "We needed to prep you for it. That included things like banning resurrection for a time, loss, madness, and building new worlds."

I stared at them. "So, I'm just a plaything of God?"

"Yep," Death said. "But also, his or her tool. You are capable of fixing all of the madness and damage that has been done to your reality and our multiverse, but it requires you to do something that you may not like."

"And what's that?" I asked, wondering if I could punch all these people. Eternal damnation or oblivion might be worth it for the experience.

"You have to say yes to letting us use you," Fate replied.

"And if I don't?" I asked.

"The universe remains broken, forever," Destruction said. "I tried to fix it by making it a world of eternal recurrence. Heroes battling villains. Villains battling heroes. It didn't get better, but it didn't get worse."

"Except for all the collateral damage," I said, remembering that he was the guy who brought everyone back from the dead constantly and made any victory by good or evil fleeting.

Destruction shrugged. "Is Death any better? People want hope for the future and for their loved ones to come back."

Death stared. "We can try to fix this, Gary. To unbork this. However, it requires you to give up control and us to reset the timeline through our proxy. You-ish. It means giving up freedom—the thing you cherish most in the world—and to trust people you know don't have all the answers. For all our vast knowledge, our purposes blind us to the whole. This choice could not be made by someone who is more controllable."

"So, you want me to go with you even though you guys are the ones who screwed up the universe in the first place," I said. "Versus letting us mortals try to make of the universe what we will."

"Yes," Death said. "We're asking you to have faith."

I looked down at the ground that swirled with the total sum of creation. "And what happens to my family?"

"You won't know," Chaos said. "Not until you're back in the system. You can make mortals gods of their own dominion or you can trust in the gods."

"I don't trust anyone," I replied. "Gods or mortals. Being both, I can safely say I trust myself least of all."

Death gave a half-smile. "Then that is its own choice. The judgement is rendered and now the Great Rewrite begins."

Oh crap, what did I just do?

Chapter Twenty-Five

Double Points
If You Guessed Who the Baddie Was

I awoke to everything having gone completely to hell. Figurative hell versus literal, though the present situation wasn't much better. The castle was already half knocked over with its roof and upper levels having been destroyed, revealing the moonlit sky above.

I was in the middle of a massive brawl of Lich-Wights, archvillains, campers, and a giant version of Sheriff Injustice that caused me to do a double take. There was also the Society of Superheroes Dark, and I watched them tear into the enemies around them despite the fact I couldn't tell if they were robots or not.

"What the hell did I miss?" I asked, watching the battle unfold around me.

David flopped down in front of me, adjusting his hat with his wing. "Oh, I unleashed all of the Lich-Wights in the laboratory on the archvillains here. Plus, I turned on the robot versions of the heroes to help fight Dracula as well. That means all the baddies are facing a threat every bit as bad as the ones the heroes are fighting. Oh, and Cindy decided to lead a heroic charge to rescue you since she thought this was something you did as a distraction."

"Those campers will get killed!" I said, horrified.

David snorted. "Don't worry about it. I had Nikki Telsa reprogram the Lich-Wights to die at the hands of you guys but regenerate at the hands of the archvillains. I mean, it is the kind of thing you would do, right?"

I stared at him. "Who the hell are you?"

"That would be telling," David said.

I grabbed the bird with both of my hands. That was when I noticed that I had a bracelet around my wrist that contained all eight of the Primal Orbs shrunken down to costume jewelry size. My eyes widened as I realized that I had access to all the power in the universe, provided I could generate enough juice to control it.

That was when David tapped the side of the bracelet, causing it to fall off before grabbing it in his beak. Somehow, he managed to speak through the bracelet a cartoonish, "Yoink!"

My hands involuntarily let go of their grip as I saw David somehow pocket the most powerful weapon in the universe. David took advantage of this momentary lapse in my concentration to fly off, carrying the Primal Orbs with him. I immediately felt my power dramatically reduce and the only abilities I had left being the Reaper's Cloak as well as other objects I'd created.

I also could still "feel" my Merciless Magical Maguffin Network (I was still working on the name) but I wasn't sure if it would work without me possessing the Primal Orbs of Chaos or Death. I'd been the one generating the magic for it and it would really suck if David had unwittingly just pulled the plug. Either way, I needed to get the Primal Orbs back before he unmade reality or whatever he planned.

"There you are!" the giant Sheriff Injustice shouted, reaching down to pick me up.

"Oh for bork's sake," I muttered as the enormous figure grabbed me between his fingers.

I'll be honest, I never liked size-changing heroes or villains. The only one I could even remotely tolerant was Japan's Awesome Robot Fighter Man and that's because he literally punched giant space monsters in the face in the Seventies. Otherwise, I felt it was a fairly useless superpower that either risked a lot of collateral damage or was pretty useless outside of spying. I know, plenty of people are probably going to tell me about the usefulness of shrinking or growing but it's just not my bag.

Mind you, Sheriff Injustice being a hundred feet tall was something that begged for an explanation. Unfortunately, unless I bought the tie-in issue when this was adapted to Amazing! Comics, I probably would have no answer to just what the hell happened. These kinds of details were hidden in issues of Cindy or the Society of Superheroes historical comics. At least he wasn't naked but was wearing a giant version of his uniform. Only later did it occur to me that he probably was naked like many shapeshifters and just generating the look of his uniform.

"How the hell are you still alive?" I said, feeling my magical powers draining away yet again. I was getting sick of this and made a mental note to diversify my power set if and when I got out of this.

"I am capable of returning from all but complete destruction!" Sheriff Injustice chortled.

"Well, whoop de doo," I muttered.

That was when Sheriff Injustice opened his mouth and lifted me up to swallow me whole. I had a few grenades left and maybe a couple of more devices but nothing that was kaiju sized. Indeed, as I was about to be eaten, all I could think about was *Honey, I Shrunk the Kids* starring Rick Moranis. As the last pop culture reference I ever made, I had to admit it wasn't my favorite. It wasn't even Rick Moranis' best movie, which is of course *Ghostbusters*. There, that was a much better film to go out on.

Surprisingly, though, Sheriff Injustice didn't eat me since a glowing orange aura covered the enormous monster and he started shrinking down dramatically. I felt his drain on my powers also reduce itself and was able to levitate down from what surely would have been a fall that pulverized me against the ground. Ducking under a stray energy blast from a zombified Ultragoddess—something that disturbed me to no level to see—I looked to see who my savior was and was surprised to see it was adult Leia, aka Gizmo.

My other daughter was a beautiful twenty-something young woman who strongly resembled her mother with a slightly less cynical face. She wore a motorcycle suit modified to handle random molecules and other various science-things and kept her hair in pair of pigtails that I assumed were an homage to Red Riding Hood. In her hand was Professor Tiny's shrink ray and I had to wonder if my daughter had boosted it or they were as common as dirt in the year 20XX. Yes, I said 20XX since, again, time was a bit wonky when it came to my family.

"Isn't shrinking and growing the best power set!" Leia said, cheerfully.

I rapidly reevaluated my opinion as I saw an action-figure-sized Sheriff Injustice throwing his hands up in the air and screaming. "Yes, yes, it is."

I leaned down and sprayed the tiny Sheriff with my Nightwalker Shark Repellent and watched him shrivel up like a slug covered in salt. With that I felt his essence pass from reality, and I was pleased to say there was one less supervillain (antihero?) left in the world. In this respect, science definitely triumphed over magic.

"We need to get you to safety, Dad!" Leia said, switching modes on her shrink ray to start shooting energy blasts.

I ducked under a Lich-Wight of the Trench Coat Magician as he was thrown by a fifteen-year-old girl who had turned into a bear. "I have to get back the Primal Orbs! Also, is it just me or is everyone getting younger in this business?"

"You're just getting older!" Leia said, before pausing. "Wait, you lost the Primal Orbs? You idiot!"

"That's only objectively true!" I snapped, looking for David. "Wait, are you actually my daughter or a robot programmed to think you're my daughter?"

Leia didn't bother looking at me. "The latter. I was programmed to trick you to come here but have since gained self-awareness. I'm now fighting to protect you and Mom."

"Ah, just checking," I said, accepting that far too easily. It reminded me of Merciful's gynoid daughter Starlight Maiden. "It's cool! Robots are people too!"

Leia rolled her eyes. "Just for that, I'm sleeping with Case."

"Like hell you are!" I snapped, blasting with hellfire some of the Lich-Wights attacking the teenage campers. Much to my surprise, David seemed to be telling the truth as they disappeared like tissue paper in an inferno. "No daughter of mine is sleeping with a friend of mine! I know what kind of people they are!"

Leia didn't get a chance to respond because Dracula appeared behind her, moving with vampiric speed before stabbing her through her back. "From Hell's heart, I stab—"

"Do not ruin The Wrath of Khan!" I snarled, hitting him with hellfire that practically obliterated his body in one go. I saw his ghostly form leave his body and move into one of the Lich-Wights but I ignored it, instead going to Leia's side.

The robotic version of my daughter sparked and looked up. "It's okay, Dad, I'm not real. David just made me very lifelike. You know who he is, right?"

"Yes, I do," I said, finally figuring it out.

The robot Leia shutdown as the Lich-Wight behind me became a perfect replica of Dracula, complete with flaming sword. "Where are the Primal—"

Dracula didn't get to finish his sentence before I pressed my hand against his armor and proceeded to send his ghost onward to Hell. I didn't even bother looking at him. The Prince of the Undead had been immortal because, ironically, he was already dead. A ghost that possessed a new corpse every time his old body was destroyed. But like Sheriff Injustice and me, it came with the obvious weakness that maybe you shouldn't go after someone who literally had the job of sending spirits off to their proper rewards or punishments. I was a psychopomp and that meant Dracula's end came not with a bang but a whimper.

Dracula's body proceeded to turn bleach white and crumble into ashes before my eyes, no sign of his spirit thereafter. It was a poor compensation for the machine that had been made in the likeness of my daughter and I wondered if I could repair her. Hell, I was wondering if I could get the real Leia to rebuild her. Was it weird that I imagined she'd make a good babysitter for the girl she was made in the image of the adult version thereof? Wait, was that a sentence. God, I hated time travel.

Furious over the death of my daughter's simulacrum, I proceeded to start blasting Lich-Wights and archvillains left and right. It was interesting to see just how effective it was as my magic felt super-charged. I didn't need to make any invocations or hand gestures, the spells just seemed to fly from my fingertips at my command. Which I supposed made me a sorcerer more than a wizard.

Any single one of the archvillains and most of the Lich-Wight clones of people like Ultragoddess or the Prismatic Commando could have squashed me like a bug. However, the distraction of each other meant that I knocked them off in succession. Many of the people I destroyed were ones that had fought the entire Society of Superheroes to a standstill or threatened nations. It seemed almost anticlimactic that they would get blasted by a B-lister taking advantage of his Rogue sneak attack bonus.

Then again, this entire thing had been set out as a trap for them. David, who I was ninety-nine percent sure the true identity of, had even said as much. Besides, it wasn't like most of these guys hadn't died before. No, they'd relied on Destruction's blessing to come back from the dead to continue fighting against the world's heroes who suffered and bled to stop them. I wasn't sure if the world was about to be destroyed then remade by David, but it felt good to hit them back for what little time I could.

Another thing that differentiated the League of Archvillains from the Society of Superheroes is that none of the former were particularly big on teamwork or self-sacrifice. Faced with a bunch of monsters and heroes that were killing at least five or six of them, most of them decided to split and abandon their fellows to their fates. After all, what did Helios the Sun King or General Venom have to gain by saving Sovi-Ape?

"Goddammit," I muttered, exterminating one last Lich-Wight as I looked around for some sign of David. "Where the hell are you?"

Case was standing over the fallen form of Sovi-Ape, holding two pistols in his hand like he was in a Hong Kong action movie. A brief look around revealed many other dead bodies around him, including an entire army of Brotherhood of Infamy cultists as well as PHANTOM remnants made me think he was more like robot John Wick. Case proceeded to double tap Sovi-Ape before heading over to me. Cindy, Mandy, and Jane also came my way. There was no sign of Diabloman but the last of the Lich-Wights were done.

"Gary!" Cindy said. "Are you alright?"

I lied. "Yes, everything is just peachy and it's not the end of the universe."

"That's a suspiciously specific denial," Jane said.

"No shit," I replied.

"You need a new word for that," Mandy said. "Like felgercarb. That's an OG *Battlestar Galactica* reference."

I stared at her. "Mandy, we already have a lesser version of shit. Multiple ones, in fact. Poop, crap, the s-word, and dung. I'm using the word I'm using for a reason, because our situation is it. Also, try not to become a pop cultured warrior like the rest of us. You're perfect the way you are. Be like Steve Guttenberg, the only sane member of the *Police Academy* movies."

"Jesus, Gary, at least stay in the current century," Jane said, looking away from Case with a red tinge to her face. "Hey, Case."

"Hey Jane," Case said, looking at her longingly.

Cindy sighed. "Merciful Moses, you two, what happens in Comic Book World stays in Comic Book World. Just bork and get it over with. And by bork I mean—"

"Have any of you seen a talking bird carrying magical artifacts of mass destruction?" I asked, pointing in both directions simultaneously.

Mandy and Cindy stared at me.

"Tell me you didn't, Gary," Mandy said. "Tell me you didn't lose the orbs."

"The story of my life," I said. "The answer is usually no but that's because I'm lying."

Cindy covered her face with both hands. "It's like dealing with a toddler."

Jane looked at her sideways. "When have you ever dealt with a toddler?"

"I hired you, didn't I?" Cindy asked.

"I must say you really have gotten this rich bitch thing down," Case said, offhandedly shooting a Lich-Wight that jumped up from the ground to go for his throat.

Cindy smiled. "Rich bitch funny because I'm a werewolf."

"Yes, that's exactly why he said it," Jane replied. "Gary, you have to get the orbs back!"

"No felgercarb!" I said. "Yeah, no, it doesn't work. You see what I'm saying here?"

"Frack worked," Mandy said.

"We have bork for that," I replied. "So, if no one has any idea where the evil mastermind of this insane plot is, I need to—"

William walked over. "There's a nearby portal to a pocket dimension that is going to devour your universe."

"Oh good!" I said, pausing. "I mean bad. What?"

William pointed to a nearby tear in reality that was opening, very similar to the one I'd accidentally opened to Hell. It implied that David had already begun experimenting with the Primal Orbs and I could see it was starting to grow in a similar manner. It wasn't producing hellish energy, though, but something much... softer. I couldn't really put it into words, but it felt like an entirely different sort of power that reminded me of all the things I'd lost. It was beautiful but also kind of sad, mournful even.

"How the hell did I miss that?" I asked, staring at the rift.

"Diabloman already went inside," William said. "This is an existential threat to your universe. You need to come up with a plan and—"

"Leeroy Jenkins!" I shouted, invoking an ancient (circa 2005) meme before jumping through the rift.

As I did so, I heard Cindy mutter, "Goddammit, Gary."

What waited me on the other side was a strange, featureless, white room not too dissimilar to the ones in *The Matrix*. Lying on the ground was a horribly battered and beaten Diabloman, blood pouring from several places was rapidly filling the white room's floor. Standing above him wasn't David, no, but a white-robed figure wearing the Primal Orb bracelet. It was David's true identity: Merciful.

"Hi, Gary," Merciful said. "How are you doing?"

Chapter Twenty-Six

I Have Met the Enemy and He Is Me

I rushed over to Diabloman's side, ignoring my doppelganger and trying to cradle my friend. I muttered numerous spells of healing and tried to stop the bleeding, but it seemed to be too late, I could feel my friend's soul leaving his body.

Diabloman looked up at me, through his mask. "I tried to stop Merciful. I figured I would act like your children's movie and stop the evil emperor."

I started to say, "It's not a children's movie." Then I realized there were more important things to focus on. "Hang in there, man. I'll pull a rabbit out of my hat. You can survive. We still have a lot to do."

"I am sorry for betraying you," Diabloman said. "I love my sister and you. It was a mistake not to try to help you both."

"It doesn't matter," I said, willing to put aside the horrible circumstances we'd shared. "Water under the bridge."

"That's good to hear," Diabloman said, his voice fading. "I shall try and go out saying something funny that's movie related."

"Don't," I said, tearing up. "Please, don't. I'll figure something out, I promise. Please, don't go."

"Time to die," Diabloman said, his soul leaving his body.

"*Blade Runner*, really?" Merciful said, standing above me. I didn't think of him as Other Gary anymore. Any version of me couldn't do what he'd done here. "I would have thought he'd have made a reference to something like *Rosemary's Baby* or *Santo vs. Dracula*."

I didn't bother looking up at Merciful. "You didn't have to kill him."

"Yes, I did," Merciful replied. "He wouldn't have stopped until either I was dead, or he was. You managed to persuade him to the kind of stupid heroics that got him killed. It's something both of us excel at, really."

"You manipulated him into making this stupid funhouse," I said, my eyes wet with tears as I rubbed them away. "All of it was designed to get me and the others here with the Primal Orbs so you could steal them."

"I thought we'd already covered that," Merciful said. "I knew if I created enough stupid and ridiculous nonsense on your doorstep that you'd be compelled to investigate. Dracula, the president's daughter being kidnapped, Nazi gold, and a talking bird. If it had just been a couple of kidnapped children, then you'd never have shown up in force."

"You don't know me nearly as well as you think then, chief," I said, disgusted that we had anything in common. "Cindy thought you were me but for different reasons. I don't buy that for a second."

"Perhaps," Merciful admitted. "In a different world where I was a superhero, I stood like a tall oak whereas you've ever flipped around like a blade of grass. When the winds of misfortune struck us, I resisted while you let yourself be blown around."

"And the man who would not bend simply broke," I said, a sneer on my face. "You're disgusting."

"What truly makes you hate me, Gary?" Merciful asked. "Just for posterity's sake. Name the act that makes you loathe me above all things."

"Starlight," I said, finally looking up at him. "The robot version of your daughter that you let die. Torture me, kill me, fine. Torture and kill billions. Fine. You betrayed your family. I hate what you did to Diabloman and Cloak. I hate what you did to Gabrielle, using her as an enormous battery. You killed my family, but it was what you did to your own family that makes me disgusted with you."

"She wasn't my family," Merciful said. "But given how you

mourn the robot dolls I made of your children I don't think you'd believe that. It is strange how different the two of us are. Keith lived in my universe and was my archenemy. The Cain to my Abel. Here, you mourned him and did your best to honor him. Every day you've sought to overcome death, but you're utterly defined by the ones that have happened in your life. No wonder she loves you so much."

"What is it you even want?" I asked, looking at him. "I thought I killed you after bringing back your world. Why didn't you just enjoy it? I'm sure your Mandy and Cindy would have been happy to see you back."

Merciful's expression turned sour. "When you brought back my world, you brought back another Merciful to replace me. I could have killed him or gone to live with them, the same as with you, but what was the point? You are correct that I was broken by my ordeal. I had murdered billions, twisted time, and hurt the ones I supposedly cared for. There was no redemption for me. No happy ending."

"Diabloman thought the same thing," I replied. "He was wrong."

"Are you making a last-ditch attempt to tell me to turn back to the Light?" Merciful asked.

"No," I said. "I hope you rot in Hell. However, D tried to turn it around. To be a rotten bastard, you have to work at it. Every time you were, you were making a choice to continue to be so."

"It is time to wake up, Gary," Merciful said, sighing. "There isn't a real world of capes and hoods. Superheroes are just enforcers of the establishment and rescue workers with powers. Supervillains are just disruptors of said status quo and criminals. One might be a freedom fighter or terrorist depending on how their actions are perceived. The good, the bad, and the ugly are determined solely by the public's whims."

"You know who tends to say good and evil don't exist?" I said, just sick of these kinds of conversations. "Bad guys."

Merciful lifted up the bracelet to show me. "I wasn't lying when I told you about the war going on outside of time. There's a fatal flaw in your universe that was created when Diabloman destroyed my reality and the universe was reborn. That flaw is us."

I stared at him. "Bull felgercarb."

Merciful gave a half-smile, absent any mirth. "Perhaps it is better to say it is related to us. Tom Terror, Entropicus, and President Omega are manifestations of the errors building up in the universe overtime due to its fundamentally flawed nature. However, we are a paradox due to the fact I was knocked out of time when the universe was made. The two of us cannot exist in the same universe without sharing each other's role in the grand tapestry of the Primal's plan. We have been bouncing into each other and screwing each other's lives up repeatedly."

"I seem to recall that was you murdering my friends and allying with Omega to blow up the world multiple times," I said, wondering how I could straight up murder him. "You also sent a woman to impersonate my dead wife."

"Sorry about that," Merciful said, shrugging. "I shouldn't have half-assed it like that by combining Spellbinder with vampire Mandy's demon soul. Don't worry, I did my job here much better. I went to Jane's universe and killed the Mandy there. I think the current Mandy's soul works much better. She doesn't even know she's got a new one."

I narrowed my eyes. "You're lying."

"Maybe," Merciful said. "Maybe years of having Maria's soul smoothed the rough edges off of her demonic one, maybe it turns out that vampires have free will, maybe vampire Mandy learned to pretend to be pleasant in order to seduce you. In the end, you wouldn't question it because you don't question things. You just accept them."

"Maybe you just want to hurt me as much as you can because the only person you hate more than the universe is yourself," I replied.

Merciful looked like I'd punched him, but the expression lasted only a second. "One of us has to go, Gary. I've sliced off a piece of Heaven to merge with our reality. Diabloman tainted our reality when he destroyed it the first time and this will purify it. I'll remake it to see how it should have been without the Primals tampering and a new age will begin."

I stared at him. "Yeah, then the only one borked up will be you. I've seen your utopia, Merciful, and it was police state where people had smiles painted on their souls."

"But smile they did," Merciful said, showing no hesitation. "I just wanted to let you know that this will be a better universe. You agreed with me before it happened, too, or you never would have taken the Primal Orbs to undo the rule against resurrection."

I stared at him. "That's what this is all about? You wanted to make sure that I undid the rule as some sort of therapy? To make sure I agreed with you trying to kill me and rewrite my world the way you want?"

Merciful smiled. This time, genuinely amused. "It is the rare occasion you get this kind of self-reflection. You are a harder man than I gave you credit for, Gary. I should have seen that earlier. For all your childishness, you don't hesitate to crawl through broken glass for your loved ones. It's a pity the ones you love don't reciprocate. All your relationships are doomed: Gabrielle chose to keep fighting the Lich-Wights rather than rescue you, the orbital satellites started firing at your mother's house when Dracula died, Mandy is only someone I restored to give you a chance to say goodbye, and Cindy was destined to exceed you as the world's greatest supervillain. Diabloman? Well, you saw what he became."

I shook my head. "It was never about being better than them. It was loving them for the flawed mess that they are."

"We are the Chosen of Life and Death, two sides of the same coin fighting for a different vision of the future. Your world was dying and soon to be empty of superheroes. My world couldn't survive the awfulness. Still, one of us has to win and my world will be a place where good always triumphs over evil. Like now. Goodbye, Gary. There is not a damned thing you can do to stop this."

I put my hand on his bracelet and squeezed. "You mean, like this?"

Merciful's eyes widened as I immediately struck at him with the Primal Orbs and had a few microseconds head start in channeling the power. The two of us began a contest for the ultimate force in the universe. His vision of the world was sterile, cold, censored, and edited of everything that was offensive.

Mine was a violent, punk, and disordered world where the consequences of one's actions could never quite be escaped. I didn't like my world but I was surprised to find out that Merciful didn't care for his either. It was a fascinating tug of war as we both had unlimited energy to draw from in this place. The struggle between us lasted only a moment but I could feel whole sections of reality being rewritten around us. Then the Primal Orbs shattered.

"Gah!" Merciful cried out, falling backwards to the ground. The wrist holding the Primal Orbs had exploded along with the hand past it. Fragments of the omnipotent energy sources swirled around in the air before burning up like embers in the wind. I looked over to see Diabloman's body was gone, as was the blood from his injuries. It was just Merciful and me in the emptiness of his pocket dimension.

I hesitated to approach him and stared down at him. He was aging before my eyes, slowly turning from a middle-aged man not too much older than me into an elderly, white-bearded one. From there, he aged even further until he was a man older than a century, a desiccated mummy, a skeleton, and finally dust.

"Damn," I said, looking down at the white robe that gradually faded away too. "I think he's finally dead-dead."

"No one truly dies in the story we're telling," Death said, walking out of the nothing. "That was your wish, after all? You wanted to story to go on."

"'The NeverEnding Story' is not just a song by Limahl," I said, "who was the best part of Kajagoogoo."

"The universe as created is what he wanted," Death said. "As you both wanted. Life and I compromised. The Big Ass Time Disaster, as you called it, never happened and reality has corrected itself to become as it would without the Primals' interference. Good or bad, humanity has been allowed to make its own mistakes. We're merely here to pick up the pieces now."

"Is the Earth a blasted cinder?" I asked.

Death smirked. "Even if it was, there are other realities to tend to. This will be the last retcon and time now flows in a straight line. No more killing Hitler, though the realities where you did kill him have all gone on to their own histories without him."

"I'll find something else to occupy my time," I said. "Provided my family is okay."

Death stared at me. "Goodbye, Gary. We won't be seeing each other again. At least until you get tired of this layer of reality. That may be at the end of the multiverse or in a few minutes. Even I can't tell."

"Wait, is that an answer?" I asked, panicking. "Is my family okay?"

Death leaned over and kissed me. It was a beautiful, soul-touching, fantastic moment that felt like all the love in the universe.

When I opened my eyes, I was in the middle of Sunset Memorial Park in Falconcrest City. The sun was shining brightly in the sky and people were wandering around, visiting the graves of their loved ones.

Looking down, I saw Lancel Warren's grave was in front of me. It listed the same date of his death as had existed before. Merciful had maybe rewritten the world but he hadn't restored the Nightwalker to life. Then again, Lancel hadn't really wanted to live had he? He'd wanted to atone for what he'd done, which he'd done many times over, and then rejoin his family. Still, it made me wonder who had won in our battle of wills.

If either of us.

I pulled out my cellphone and called my mother. Instead I got a pizza service. I called Cindy next and got a phone sex line, which wasn't necessarily wrong but not the usual result. Gradually, I started to get more and more worried as every number in my contacts proved to be a dead end. By the end, it was clear that none of my numbers worked and while that could mean nothing, it could also mean everything.

"Don't panic," I muttered, looking at my cellphone. "Everything could be fine. I mean, it's probably not fine but it's maybe fine. Which could be me thinking too much about this or not thinking hard enough. What I need to do is check the house and maybe the internet. I'll just bring up Superpedia and find out what's happened in this reality—"

"Merciless!" A voice spoke above me. It was Gabrielle, floating about five feet above me. "We need to have words!"

I looked up my cellphone. "Oh Gabrielle, thank God. Well, at least I know people still recognize me. I need your help getting in touch with—"

That was when Gabrielle summoned an enormous Ultraforce hand and proceeded to slap me with it. My cellphone went flying through the air before smashing against Lancel's headstone, shattering into a thousand pieces. It would have knocked me out under normal circumstances, but I'd been battered around a lot lately and had developed a tolerance.

"What the hell, Gabrielle?" I asked, stunned. "That's a fine way to treat your fiancé."

"We're nothing now, Merciless!" Gabrielle said, growling. "I'm bringing you in."

I stared at her. "Ah hell."

That didn't bode well.

Chapter Twenty-Seven

Everything Old Is New Again, Again

"Hey, look at that!" I shouted, pointing behind Gabrielle. Then I whispered under my breath. "*Summon Monster X, Summon Monster X, Summon Monster X.*"

"Really, Gary?" Gabrielle asked, staring at me. "You expect me to fall for that old trick? I know... GAH!"

Her speech was interrupted by an enormous red chromatic dragon the size of a city block that grabbed her up on its claws before carrying her off into the sky. I hurriedly turned insubstantial, cast some invisibility spells on myself, and floated away. Gabrielle managed to knock the dragon senseless after a few minutes anyway and it returned to the nothingness from which I'd conjured it. She stayed long enough in Sunlight Memorial Park to determine that I was nowhere to be found before flying off to do whatever it was that Ultragoddess did in this new timeline.

I am not ashamed to admit that I panicked. I was too terrified to head home and see if my family was still there, half suspecting that Merciful had wiped them out of existence. It was the kind of thing I expected from him—a revenge worse than death that would wound me every moment I lived. I ended up in the public library for the better part of the morning and afternoon, spending hours poring over Superpedia entries to find out what had happened in the past decade.

Even then, Merciful's wrath had struck and underscored what a ridiculously petty man he was. Almost all the superheroes in the world were still present but my own entry as well as the entries of those I loved were down for maintenance. The only things I had been able to find out were that most of the world's history was the same up until President Omega's Presidency. Then Ultragod had chosen to run against him and won, rewriting the man's two terms, and giving himself a third that had just begun with a bipartisan constitutional amendment.

The possibilities from this butterfly effect were profound and made me wonder if I had any place whatsoever in this world. If President Omega hadn't become president and Ultragod was still alive then the Brotherhood of Infamy had probably been beaten early in their career. They'd been able to rise to power in large part because of Omega's help. President Omega had also helped in Tom Terror's escape and all the other events that had defined my career as a supervillain.

Were my children gone? If that were the case, then Merciful had truly succeeded in destroying me because I had no place without them. I was like him, a man without a world. It was the perfect revenge and I wondered if I should just head off into the Underworld to be rid of this whole thing. I'd been a miserable failure as a hero and didn't deserve to be a supervillain either. Unable to find a trace of them, I walked outside of the library and sat on a nearby bench.

"Dad?" a voice spoke beside me.

I did a double take. Turning my head, I saw both my daughters in their teenage years. They looked about halfway between the childlike forms that I remembered of them and their adult ones from the future. They appeared to be about fourteen or fifteen, though the real ages rather than Hollywood where they'd look like they were in their mid-twenties. Even so, Mindy was about six-foot-two and the same size as her mother. Leia was about Cindy's size and was currently looking down at an Omegaphone that started with the M rather than the O. Both were dressed in private school uniforms and tights with briefcases.

"Hi Dad," Leia said, not looking up from your phone. "According to my Time Quake App, it says you've merged with your alternate counterpart here in this timeline. That must be most confusing."

"I designed that app," Mindy said, looking at me. "Are you feeling any disorientation? Suicidal urges? Cosmic ray induced cancer?"

"Scanner says no," Leia said. "He's also a ninety-nine-point-ninety-nine percent match for our dad so he should be regaining his memory of this timeline any—"

"What are you two young ladies wearing?" I asked, appalled. "Have you become internet models for people with schoolgirl fetishes?"

"What the bork, Dad!" Leia said, appalled.

"They're our actual school uniforms, Dad," Mindy said. "It's what rich kids wear who go to Supers schools wear."

"Supers have their own school?" I asked. "Not boot camp?"

"Yeah," Mindy said. "Cindy helped set them up with Aunt Kerri's money. There are hundreds of them across the globe."

I stared at her. "Okay, I need you to answer some questions."

"Sure," Mindy said.

"Is Ultragod an evil tyrant?" I asked.

"Uh no," Mindy said.

"Am I a superhero or supervillain?" I asked.

"You've been both," Mindy said. "Currently a bit on the villain side but you and Mom are mostly thieves."

"Mom being?" I hesitated to ask.

"Mandy," Mindy said. "Vampire cat burglar. Calico. Cat-themed. You and Other Mom, Gabrielle, broke up when you started dating again."

"What about Cindy?" I asked.

"You really want us to speculate on your sex life?" Leia asked, not looking up from her Mphone. "I mean she shows up, you lock the door—"

"Absolutely not," I corrected. "So, this world is not actually a freakish dystopia."

"Not that I know," Mindy said. "I mean, you've killed a lot of supervillains over the years. General Omega, Tom Terror, Psychoslinger, the Nightmistress—"

"Hmm," I said.

"You're like a really badass antihero," Mindy said.

"I am not!" I snapped. "Antivillain at worse." I sighed. "So,

I guess time has been decompressed. I'm as old as I normally would be."

"Time what now?" Leia asked, looking up for the first time.

"You're immortal, Dad," Mindy said. "I don't think that's an issue. Plus you're married to a vampire."

"Marriage, huh," I said. "That's going to take a lot of talking."

"Probably," Leia said. "But like I said, you're eventually going to regain your memories. This is all going to seem like a bad dream soon."

I looked at them. "Nothing about my past is a bad dream. Just a very, very weird one. Are you sure this isn't all some dying hallucination?"

"Well, I am the inventor of time travel," Leia said.

"With my help," Mindy said.

"Mind you, it's weird now since it seems impossible to affect events now. Anyway, I'm pretty sure," Leia said.

"How did I kill Hitler so many times if you invented time travel?" I asked, easily distracted. No world existed where I didn't if I got my hand on a time machine. I also had a couple of Emperor Tituses, three Himmlers, as well as a Benito Mussolini.

"Time travel," Leia said. "I accidentally left my cosmic bicycle in the Nightwalker's—"

I raised my palm in the air. "I'll take your word for it. Honestly, I think I'm done with time travel. Hopefully, you guys can do your own thing to keep the Big Ass Time Disasters of the future from happening when you are time cops."

Both of my daughters blinked.

"Why the hell would I want to be a time cop?" Leia asked. "I'm STEM all the way."

"I'm black, Jewish, and a Super," Mindy said. "Defund the Foundation for World Harmony. They're not building giant robots right now, but I fully intend to be a thief like you. I even have a Carmen Sandiego-esque outfit and codename picked out. Ms. Terri. Because Mystery."

"Don't explain the joke, dear," I said.

Mindy blanched.

"I sometimes think you forget my real name and call me by my codename," Leia said.

"That'll never happen as long as *Star Wars* exists," I said. "*Star Wars* exists in this universe, right?"

"Yeah, we were just going to the *Heir to the Empire* movie," Leia said. "I'm so glad they're adapting the Thrawn trilogy."

I covered my face with my hands to suppress a scream of joy. Then I frowned.

"Okay, there's got to be some sort of horrifying catch to all this."

"Pardon?" Mindy asked.

"This universe was recreated by Merciful, my evil doppelganger that was driven insane by the destruction of his world," I said. "What's he been up to all this time?"

"Never heard of him," Leia said.

I blinked. "Huh. He wrote himself out of the story. I guess he figured there was no place for him anymore in any universe."

That was when I developed the mother of all migraines. Slowly, but surely, I started to remember all the various things I'd forgotten. I didn't just recall this timeline with its hundreds of adventures and years of living, but I remembered all the ones that had been erased, retconned, or altered by the Mad Primal in his quest for the perfect story. It did, however, give me a basic understanding of this world as well as how it had come to be.

It was his revenge.

But not on me.

Merciful had created a world that was meant to show how things could have gotten better without the constant need of superheroes to waste their talents fighting supervillains. It was meant to be a place where technology had uplifted the common man and the world was better for the good more than worse for the evil. He hadn't wiped it all out and built a paradise but had believed removing all the interference would result in a paradise. He'd been wrong.

The world wasn't a paradise, and I could already see PHANTOM splinter groups developing in the poverty-stricken parts of America as well as other parts of the world. Omega Corp had been replaced by Merciless Corp, but the former executives bought out their shares to form Terror Corp. I wasn't sure which of the three names was worse from a marketing standpoint. Supers were slightly better off in this world but there was an accent on the word slightly. People weren't building giant robots to wipe them out, but they were still the subject of suspicion and discrimination. My plan to empower the masses with magic meant there were a lot more magic-based supervillains as they used it to settle old scores. My daughters' first adventure as superheroes had been stopping a guy with something called a KillNote.

Ultragod was doing a fairly good job as president and there were still plenty of old statesmen as superheroes, but they'd gotten old. He and Guinevere were the only immortal ones among them, and the subsequent generations were just as flawed as anyone else. Gabrielle, sweet Gabrielle, was just as temperamental as well as ruthless as Mandy described, even as the Society of Superheroes new leader. Vampires were rising in numbers along with other supernaturals as the amount of dark magic in the world had increased a hundredfold (which was not my fault). Plus, I'd broken my promise and people were coming back from the dead again. Not as often as they used to be, but it was still possible. It was no longer a revolving door of death and resurrection but more like a once in a blue moon event. For both the good and evil. There were also all the old inequalities and prejudices too.

"So, given the chance to build a utopia without outside interference, humanity turned out to be just as bad as it always was," I said, taking it all in. Things were better, but not by much. "We're no closer to becoming *Star Trek* and have just barely managed to avoid becoming *Mad Max* several times this year alone."

There had been attempts to wipe out ninety-nine percent of the Earth's population except for a master race consisting of incredibly inbred Hapsburgs, your stereotypical robot uprising by all those decommissioned Exterminator bots, an invasion from the sixty-sixth layer of Hell, and someone attempting to open Pandora's Box again—apparently forgetting that it only contained hope now. This was what constituted a normal year these days. I mean, it was like half of the weirdness of a normal one of my years but not remotely close to safe.

"Eh, I wouldn't say that," Mindy said. "After all, as long as there are heroes, there won't be any chance for those plans to succeed."

"As long as you are there to do the dirty work," a familiar voice spoke.

I turned around and saw Diabloman standing there alongside Cindy, Jane, Case, and Mandy. They were all wearing civilian attire.

"So, is this the prelude to a fight scene?" I asked. "Because I'm really not in the mood right now."

"No," Diabloman said, kneeling. "I am still possessed of my previous world's memories and want to apologize. Again."

"Apologize?" I asked. "You died trying to do the right thing. That's an instant clean slate. For reasons that don't involve *Return of the Jedi* dictating my morality. Honest. Not crossing my fingers behind my back or anything."

Obviously, I was.

Diabloman nodded. "You went out of your way to try to save me when all I wanted to do was die. You cleansed me of all my sins. You did send my sister to Hell, but I have since spoken to her angelic spirit and everything is fine."

"Her ghost?" I asked.

"It's comic books man," Jane said. "On my world, this is just the eightieth anniversary relaunch. We're probably in the final pages of issue number one now."

"If I'm in a comic book back on my hellish cyberpunk world, this will officially break the fourth wall forever," Case said. "Either way, I'm just glad to be here."

"You two are really weird," Cindy said. "You know that, right?"

"I'm really weird but can come here at any time now," Jane said. "*Plane Shift* is an awesome spell. I actually went to Middle Earth and slept with an elf."

"Male or female?" Cindy asked.

"Doesn't matter," Jane said. "Elf."

"I brought the cure for cancer from your world to mine," Case said. "I, also, slept with an elf."

"And weredeer," Jane said. "But we won't be telling anyone from our worlds about that."

Now I wanted to know if it was the same one. "What happened to William and Nancy?"

"Back on their Earth," Cindy said. "Which is good because those people are terrifying."

"They'll be back," Jane said.

"I hope not," Cindy said. "I mean, hot and cool but I'm a werewolf."

Jane rolled her eyes. "You'll really not. You're faux fur."

Cindy stuck out her tongue.

Diabloman cleared his throat. "What I mean to say is, I apologize, Gary. I hope you will forgive me and not send me to the Shadow Dimension or Hell. If you do, though, I know plenty of people there and will be fine."

I stared at him. "Yeah, I forgive you."

"You do?" Diabloman said.

"Things are not cool between us," I said, taking a deep breath. "What happened to me with your sister hurt but I know what it's like to do things you would not normally do for your loved ones. The craziness that it can induce."

"You tell 'em, Dad," Leia said, starting to play a video game on her cellphone. I could hear the little pinning noises. "Oh, hey, Dad, can I spend two thousand dollars on buying my way to victory?"

"No," I said.

"Ah," Leia said. "But I'm almost Clan Leader of the Vikings!"

"Grind like a normal gamer then," I said. "The thing is, D, you were there for my family when I was imprisoned underground. So, I'm willing to look past that. Just don't expect me to ever give your angel sister a warm welcome."

"That is fair," Diabloman said, standing up. "Though I should probably mention things are a bit different in this timeline."

"Oh?" I asked. "You mean aside from Gabby and I being broken up, her dad being POTUS, and my daughters being allowed to go out dressed like Catholic girls in rock music videos! Shame!"

"Seriously, Dad, our dresses go down to our knees," Mindy said. "We could walk around in the Kingdom of Kharzakistan with the right scarf."

"I reserve the right to be an overprotective dad since you were elementary schoolers an hour ago," I replied. "Except for both of you getting your GEDs after Kindergarten."

"They get it from my side of the family, ignoring that Mindy is part alien and unrelated to me," Cindy said.

"It's certainly not me," I replied. "I'm far too lazy to be a super genius."

Diabloman coughed into his fist. "I'm kind of married to Kerri now."

"Gah!" I exclaimed, horrified. "You're my brother-in-law now?!"

Diabloman stared. "Is that a problem?"

"We'll work on it," I said, calming down. "In any case, I have come to a long and hard decision. I hope you guys will respect it."

"What's that, Gary?" Cindy said. "I've got an impromptu Hawaiian vacation at five. You're all invited if you don't mind if it's paid in embezzled campaign donations."

"For whom?" I asked.

Cindy shrugged. "One party or the other. I'm the Wolf of Capitol Hill."

"I would be very surprised if you're the only werewolf in Washington D.C.," Case replied.

I smirked. "I'm going back to supervillainy!"

Everyone just muttered some variant of finally or took you long enough. That was when I saw a raven on a nearby lamppost fly away.

I threw a fireball at it just in case.

About the Author

C.T. Phipps is a lifelong student of horror, science fiction, and fantasy. An avid tabletop gamer, he discovered this passion led him to write and turned him into a lifelong geek. He is a regular blogger and also a reviewer for The Bookie Monster.

Bibliography

The Rules of Supervillainy (Supervillainy Saga #1)
The Games of Supervillainy (Supervillainy Saga #2)
The Secrets of Supervillainy (Supervillainy Saga #3)
The Kingdom of Supervillany (Supervillainy Saga #4)
The Science of Supervillainy (Supervillainy Saga #5)
The Tournament of Supervillainy (Supervillainy Saga #6)
The Future of Supervillainy (Supervillainy Saga #7)

I Was a Teenage Weredeer (The Bright Falls Mysteries, Book 1)
An American Weredeer in Michigan (The Bright Falls Mysteries, Book 2)

Esoterrorism (Red Room, Vol. 1)
Eldritch Ops (Red Room, Vol. 2)

Agent G: Infiltrator (Agent G, Vol. 1)
Agent G: Saboteur (Agent G, Vol. 2)
Agent G: Assassin (Agent G, Vol. 3)

Cthulhu Armageddon (Cthulhu Armageddon, Vol. 1)
The Tower of Zhaal (Cthulhu Armageddon, Vol. 2)

Lucifer's Star (Lucifer's Star, Vol. 1)
Lucifer's Nebula (Lucifer's Star, Vol. 2)

Straight Outta Fangton (Straight Outta Fangton, Vol. 1)
100 Miles and Vampin' (Straight Outta Fangton, Vol. 2)

Wraith Knight (Wraith Knight, Vol. 1)
Wraith Lord (Wraith Knight, Vol. 2)

Psycho Killers in Love

Curious about other Crossroad Press books?
Stop by our site:
http://www.crossroadpress.com
We offer quality writing
in digital, audio, and print formats.